# FLASHPOINT

## Book Eight
## of
## The Commitment Series

A BADGER BLISS BOOK

By

# Karen D. Badger

Karen D. Badger

# DEDICATION

Although this book was penned several years ago, it is coincidently being released in November-December of 2018, at a time when wildfires are running rampant across Northern California. Countless people have fallen victim in their wake. Many have lost possessions, livelihoods, and in some tragic cases, loved ones.

Wildfires are nothing new to California. They have historically cost the state more than $800 million dollars a year, however, the more global warming pollution that is emitted into the atmosphere, the more wildfires we can expect to see in California. If the average temperatures continue rise by as little as 5.5 degrees to 8 degrees F, by mid-century, the risk of wildfires in California is expected to increased by 20%...and by the end of the century, that increase is expected to approach 50%.

I dedicate this book to the victims of wildfires everywhere, to the dedicated scientists and environmental activists who strive to understand and to inhibit the growth of global warming trends across the world, and to the smoke-jumpers and hotshots who risk their lives on a daily basis to minimize the consumption of lives and land by fire. Don't ever stop trying...and don't ever stop caring. The world needs you.

ALSO WRITTEN BY KAREN D. BADGER AND
AVAILABLE FROM BADGER BLISS BOOKS:

ON A WING AND A PRAYER
YESTERDAY ONCE MORE
THE BLUE FEATHER
ALL MY TOMORROWS
1140 RUE ROYALE

The Billie/Cat Commitment Series:
IN A FAMILY WAY
UNCHAINED MEMORIES
HAPPY CAMPERS
COLLECTIVE IDENTITY
SWEET ANGEL
RELATIVE-LY SPEAKING
TAILSPIN
FLASHPOINT

www.badgerblissbooks.com

# FLASHPOINT

## Book Eight
## of
## The Commitment Series

A BADGER BLISS BOOK

By

# Karen D. Badger

This is a work of fiction. All characters, locales, and events are either products of the author's imagination or are used fictitiously.

FLASHPOINT

Cover design by Karen D. Badger

A Badger Bliss Book
Published by Badger Bliss Books
Georgia, VT 05468

www.badgerblissbooks.com

Print-Book ISBN 13: 978-1-945761249
Print-Book ISBN 10: 1-945761-24-5
E-Book ISBN 13: 978-1-945761256
E-Book ISBN 10: 1-945761-25-3

First Edition, December, 2018

Printed in the United States of America and in the United Kingdom

# ACKNOWLEDGMENTS

As always, I want to acknowledge my wonderful beta readers and editors, Carol Poynor (Chief Eagle Eye), Eleanor Atherton (my Mom and number-one fan), and my amazing wife, Barbara Sawyer (who once again, endured writer's widowhood while I worked to get this book out). These ladies work especially hard to provide feedback and detailed corrections that may have otherwise detracted from the storyline. I value each and every one of them, and I am proud to be part of their lives.

A big shout out to several dozen Facebook friends who, through multiple rounds of voting, helped me to settle on the final book cover. I hope you all like it!

A special thank you to the die-hard fans of Billie and Cat Charland, who are always asking when the next installment will come. The ladies have a lot more to say and share, as long as there is interest! I am seriously considering my hand at penning a young adult story next. Tara Charland is an interesting young lady whose story is longing to be told!

Now, grab a hot chocolate (or a hot Toddy if that is more to your liking), sit back, put your feet up and enjoy this eighth installment of the Billie/Cat Commitment Series!

# CHAPTER 1

"My God, you're going to kill me one day," Billie exclaimed. She struggled to regain her breath.

"Whadda ya mean?" Cat rolled onto her back and stretched her arms high above her head.

"Just when I think you've outdone yourself, you hit me with something like *that* and totally blow me away," Billie replied.

Cat smiled coyly. "I don't know what you're talking about."

Billie rolled over and pinned her wife to the bed, completely covering Cat's body with her own. "Don't give me that innocent act, Red. I haven't experienced a climax like that since...since..." Billie tried hard to remember the last time they had enjoyed such uninhibited love making.

Cat tucked a stray lock of hair behind Billie's ear. "Since before the breast cancer scare?" she suggested.

Billie's eyes softened and she recalled the past couple of weeks of anxiety and strife they lived through while they waited for biopsy results for a lump found in Cat's breast. For the billionth time, she thanked their lucky stars that it was benign. It was the most harrowing experience she had ever lived through. Billie nodded slightly. "Yeah—since then." She rolled onto her back and lay next to Cat. Billie fell silent and stared at the ceiling.

During the last two weeks, Billie had spent countless agonizing hours fretting over what her life would be like without Cat. Surely, she would go on. She would have to. The kids needed her, but without her soul...without her heart...without Cat's presence in her life, it would barely be worth the effort. Luckily the lump was not cancerous. Once more, she thanked the heavens above for smiling down on them and for giving them more time to live and love.

Cat shifted to her side, and with her fingertips, traced the worry lines that were newly evident around Billie's eyes, and in the process, wiped away the lone tear that had escaped the corner of her wife's eye. She placed a gentle kiss where the tear had been. "I'm sorry," Cat whispered softly.

Billie's head snapped up. "For what?"

"For taking you to hell and back."

Mirroring Cat's earlier move, Billie rolled onto her side to face Cat. She ran the back of her fingers across Cat's cheek. "Kitten, that wasn't your fault. You have nothing to apologize for."

"I know," Cat began, "but still, it was a nightmare neither of us needed."

"I agree, but it's over, and with a little luck, we'll never have to live through that again. One thing the experience taught me was to enjoy every moment we have together and *not* to fret about the future. Cat, we made it through, *and* we came out stronger in the end. Together we are invincible. Our love makes that possible. Promise me you'll let it go," Billie demanded passionately.

Cat closed her eyes and squeezed out a tear that rolled down her cheek and onto the pillow.

"Hey, none of that," Billie said. "The time for tears is over. We have our whole lives ahead of us. We have three amazing kids to raise. We have jobs to do, friends to spend time with and grandkids to meet some day."

Cat's eyes flew open. "Grandkids? Not for a while I hope. I'm not ready to be a grandmother."

"Well, considering Seth is only seventeen, and Tara and Skylar are even younger than that, I'd say it's pretty safe that it will be a while before that happens…but the fact is, we will be here to see it, and enjoy it—both of us."

Cat smiled. "I bet you'll be a fun Grandma."

"Fun? Like Grandma Jo?"

"Lordy, no! Bite your tongue, woman! Grandma Jo is quite a handful. I don't know how Grandma Alex puts up with her.

Sheesh! What I meant is that you are the fun mom, and I'm the scary mom, so I expect it to carry over to the grandkids."

"You are not scary, Cat. You're a bit stricter than I am maybe, but definitely not scary."

"Well someone has to be the disciplinarian. You are such a pushover. The kids know they can walk all over you."

"I don't think Seth would agree with you after I pulled him out of the driver's seat and laid him out across the hood of his car that time he drove drunk."

"You had good reason to be angry with him, Billie. He's lucky he got off so easy. You scared him rather than hurt him."

"And he lost his car for an extended period of time," Billie reminded her.

"Okay. I take it back. You are strict when you need to be, but you have to admit that you are the first one to jump into a wrestling or tickling match with the kids...not to mention impromptu dance parties whenever you hear music playing. Sometimes I don't know who the bigger kid is—you, or Skylar."

"So, maybe I'm more like Grandma Jo than I realize," Billie pointed out.

"Heaven help us!" Cat laughed.

"I like the sound of that," Billie said.

"What's that?" Cat asked.

"Your laughter. It makes me feel good."

"It makes me feel good too, Billie. Thank you for never giving up hope."

"I will never give up on you, Cat. I need you around for a long time to come. I'm not sure I can handle a boatload of grandkids by myself!"

"Well, you won't have to if I have anything to say about it."

"Promise?"

"I promise," Cat replied.

"I'll hold you to that. So, it's Saturday. What would you like to do today?" Billie asked.

Billie watched Cat's brow knit in thought.

"I know!" Cat exclaimed. "Let's plan a vacation."

Billie was a bit taken aback by the suggestion. "A vacation? What did you have in mind?"

Cat sat up and crossed her legs in front of her. "I'm not totally sure yet. Something fun. After all, we have my test results to celebrate. Let's do something that will make us appreciate life. Maybe something with a nature theme," she suggested.

Billie jumped off the bed and stood with her feet apart and hands on her hips. "No way am I doing the camping thing, Cat. Happy Trails Campground is still pretty fresh in my mind. I will not live that nightmare again!"

Cat tilted her head back and laughed.

"I fail to see what is so funny," Billie stated indignantly.

Cat leaned forward and rested her elbows on her knees. "You are just so damned cute!"

"Cute? Cute?" Billie exclaimed in disbelief. "I wasn't so cute at Happy Trails when I was covered with poison ivy and mosquito bites…or when I spent the night at the campground all alone after being sprayed by that skunk, while you, Jen, Fred and the kids went to a hotel!" Billie reminded Cat of just a few of the many disasters the family endured while camping with their friends Jen and Fred Swenson and their children a few years earlier.

"Billie, it won't be like that," Cat defended.

"You're damned right it won't, because I'm not going!" Billie began to pace back and forth across the room.

Cat struggled to hide a grin. "Not even if we rent a fully furnished cabin?" she asked.

Billie stopped "Cabin?" she said. "I'm listening."

"Fully furnished cabin, with running water, cooking facilities, bathroom, rain-proof, bear-proof and disaster-proof." Cat listed the possible amenities that would allow them to avoid the Happy Trails Campground disasters they had all lived through. "In short, all the comforts of home."

"Disaster-proof?" Billie repeated. Her eyebrows were perched high on her forehead.

"Disaster-proof. I guarantee it. So, how about it?" Cat asked.

"Go on." Billie sat on the edge of the bed to wait for the details. After a moment or two of looking at the blank expression on Cat's face, Billie became impatient. "Well?"

"Well what?" Cat replied.

"Details?" Billie impatiently waved her hands in front of her.

"I don't know. The thought just came to me a moment ago. I don't have it all planned out yet," Cat replied. "We'll need to do some research online before settling on a destination."

"Okay. Fair enough." Billie rose to her feet and collected the clothes she had discarded around the room at the start of their lovemaking earlier that morning. She pulled a T-shirt over her head. "I'll go power up the computer." She stopped in the bedroom doorway. "What time did Jen say she'd send the girls home?" she asked.

Cat looked at the clock on the bedside table. "Jen said yesterday that she was going to take them to a movie and then out for ice cream this afternoon before dropping them off at the mall. I suspect it will be a few hours yet. Why?"

"I want to get the kids' input on our trip."

"That's a good idea."

Billie made another move toward the door, but stopped once more. "Should we invite the Swensons to go with us?"

Cat bit her lower lip and frowned. "Billie, you know I love Jen, Fred and the kids like they were my own family, but I'd really like this trip to be about us. Am I being selfish?"

Billie smiled and thought about their best friends, Jen and Fred Swenson. They hadn't always been friends. In fact, when they first moved into the neighborhood several years earlier, all the neighbors shunned them when they realized the nature of their relationship. It wasn't until the Swenson's home caught fire one night, and Billie risked her own life to pull Fred and their two children, Stevie and Karissa from the burning house, that they became friends. Since then, their friendship had grown into something much deeper than would be normal between neighbors. Fred made it a point to become their advocate for the rest of the neighborhood, and soon, they were widely accepted as valued members of the community. They considered the Swensons family…family you choose, rather than family you're born into. Thinking about Jen and Fred made her smile. Jen was brash and outgoing, bold and opinionated, while Fred was laid back and a bit goofy by nature. They were perfect for each other. Their children, Stevie and Karissa were the same ages as Seth and Tara and had become best friends as well.

Billie snapped out of her reverie. "You're not being selfish at all, Cat. I agree. Let's make this about us and the kids. Heaven knows, the cancer scare affected all of us as a family. We need time to be together and to reconnect without other people around. Maybe we can do something with Jen and Fred later. I'm going to check out possible destinations online," she said over her shoulder and then disappeared through the doorway.

Cat grinned from ear to ear and leisurely climbed off the bed to collect her clothes. She marveled at how Billie could go from stubborn and defensive one moment to excited and cooperative the next.

"Don't ever change, Billie Girl. I love you just the way you are," she mumbled under her breath and she followed in the wake of her excited wife.

# CHAPTER 2

Billie sat in front of the computer, pressed the power button and waited for the desktop unit to come alive. Moments later, she clicked on the icon for her favorite search engine.

"Okay, what should I search for...campgrounds, National parks, amusement parks?"

Billie settled on National parks and pressed the enter button. Within seconds she was presented with a long list of websites.

"Damn! I didn't realize how many National parks there are in the country. It'll take me all day to go through these." Billie sat back and fought the feeling of overwhelming helplessness that crept into her consciousness. "Maybe Cat can help me narrow down the search."

Billie made her way to the kitchen where she found Cat at the counter with her back to her. From her position she watched Cat wipe her eyes with the back of her hand and sniff loudly. She was obviously crying. A gut-wrenching anxiety immediately gripped Billie's stomach.

Billie approached Cat and placed her hands on Cat's shoulders. "Cat! Honey, what's wrong?"

Cat turned around and sniffed once more. "Onions!" she exclaimed. "I decided to start a spaghetti sauce for dinner."

Billie raised one eyebrow to Cat. "Onions?" she asked.

Cat sniffed again. "Yeah. Wanna help?"

"You actually want *me* to help you cook?" Billie asked in disbelief.

An expression of sudden panic crossed Cat's face. She slapped her own forehead with the heel of her palm. "Jesus! What was I thinking?" she exclaimed in an exaggerated tone. "You're right. We want this to be edible."

"Hey! Do you have to be so brutally honest? Can't you just humor me for once?" Billie feigned mock indignation.

Cat smiled and gently touched the side of Billie's face with an open palm. "Dear heart," she began, "have you ever had food poisoning? Trust me—it's not fun. No, I think I've got this one covered."

"Good, because I'm actually in the middle of an Internet search for campgrounds and I need some advice," Billie explained.

Cat turned back to her cutting board and reached for a large clove of garlic. She peeled the skin from the fragrant clove while she talked. "Okay, shoot. What can I help you with?"

Billie reached for the wooden spoon on the stove beside the frying pan where Cat had ground beef and onions browning. She absently stirred the mixture and explained her dilemma to Cat. "Well, I entered 'national parks' into the search engine and over 25,000 websites were returned. I need to narrow down the search. Got any suggestions?"

"Why did you choose national parks?" Cat asked as she chopped the garlic.

"I don't know. I guess it sounded like a good place to start. National parks are usually pretty well maintained, and there are some really great parks to choose from...Acadia, Yosemite, The Grand Canyon, among others. I thought it might be good for the kids to see some of the national landmarks." Billie tasted the browning meat and onion mixture. "Yum. This is good. "

Cat scraped a large pile of chopped garlic into the pan and watched Billie diligently stir the small white slivers into the meat. "National parks sound good to me. We can use the trip to expose the kids to some of the natural treasures of this country. Do you have a particular area of the country you'd like to go? "

"That's part of the problem. There are at least sixty parks in the US, and they are everywhere, although I think most of them are in the Midwest. I guess it depends on how far we want to travel."

"I think we can safely eliminate the parks in Hawaii and Alaska. That should knock a few off the list, don't you think?" Cat suggested.

"Actually, that eliminates about a dozen if you include the ones in American Samoa and the Virgin Islands."

"There—now you're down to only four dozen," Cat pointed out.

"That's still a lot of parks to choose from," Billie complained.

"Why don't you do a search within results using the word 'landmarks'?" Cat suggested.

Billie spooned another scoop of the meat mixture into her mouth.

"Hey! You're gonna eat it all before I add the sauce if you keep that up," Cat exclaimed.

"I can't help it. It tastes so good." Billie inserted the spoon in the meat mixture once more before Cat suddenly snatched it out of her hand.

"Enough!"

"Okay! Okay!" Billie stepped back from the stove. "So I should narrow the search using 'landmarks', huh? I'll try that. Thanks!" Billie leaned in to kiss Cat. "Hmm. I don't know what tastes better—you or the meat mixture!" Billie jumped out of the way just in time to avoid the rolled up towel that Cat snapped in the direction of her rear end.

"Gee thanks! It's not every day someone tells me I taste like chopped meat!" Cat threatened Billie with the rolled up towel once more and effectively chased her out of the kitchen.

Billie chuckled and made her escape back to the office. She sat down in front of the computer again and changed her search criteria to national parks in the contiguous United States, with landmarks. The refined sort criteria narrowed the field from more than 25,000 to just under 3,000 websites.

She looked at the thousands of sites presented to her. "Humph! Well, I guess I've still got my work cut out for me."

Billie stared at the screen for a few moments and then decided to make a list of all the amenities she thought would make their vacation comfortable. After a half hour, her list included the words landmarks, cabin, electricity, plumbing, swimming, hiking, horseback riding, kayaking, fishing, biking, and of course, for Cat's sake, shopping. "That should eliminate a few sites," Billie murmured. She typed the new search criteria into the search field and pressed the enter key. The resulting search yielded 213 sites.

"Yes!" Billie shouted. "*That,* I can manage!"

Two hours and 213 sites later, Billie once again sat back and looked at the list of notes she had handwritten on the pad of paper by her side. Quite satisfied with her progress, she leaned her head back, stretched her neck back and forth and then closed her eyes. Seconds later, her eyes snapped open as her mind registered the enticing aroma wafting from the kitchen.

Billie rose to her feet and followed her nose straight to the pan of spaghetti sauce that was simmering on the stove. She lifted the cover, inhaled deeply and then lowered the spoon into the rich carmine sauce. A look of pure anticipated bliss graced her features as she brought the treasure to her lips.

"Caught ya red handed!" a voice said from the doorway to the basement.

Billie jumped two feet into the air and dropped the spoon into the sauce and the cover of the sauce pan to the floor.

"For crying out loud, Cat! You scared the shit out of me!" Billie reached for a paper towel to clean up the sauce that had splattered to the floor from the inside of the lid.

Cat stood there with one hand hiding the grin forming on her mouth. "Serves you right," she said. "If you had your way, the sauce would be gone before dinner time."

Billie discarded the soiled paper towel into the trash and then looked at Cat with an exaggerated pout on her face.

Cat narrowed her eyes at Billie. "Don't you dare use that pout with me, Billie Jean Charland!"

Billie continued to pout...and soon added puppy dog eyes to the fray.

Cat spared one glance at the pitiful look on her wife's face then threw her arms into the air. "Okay! Okay! You win. Help yourself." She gestured toward the stove.

Billie grinned broadly and retrieved the spoon that had fallen into the pan. Within seconds, an orgasmic look crossed her face as she savored the spicy red sauce. "Damn, you're a good cook, Cat."

Cat wrapped her arms around Billie's waist. "That response is worth allowing you to cheat."

"There are three things that will cause my eyes to roll into the back of my head. One—a good back scratch. Two—your cooking, and three—well, you know what number three is."

"I do indeed," Cat planted a kiss in the 'vee' above Billie's breasts and then laid her head in the spot vacated by her lips.

Billie's arms made their way around Cat's shoulders and held her in a firm hug for several moments.

"Hmm, this feels good," Cat purred.

Billie laid her cheek on top of Cat's head and closed her eyes. "Yes it does."

Billie held Cat in her arms for a few moments before she abruptly broke contact. "Ooh! I almost forgot. Want to see what I've come up with for possible vacation destinations?"

"So you've made a decision?" Cat asked.

"No. I've just narrowed down our options. I'd like everyone's inputs before making a final choice. Come on."

Billie took Cat's hand and led her into the guestroom that doubled as an office.

Upon entering the room, Cat sat on the edge of the bed while Billie retrieved her notes from the desk. Billie motioned for Cat to scoot over to make room for her to sit. Rather than move over, Cat climbed onto the bed and lay down with her head on the pillow and made room for Billie to join her. Lying side by side on their backs, they reviewed the notes Billie had taken during her Internet search.

"So, I've narrowed down the possible destinations to Acadia National Park in Maine, Yellowstone National Park in Wyoming,

Redwood National Forest in California, Yosemite National Park in California and the Grand Canyon in Arizona," Billie began.

Cat followed along while Billie read from the notes she held above them. "That's a pretty diverse list. What made you choose those locations?"

"I was looking for places where there was enough to do to keep everyone busy. You know, things like hiking, kayaking, horseback riding, fishing, biking..."

"And, shopping!" Cat quickly added.

"And, shopping," Billie confirmed. "In fact, one of the major attractions of Acadia in Maine was the antique shops all along the east coast, as well as the lighthouses. Apparently, there are dozens of them along the coast of Maine."

Cat looked the list over once more. "Cool! Are you leaning more toward one than the others?"

Billie laid the list of notes on her stomach and crossed her fingers over them. "For starters, this needs to be a family decision. I have my preference, but I really want to get everyone's input before settling on one. I'm open to other destinations that aren't on the list as well. Any thoughts?" she asked.

"Before I put my two-cents in, I'd like to see more information on each of these parks," Cat replied.

"Fair enough. I'll print out a package on each and then we can review it with the kids during dinner."

"Sounds like a plan." Cat rolled to her side to face Billie. She traced the side of Billie's face with her index finger and smiled broadly at her.

"What's that smile for?" Billie asked.

"You're such a nerd," Cat commented teasingly.

Billie's eyebrows shot into her hairline. "Nerd?" she replied incredulously.

"Yeah. I mean, look at your notes. They're so complete and orderly."

Billie looked at her notes and realized Cat was right. She grinned sheepishly. "Okay, I admit it. I'm a nerd. Got a problem with that?" she asked.

"No! Not at all. Nerds are good. Especially sexy nerds." Cat placed a kiss on the end of Billie's nose.

Billie rolled over to lie partially on top of Cat. "Sexy, huh?" She lowered her lips to Cat's.

"Hello there!" The loud voice came from the kitchen.

Billie's head snapped up as she strained to look over her shoulder. "Great!" she cursed under her breath. "That woman has remarkable timing."

Cat chuckled.

Billie rolled off her wife, threw her long legs over the edge of the bed and sat up. "In the guest room, Jen!" she called out loudly.

Seconds later, a curly, blond head appeared in the doorway. "Why is it every time I come over here, you two are in a bedroom?" Jen asked.

"Whatever do you mean?" Cat asked innocently.

"What do I mean? What do I mean? Really? Does this sound familiar? 'Oh my God, Cat. Harder! Harder!' 'Billie! Billie! Baby. More—please!'" Jen said in a loud and orgasmic voice as she ran her own hands up and down her body to exaggerate her point.

Billie's and Cat's eyes met; each one's face beet red with embarrassment.

"Ah, I hope you're making that up, Jen," Billie said, unable to look at her friend's face.

"Nope! On the way to the movies, I stopped in to see if you wanted to go with us, and when I came into the house, the two of you where nowhere in sight. I walked through the kitchen and living room looking for you, and by the time I reached the bottom of the stairs to the second story, the sound of your little play time hit me square in the face. Thank God the kids waited in the car! Geesh! Is that *all* you two do when the kids aren't home?" she asked, teasingly.

Billie and Cat's discomfort increased tenfold when they realized their friend really did eavesdrop on their lovemaking earlier in the day.

Cat scurried off the bed and stood her ground in front of their friend. "You're just jealous," she said in an attempt to make the best of an embarrassing situation.

Jen threw her hands into the air. "You're damned right I am! How do you two do it? Tell me your secret! Please! I'll pay anything!" Jen fell to her knees and clasped her hands in front of her as though in prayer.

"Our secret? That's easy. Cat is a nymphomaniac," Billie said.

Billie's comment drew a wide-eyed, shocked expression from Cat as well as the back of Cat's hand landing firmly in her midsection.

"Nymphomaniac?" repeated Jen. Disbelief tinged her voice.

Cat fell easily into the teasing.

"Oh, yeah," Cat admitted. "I'm a big-time nympho. Gotta have it at least four or five times a day. Luckily, Billie is up to the challenge."

Jen looked back and forth between her friends. "So, is it contagious?" she asked hopefully.

"Nope. You gotta be born with it," Cat replied.

"Well that sucks! Can it at least be learned?" Jen asked.

"That depends on who the student is—you or Fred," Cat answered.

"Fred. Definitely Fred," Jen quipped. "I have no problems in that arena. After all I'm approaching forty, and you know what they say about a woman's sex drive at forty. Fred, on the other hand, like most men, reached his sexual peak in his twenties!"

Billie draped her arm around her friend and they walked together into the kitchen. Cat followed close behind. "Jen, my friend, you don't need nympho lessons. What you need is a woman," she said.

"Got anyone in mind?" Jen asked jokingly.

"Billie!" Cat scolded her wife for what seemed like the hundredth time for urging their *heterosexual* best friend into a lifestyle that didn't suit her.

"Hey, what's wrong with that suggestion? Think about it. Two women approaching forty at the same time. Can't get any better than that!" Billie cast a meaningful look at Cat that caused her to blush to the roots of her hair.

"Sounds tempting," Jen said. "But to tell you the truth, Fred's kind of grown on me over the years, and as goofy and bumbling as he can be, I love him dearly."

"Yeah, he's a good guy. He's kind of grown on us too," Cat added.

"He sure is fun to be with. Speaking of which, we are planning another camping vacation and we were chatting earlier about how much fun we had on the last trip to Happy Trails Campground."

"Fun? You call that disastrous trip to Happy Trails, fun? I'm surprised you agreed to go, Billie. I got the strong impression that you'd never go camping again after that experience." Jen helped herself to a spoonful of Cat's spaghetti sauce. "Umm, this is good, Cat."

"Why do you assume Cat made the sauce?" Billie asked.

Jen raised her eyebrows at Billie. "Do I really need to answer that question? So I'll ask again—are you out of your mind for planning another camping trip?"

"It will be nothing like Happy Trails," Billie said. "I can assure you if there was any chance at all it would be even remotely like that, I wouldn't be going. Cat promised me it would be disaster proof."

"Disaster proof, huh? How so?" Jen asked.

Cat turned around and leaned her backside against the countertop as she watched the interaction between her wife and friend.

Billie put a pod into the coffee pot and turned on the switch before answering. "Picture this," she made a picture frame with her hands. "Cabin, plumbing, electricity, rain-proof, bear-proof, swimming, hiking, kayaking, horseback riding..."

"Whoa! Stop right there. Horseback riding? My ass *still* hurts from that God-awful ride I took at Happy Trails!" Jen said. "When are you planning to go on this trip?"

"Well, Billie starts a new case this week that should wrap up in early August. So we'd like to take the trip a week or two before school starts again," Cat replied.

"Damn! Bad timing" Jen said.

Billie looked uncomfortably at Cat. "What do you mean?"

"Well, you know I start my new teaching position when the school year begins, right?" Jen asked. "I learned this week that my final class to be certified to teach again begins on Monday and literally ends just two days before school begins. Darn! I really would have loved to go, but I'm afraid we'll have to pass this time," she explained.

Cat walked over and hugged her friend. She looked at Billie over Jen's shoulder; a look of relief flooded her face. "That's all right, Jen. There'll be plenty of opportunities to vacation together during school breaks, or next summer."

"Damn!" Jen said again. "I'm really sorry."

Billie placed three cups of coffee on the table and retrieved the cheesecake from the refrigerator. She placed it in the middle of the table. "No problem, Jen. Like Cat said, there'll be plenty of chances to vacation together later. Cat, I'll get the plates if you want to cut the cake."

After collecting plates and forks from the cupboard, Billie pulled out a chair and sat down to help Cat dish out the dessert.

"So where are you going?" Jen asked."

"We're looking at several places..." Billie kicked off two hours of dessert and lively conversation.

# CHAPTER 3

Billie spent the rest of the afternoon gathering information online for the pared down list of five potential vacation destinations while Cat lazed in the overstuffed chair in the living room, reading a book. Every now and again, Cat raised her head and smiled in the direction of the guest room as various exclamations reached her ears; exclamations ranging from impatient curses to gasps of surprise when something unexpected or exciting appeared on the computer screen.

Cat thought back to the day eleven years earlier when she first met Billie. She joined an aerobics class on a whim, with the intention of de-stressing after a long day at work as an anesthesiologist. What she didn't realize is how her life would change when she first walked into the class and came face to face with the tall-dark aerobics instructor, Billie Charland. She totally lost what little coordination she had and in the midst of performance anxiety, she fell flat on her face in the middle of class. Her first instinct was to cut bait and run, but Billie intercepted her after class and offered her personal lessons a few times a week in the mornings.

Her relationship with Billie developed into a deep friendship and soon, they were seeing each other on a daily basis. However, there were secrets on both sides that threatened to destroy their budding friendship. For starters, Cat had a four-year-old daughter, Tara, who Billie found out about quite by accident. Cat hadn't shown up for class and when Billie went looking for her, her daughter, Tara, answered the door.

Billie had a secret of her own. The only thing that made Cat uncomfortable in their relationship was the fact that Billie refused to commit to anything in the evenings. At some point, Cat convinced herself that Billie was engaged in another relationship on the side. A confrontation ensued after which Billie dragged her to the hospital to introduce her to her then six-year-old son, Seth, who was in a coma in the hospital. Cat felt horrible for not trusting her, and she felt even worse when she realized Billie kept her son a secret for fear of rejection.

That was eleven years ago. A little more than a year after they met, they had a third child, now, ten-year-old Skylar...a product of rape. But not just any rape. It was rape by Seth's biological father, Brian, who was determined to make Billie suffer for ruining his life. He went to prison because of that crime while Billie and Cat worked to restore a sense of normalcy to their lives.

As horrid as her beginnings were, Skylar was the bond that drew them together as a family. It was a bond that would be sorely tested when Skylar developed leukemia at six years old and they nearly lost her to the disease. They thanked the heavens above every day that she was in remission and continued to be healthy.

It seemed to Cat that as one disaster resolved itself, another arose throughout their relationship. She and Billie were not immune to their own life-threatening experiences. After Skylar's birth, Brian was released from prison, and took Cat, and the children hostage. Billie did her best to rescue them, but ended up shot in the head and spent the better part of the next year regaining her health and her memory. There was a time when she did not even know who she was...or who Cat and the children were.

Their family was nearly torn apart by that life threatening experience and it left Billie with a form of epilepsy that caused her to become aggressive and angry. It took brain surgery to remove scar tissue to relieve the almost constant pressure and headaches she suffered through, and to restore to them, a sense of hope for the future.

Cat had her own health scare when a breast lump was discovered during a normal physical. The lump turned out to be benign, but it was a very terrifying and sobering experience for all of them.

Cat sighed and smiled. She wiped a lone tear from the corner of her eye as she allowed feelings of extreme happiness to fill her heart, knowing her family was together and the future looked promising.

***

"Finally!"

With a stiff neck and sore lower back, Billie called it quits and shut the computer down. She retrieved the stack of information she'd sent to the printer from various Internet sites and carefully collated and stapled each packet in preparation for their discussion with the kids at dinner that evening. She felt a sense of excitement at the idea of a relaxing and fun-filled week alone with her family in the woods. Her only regret was that they still had two weeks to wait before they could go. It would be a long two weeks.

Billie rose from her seat at the desk and raised her arms high into the air. She clasped her hands above her head and stretched from side to side while she enjoyed the muted sound of vertebrae cracking into place and the mild rush of heat that followed in its wake. Feeling relaxed after her stretch, she gathered her papers and went in search of Cat, who she spotted as she entered the living room.

"Hey, there." Billie reached Cat's chair and leaned over to tenderly kiss her wife.

"You look very pleased with yourself," Cat observed.

"I am." Billie sat on the arm of Cat's chair. She fanned the stack of papers in her hand. "I found all sorts of exciting information about all five national parks. It's going to be a tough choice."

"Can I see?" Cat reached for the papers.

"Sure." Billie handed the stack of papers to Cat and then rose to her feet. "Want something to drink?" she asked as she headed into the kitchen.

"Tea sounds good." Cat replied without looking up from the papers she was reading.

"Tea it is! I'll be back in a few."

As soon as Billie entered the kitchen, she spotted the spaghetti sauce simmering on the stove. As she approached the stove, she forced herself to reach over the sauce pan for the tea pot which rested on the burner behind it. With all the willpower she could muster, Billie turned away and headed to the sink where she rinsed, then filled the teapot with water before placing it back on the burner. Suddenly, all resolve drifted away as the enticing aroma wafting from the mixture of sauce and herbs rose to her nostrils and rendered her totally incapable of resisting. Sparing a quick glance toward the living room, she lifted the lid from the pan and nearly fainted as a rush of spicy Italian aroma assaulted her senses. She reached for the spoon, dipped it into the sauce and brought it to her nose, intending to savor every moment before treating her taste buds to the flavorful sauce.

Just as she was about to taste the liquid ambrosia, the kitchen door swung open. "Hi, Mom!" Tara quipped as she entered the room. "Hmmm! What smells so good?" She dropped her shopping bag on the floor by the door and headed straight for the stove.

"My spaghetti sauce. Want a taste?" Billie asked seriously.

"*Your* spaghetti sauce?" Tara said in disbelief. "Get out! *You* made spaghetti sauce?"

"Hey! It could happen!" Billie replied with mock indignation.

"Is it edible?" Tara eyed the rich red mixture on the spoon suspiciously.

"It's great. Here, have a taste," Billie urged, the hint of a grin showing on her otherwise serious face.

Tara looked doubtful, but hunger overcame reason as she agreed to taste the sauce. Hunger was quickly overcome by surprise as she realized how succulent and savory the sauce was. "Holy shit, Mom! *That* is good!" Tara exclaimed.

Billie narrowed her eyes at Tara. "Holy shit indeed! Don't let your mother hear you talk like that or both our hides will be hanging on the line—yours for swearing, and mine for letting you!" Billie quickly regained her composure. "So you like it, huh?"

"Like it? I *love* it!" Tara exclaimed.

"Love what?"

Tara and Billie both turned to see Skylar straggling in through the kitchen door from shopping at the mall with Tara and Karissa. Billie had all she could do not to burst out laughing as she noticed the exaggerated makeup on her ten-year-old daughter's face. It was so poorly applied it closely resembled a clown's face.

Billie looked at Tara and tried hard to contain herself. "So, who did your sister's makeup?" she whispered to the fifteen-year-old.

Tara saw the twinkle in her mother's eyes and immediately recognized her attempts to stay composed. "Actually, she did it herself," Tara explained. "They had a sale on makeup at the boutique and they allowed the customers to try it on before buying it."

"Oh, I see," Billie said, at a total loss for words. She turned so that Skylar couldn't see her face and whispered to Tara, "You actually *let* her walk around the mall like that?"

Tara grinned. "Karissa and I made her walk way ahead of us so no one would know she was with us," the teenager hoarsely whispered to her mother.

"What's cooking? It smells really good!" Skylar was totally oblivious to the discussion between her sister and mother on the topic of her cosmetic makeover.

"Spaghetti sauce. Mom made it," Tara answered.

"No way! Mommy can't cook!" Skylar exclaimed loudly, not even thinking about hurting her mother's feelings.

Billie suddenly realized that her younger daughter had returned a quip for a quip as they traded unintentional barbs—Billie about Skylar's makeup, and Skylar about Billie's cooking ability.

*Well, turn about is fair play*, Billie thought and she turned to answer her daughter. "You know I'm not a totally rotten cook," she said. "Here, have a bite." She spooned another taste of sauce from the pan.

Skylar backed away. "I'm not eating that!" She was convinced it would be the next closest thing to eating doggy poop.

"I'll eat it!" Tara offered and she took the spoon from Billie and licked it clean.

"Billie? Billie, honey, would you please stir my spaghetti sauce while you're in there?" Cat's voice was heard from the living room.

Tara and Skylar looked at each other and then at their mother, whose face very clearly showed her guilt.

"You lied!" Tara exclaimed. "Get her!" she shouted and both girls chased Billie into the living room where she hid behind Cat's chair.

Billie pointed at her daughters. "Ah, don't forget the cook is my girlfriend."

Cat immediately rose to her feet and looked at Billie like she was growing antennae from her forehead. She spared a glance at her daughters and nearly forgot what she was about to say when she saw Skylar's makeup. She quickly regained her focus. "What's going on here?" She stood between her daughters and her wife.

"Mom said *she* made the spaghetti sauce!" Tara pointed to the guilty-looking Billie cowering behind Cat's chair.

Cat's hands immediately went to her hips and she looked at Billie with raised eyebrows. "Oh, really?" she asked. She looked back at her daughters, stepped aside and gestured toward Billie with both hands. "Have at it, girls!" Cat grinned from ear to ear as the two young ladies wrestled Billie to the floor and administered tickle torture until she surrendered.

"Okay, that's enough. Why don't the two of you head upstairs and wash up before dinner. I'll put the spaghetti on to cook in a few minutes. Okay?" Cat suggested.

The girls immediately abandoned their perch on top of Billie and did as their mother asked while Cat stood over Billie, hands once more on her hips. She shook her head in disbelief. "You'll never learn will you?" she said jokingly and reached down to help Billie to her feet.

"So much for, 'the cook is my girlfriend'!" Billie deadpanned. "I could have used some help here, you know."

"You're lucky I didn't join them. Did you really think you could fool them into thinking you cooked dinner?" Cat asked.

Billie looked insulted. "You make it sound like I can't cook at all, Cat," she pouted.

Cat's eyebrows once more took up residence in her hair line as she looked at Billie.

Finally, the obvious became unbearable. "Okay! Okay! I admit I can't cook, but a girl's gotta have a little fun now and then, ya know?"

Cat stood on tip toes to kiss her tall wife. "You're lucky you're cute," she said. "Oh, and by the way, what's up with Skylar's makeup?"

Billie was only half listening as she heard a sound coming from the driveway. "Seth is home from work!" She ran into the kitchen and directly for the pan of spaghetti sauce where she stood stirring it—a look of pure mischief on her face.

Cat stood in the kitchen doorway to watch her wife's antics and shook her head from side to side; a wide grin on her face.

Seth came into the house and immediately stopped short to take a deep breath. "Don't tell me—spaghetti for dinner, right?" he asked hopefully.

"Oh, yeah," Billie said. She scooped a spoonful of sauce from the pan and held it out to her son. "Come have a taste of my sauce. You're gonna love it."

At seventeen, Seth was taller than Billie by at least three inches. He stopped in front of his mother and cocked his eyebrow with a look that was 'so Billie', Cat had to stifle a laugh from her position in the doorway. "*Your* sauce?" he asked before devouring the contents of the spoon.

He never broke eye contact with his mother when he patted Billie on the side of the face. "Nice try, Mom. Nice try." Seth walked through the kitchen toward the living room and stopped in front of Cat, who was still in the doorway. He leaned down and placed a kiss on her cheek. "Great sauce, Ma." He then winked and walked away. "I'm gonna shower before dinner. I'll be down in a few."

Billie turned toward Cat with an astonished expression on her face. She was totally at a loss for words at her son's obvious betrayal.

Cat smiled ear to ear. "They know you so well, my love. They know you so well!"

Suddenly the whistling sound from the tea pot announced its presence as the ladies dissolved into laughter.

# CHAPTER 4

"Ma, you've outdone yourself," Seth exclaimed between bites. "This spaghetti is the best."

"Yeah, *Mama,* it's really good," Tara stressed the word 'Mama'.

Cat smiled as she caught Tara's intimation.

"What about you, Sweet Pea. Do you like it?" Billie asked her youngest daughter. Skylar had stuffed her mouth so full of spaghetti; all she could do in reply was to nod vigorously.

Cat reached for a piece of garlic bread. "How was work today, Seth?" she asked.

"It was okay. Really busy, but okay. We were out straight all day. I spent the whole day bagging groceries. My boss said it will slow down as school gets closer to starting," he explained.

"I hope it slows down enough for you to get a week off in the middle of August," Billie said.

Seth frowned. "Why would I need a week off?"

The turn in the conversation caught the attention of the two girls who waited attentively for Billie's reply.

"Mama and I were thinking that we need to celebrate her test results by taking a vacation. What do you think?" She looked around the table at the children.

"Where are we going?" Skylar asked.

"Well, that's what we'd like to discuss with all of you," Cat answered. "Mom spent hours online today looking up a few spots. We have some suggestions, but we'd like to hear your ideas as well."

"What kind of vacation are we talking about?" Seth asked. "I mean...are we going to an amusement park, or on a cruise, or something like that?"

"We were thinking more along the lines of a camping trip," Billie replied.

"I thought you said you'd never go camping again," Tara interjected.

Cat smiled and she sat back to watch Billie wriggle out of this one.

"I know I said that, but this won't be like the last camping trip we went on. First, we need to make sure the weather is cooperating, then we need to pick a place that has cabins so we don't have to camp out in tents and have to worry about rain and bears," Billie explained.

"It sounds kind of boring. What's there to do in the woods?" Tara asked.

"Depending on where we go, there are plenty of things to do to keep us all busy," Cat replied.

"Like what?" Skylar questioned.

"Well, there's hiking, kayaking, fishing, biking, horseback riding...and depending on where we go, there will be things to see in the surrounding communities. We might even camp somewhere close to that amusement park Seth was talking about," Billie explained.

"Sounds cool! When do we go?" Seth asked.

Billie smiled at her son's willing and cooperative nature.

"I still think it sounds boring. Can Kelly come with us?" Tara asked.

Cat and Billie exchanged a contemplative glance in response to Tara's question.

Kelly was Tara's age and the daughter of a military officer. Throughout her father's career in the Marine Corps, she had lived in numerous places around the globe. She moved into the neighborhood several months earlier and soon hooked up with Tara through mutual friends. The two girls seem to hit it off immediately, although Cat thought that Kelly's more stiff military-type mannerisms (no doubt learned from her father) made her an odd bedfellow for Tara's more laid back style.

"We were kind of hoping to make this just a family trip, sweetie," Cat explained. "Not even the Swenson's are coming this time."

"Oh, man!" Tara whined. "It's *really* going to be boring without Kelly *or* Karissa."

"If Kelly goes, can Missy come too?" Skylar asked hopefully.

Billie made a 'T' with her hands. "Okay, time out. Like Mama said, this is supposed to be a family camping trip. We rarely spend time with just each other these days, except at the dinner table. As you three get older, it will get even worse. Heck, Seth will be in college soon and will be gone most of the time. We want this to be a *family* trip. That means the five of us. This will be fun if you give it a chance. Okay?" Billie looked around the table and waited for responses.

Tara crossed her arms in front of her and pouted.

"I'm willing, Mom," Seth said.

"Me, too! I like horseback riding," Skylar added.

"Tara?" Cat prompted her daughter.

"Come on, Tare. It'll be fun," Seth playfully punched his sister lightly on the arm. "Kelly won't mind. It might even do you two some good to be apart for a week," he added.

The contemplative gaze shared earlier by Billie and Cat became adorned by a frown on Cat's face, and one raised eyebrow on Billie's as they absorbed Seth's remark.

Tara looked at her brother and begrudgingly smiled at the puppy-dog face he was giving her while silently pleading with her to go along.

In exasperation, and as a way of surrendering without losing face, Tara threw her hands into the air. "Okay. Okay. I'll go. Sheesh!" she exclaimed.

"Great!" Billie said. "So the next question is, where?"

"Mama said you did some research on a few places. What did you have in mind?" Seth asked.

Billie excitedly jumped to her feet and retrieved the stack of papers from the counter top that she printed out earlier. She tossed the packets on the table. "Take a look," she said.

Billie paced around the table while the kids browsed the packets and excitedly talked about each potential destination.

"I thought it might be fun to visit a national park and see some of the things we only hear about on TV or in books. For example, the Old Faithful Geyser in Yellowstone, or maybe the Grand Canyon, or maybe even the huge redwood trees in California. Of course, we could go somewhere else if you've got other ideas," Billie offered.

"I like Yellowstone. Don't Yogi Bear and BooBoo live there, Mama?" Skylar asked her mother.

Cat tilted her head back and laughed. "I think they live in Jellystone National Park, sweetie."

"Yellowstone sounds okay to me," Tara said. "It might be cool to see Old Faithful."

"Seth?" Billie waited for her son's input.

"The Grand Canyon sounded good to me, but now that I think about it, there's probably more to do at Yellowstone, so I guess you can count me in too," he replied.

"Mama?" Billie looked at Cat for her suggestion.

Cat smiled at Billie. She knew her reply was simply a formality, as Billie had confided to her earlier that Yellowstone was her first choice as well. "I think the kids have made an excellent choice."

"Jellystone it is. Yogi, here we come!" Billie exclaimed as Skylar's giggles filled the room.

***

Billie and Cat lay side by side in their bed; Billie with her hands locked behind her head, and Cat with hands clasped on top of her stomach. Both women looked straight up at the ceiling. The house was quiet. Skylar was sleeping soundly in her bed, and Seth and Tara were watching a movie in the family room. The time on the clock read 11:48 p.m.

"I'm glad the kids picked Yellowstone," Billie said. "That was my choice as well, but I really didn't want to influence the decision unless it was deadlocked."

"Yellowstone will be fun," Cat agreed, albeit a bit distractedly.

Billie noticed that Cat had become emotionally distant shortly after their discussion with the children at dinner. Knowing that Cat sometimes needed her own space, she didn't press the issue during the evening, but now, at nearly midnight, and with the children out of hearing range, she called the red haired woman to task on her remote behavior.

"Cat, are you all right?"

Cat spared a glance at Billie. "I'm fine. Why do you ask?"

Billie unlocked her hands and rolled onto her side. She propped herself up on one elbow, and with her free hand, traced a path from Cat's shoulder to wrist with her fingertips.

"You seem distracted," Billie stated. "Especially after our discussion with the kids at dinner. Are you sure everything is all right?"

Cat returned her gaze to the ceiling and avoided Billie's eyes. She remained silent for longer than Billie could bear.

Billie placed her palm on Cat's cheek and gently turned her face toward her. "Kitten," she said softly. "Please tell me what's bothering you."

Billie's piercing blue-eyed gaze held Cat captive and compelled her to speak her heart. "Billie, I'm worried about Tara," she admitted.

"Tara? I don't understand."

"Didn't you hear what Seth said to her tonight?" Deep concern tinged her voice.

"Seth said a lot of things to her tonight," Billie answered. "I'm not really sure which part of the dinner conversation has upset you."

Cat scrambled to her knees on the bed and faced Billie. "I can't believe you missed it."

Billie frowned. "Cat, I caught everything that was said. What I don't know, is which part has upset you." Billie was starting to become irritated.

Cat covered her face with her hands and inhaled deeply, then slowly exhaled to regain her composure. Finally, she dropped her hands from her face and looked at Billie once more. "I'm talking about the comment Seth made concerning Kelly," Cat explained. "Didn't you think that was kind of odd?"

Billie maneuvered herself into a cross-legged seated position in front of Cat and rested her elbows on her knees. She looked directly at Cat. "I found the comment enlightening, but not odd." Billie watched a look of disbelief flood Cat's features.

Before Cat could speak again, Billie continued. "Cat, if the comment truly meant what we think it did, you shouldn't be surprised. Shannon and Julie speculated as much several weeks ago after meeting Tara just once," Billie reminded Cat of the comments her clients Shannon and Julie Nash had made during a cookout. They had basically assumed Tara was gay, and also assumed that Billie and Cat were aware of that fact.

Cat's demeanor deflated visibly at Billie's words.

Billie lifted Cat's chin so that their eyes met. "Cat, honey, talk to me."

Billie watched a collage of emotions cross Cat's face as she obviously struggled to voice what she was feeling.

"Billie, I don't know how to deal with this. I mean, it's such a paradox to *not* want for our daughter, the very thing that has made me—has made *us*—so happy all these years."

Billie remained silent in the hopes that Cat would say more. Instead, Cat spent the next few minutes avoiding her gaze and fidgeting excessively. Finally, Cat climbed off the bed and paced back and forth across the room with one hand on her hip, and the other worrying the bangs on her forehead.

Billie needed to get to the root of Cat's behavior. She scurried off the bed and stood directly in Cat's path...effectively stopping her in her tracks. She took Cat firmly by the shoulders. "Cat, you're about to explode. Now talk to me."

Tears filled Cat's eyes and her body visibly shook. "Billie, I don't want Tara to be gay."

Billie took Cat into her arms and held her close until the trembling subsided. Finally, Billie held out her hand to Cat and led her to the bed where she once again took her into her arms. After several moments of silently communicating through their closeness, Billie broke the spell.

"Cat, we need to talk about this. Please tell me why you don't want our daughter to enjoy the kind of love you and I share."

"Billie, I love you with everything that I am. I would never change one thing about our lives together. And I would give my life to guarantee all three of our children enjoy the depth of love and devotion we share. Honey, it has nothing to do with the potential happiness Tara could experience in a relationship such as ours," Cat replied.

"I don't understand, Cat. On one hand you say you don't want Tara to be gay, yet on the other, you want her to be as happy as we are. She *can* have both."

Cat removed herself from Billie's embrace and sat up. She swung her legs to the side of the bed and sat with her back to Billie. Billie propped herself up on one elbow and waited for Cat to speak. After several moments of contemplative silence, Billie placed her hand on Cat's shoulder. Cat jumped at the unexpected contact.

"I'm sorry, love. I didn't mean to startle you," Billie apologized.

Cat rose to her feet and turned to face Billie. She folded her arms around her middle and hugged herself to ward off the anxious feelings that were rising within her chest. "No, that's all right. I'm okay." Cat paced across the room once more.

This time, instead of stopping her, Billie remained where she was on the bed. She sensed Cat had something important to get off her chest.

Cat paced back and forth and rubbed her hands nervously up and down her own arms as she cast uneasy glances at Billie.

"Billie, I have told you before that growing up gay wasn't easy for me," Cat began. "Sure, my family embraced me with open arms. Mom and Dad, and all three of my sisters accepted me unconditionally. And of course, Grandmas Jo and Alex…well, I guess their relationship states the obvious. But beyond my family circle, things weren't as nice. I was ridiculed at school, and made to feel dirty and broken by our church. Yes, believe it or not, at one point, my whole family was church goers, but when it became obvious that I was being cast out because of the church's narrow minded view of what is normal, my family chose to stand by me."

Billie repositioned herself on the bed so that she sat upright with her back against the headboard as she watched Cat pace.

"High school had its rough moments. Twenty years ago, there was no such thing as gay/straight alliances at school. There was no protection from the students *or* the administration. As horrible as it sounds, I was actually ridiculed by teachers," Cat continued.

"But Cat, that was twenty years ago. Things have changed. Society overall is more accepting now," Billie argued.

Cat stopped pacing and looked at Billie. "Yes, things *have* changed over the past twenty years; however, homosexuals will never be totally accepted in society. It may look like things are getting better, but the haters are still out there, lurking under rocks, just waiting to emerge. So many communities maintain a strong sense of insiders and outsiders. People who are different in some way from the rest of the community are marginalized and discriminated against by everyone. Hell—look at what happened when we moved into this neighborhood. The kids suffered that discrimination right along with us. I don't want that for Tara ever again. I don't want that for *any* of our children ever again."

"Tara doesn't strike me as someone who will accept second-class citizen status, Cat. She is strong enough not to allow herself to be discriminated against," Billie pointed out.

"You are right. Tara *is* strong; however there will always be individuals who live in the Stone Age who will strike without warning. There will always be a Gerald Manning lurking nearby to torture, maim and punish those he feels don't fit his warped sense of morality." Cat's voice rose to near hysteria by the time she finished her speech.

Billie was confused by the name Gerald Manning, but she knew instinctively that he was connected to some traumatic event in Cat's life. Billie scrambled off the bed and took Cat into her arms. "It's all right, Cat. I've got you, baby. Let it go," she purred into Cat's ear.

Cat wrapped her arms around Billie's waist and squeezed tightly. "Billie, there is something I've never told you. Something that happened to me in college."

"Shhh, it's all right. You don't have to tell me," Billie placed a kiss on the side of Cat's head.

"No, Billie. The memories have been haunting me for years. It's time to let them go." Cat broke free of Billie's embrace and walked a few steps away. She wiped the tears from her face and inhaled deeply before continuing. "A man named Gerald Manning attacked me when I was in college," she began. "And I wasn't his first victim."

Billie felt the beginnings of confusion and rage swell in the pit of her stomach and she had to force herself to remain calm. She walked to the bed, sat down and placed her hands on the comforter on either side of her. "Go on," she encouraged Cat.

Cat retrieved the chair from the vanity and pulled it over so she could sit directly in front of Billie. She sat, folded her hands in her lap and looked at the floor. She tried desperately to compose her thoughts before beginning. A few moments later, she looked into Billie's eyes and almost lost her resolve as she saw fear and anger in the sky blue depths.

Cat took a deep breath and began. "Gerald Manning was a Neo-Nazi." Cat paused slightly when an audible gasp escaped Billie's lips. She composed herself once more before she continued. "He was actively involved in a group on campus that among other things, believed gays and lesbians were subhuman. Their convictions included beliefs that homosexuals were trying to destroy the moral fiber of the American family, that they are child molesters, immoral, and intent on spreading diseases such as STD's and AIDS. They ranked us on the same level as prostitutes and murderers. Their minds and hearts were black with hate, Billie, and in their warped way of thinking, they felt morally responsible for eradicating our kind from the face of the earth."

Billie rose to her feet and walked to the opposite side of the room. She stood with her back to Cat for several long moments before she turned round to face her. "Cat, how can an educational institution allow such a group to exist on campus?"

"Billie, part of what makes America so great is our right of free speech. If the university banned them, then they'd also have to ban other groups…even the good ones. The college had no recourse but to allow them to exist as long as they did nothing to harm other students. Most of what they did was hold rallies and post proclamations of hatred. Gerald Manning was a renegade. He pushed the limits. He acted with the full support of the group, but when push came to shove, they denied all knowledge and responsibility for his actions," Cat explained.

Billie leaned against the wall and slid her backside down until she sat on the floor in front of it with her knees bent and her forearms resting on top of them. "Cat, you said you weren't Manning's first victim," Billie prompted.

"His first victim was a gay man named Josh. Manning charged that Josh made a pass at him and that he was defending himself. He nearly killed Josh," Cat explained.

"Why wasn't his hate group expelled from campus after that first incident?" Billie asked.

"Because his victim's family chose not to press charges and the police dropped the investigation. It was never proven that their group was responsible for the attack," Cat said bluntly.

"What? He beats the shit out of someone and they don't press charges?" Billie asked. Disbelief was evident in her voice.

"Josh's family was ashamed of their son's sexuality and chose not to press charges in order to keep the incident out of the news. Apparently his family was also pretty wealthy and influential with the administration because the incident was pretty much hushed up. The gay/lesbian community knew about it because of the victim's ties with us, and of course, I had firsthand knowledge of Manning's potential danger through my personal encounters with the bastard," Cat explained.

"You said you had more than one encounter with Manning?" Billie asked.

"Yes I did. Just before he nearly beat Josh to death, he started pursuing me. It started out with him making a pass at me, and of course, I wasn't interested, and I told him as much. Finally after the fourth time I turned him down, he pinned me against a wall and asked if I was a lezbo, or something along those lines. He just couldn't understand why I didn't want to have sex with him. That's when I finally admitted to him that he had the wrong equipment, and that yes, I preferred women. It was at that point that the serious harassment began," Cat recalled.

"Serious harassment?" Billie asked from her position on the floor.

"After the incident with Josh, the school quietly expelled Gerald, but that didn't keep him away. He felt invincible. He had literally gotten way with nearly killing Josh, so he continually violated the restraining order the university had placed on him to keep him off campus. He began stalking me. He followed me from class to class. He left nasty, homophobic sexual notes taped to my dorm room door. I reported him to campus security, but he always seemed to carry out his harassment undetected. Finally, the university assigned a security guard to escort me from class to class and after a while the harassment seemed to stop…that is, until one night he caught me alone, while walking from the library to my dorm at dusk." Cat paused and a shiver ran through her as the horrific memories of that night returned.

Cat's emotional state was obviously fragile. Billie crawled over to Cat and placed her head in Cat's lap. Cat bent at the waist and lowered her own head to rest on Billie's as they held each other for several moments. Finally, Cat sat erect again, which caused Billie to raise her head and to sit back on her knees.

Cat once again wiped the tears from her face before continuing. "That night, I called campus security when I was ready to leave the library and then waited in the doorway for the guard to arrive. I waited for nearly an hour, and when he didn't show, I decided to chance the short distance between the library, and my dorm. It was no further than Jen's house is from ours, so I thought I could make it safely. Unfortunately, the shortest route called for me to pass through a narrow gap between two buildings. It was in this tight, secluded space that Manning caught me. He had apparently been watching as I waited for the guard, and then followed me when I attempted to make it home safely on my own. He beat me to within an inch of my life—especially after I kicked him in the groin. I was lucky enough to escape rape—that well-placed kick assured as much—but the beating was enough to put me in the hospital for a week. Security finally showed up and arrested him, but not before the damage was done."

Cat sat back in her seat and closed her eyes. She only opened them again when she felt Billie's hand on her thigh.

"Cat, you don't need to say any more. I understand your feelings about Tara now," Billie said.

Cat began to cry as Billie's comment instantly reminded her of how this discussion had begun.

Billie stood, bodily lifted Cat from the chair and then carried her to the bed where they laid together in a tight embrace while sobs wracked Cat's slight frame.

"Billie, I can't bear the thought of Tara living through that nightmare," Cat cried. "No one should have to experience that. As much as society has changed, there are still sick people out there that believe all homosexuals should be exterminated. There are still zealots who hide behind the guise of their religion to justify the brutal torture and murder of someone simply because they differ from the norm. Billie, I don't want our daughter to become one of their victims. I don't want her to become the next Matthew Shepard." Overcome with emotion, Cat buried her head in Billie's shoulder and cried.

Billie kissed Cat on the forehead. "Neither do I, Kitten. Neither do I, but we can't do anything about Tara's sexual orientation. Only Tara knows where her heart lies, and we both know if she denies her true nature, she will never be happy. Do you understand?" she asked.

Cat nodded reluctantly. "I do understand, Billie, but I'm still terrified that some day she may have to live through the pain and humiliation brought on by a society filled with fear of our kind. Make no mistake—fear is what drives that type of behavior—fear and ignorance," Cat exclaimed.

"Sweetheart, we don't even know for sure that Tara is gay. In fact, *she* may not even know for sure. But in the event that she is, we should probably start by educating her on how to protect herself. Let's talk to Tara about this while we're on vacation, okay?" Billie suggested.

Cat nodded silently and snuggled in closer to Billie.

Billie kissed Cat's forehead and then turned off the light on the nightstand. "I love you, Cat," Billie said.

"I love you too, Billie."

# CHAPTER 5

Billie loved Sunday mornings. She normally rose before the rest of the family and typically completed a five-mile run through the park with Jen followed by a stop at the local coffee shop for a beverage and pleasant conversation with their best friend before returning home. On this morning, she was somewhat preoccupied while she and Jen sat in the coffee shop to enjoy their beverages.

"Are you okay, Big Guy?" Jen asked.

"What do you mean?" Billie replied.

"You seem a little distant this morning. What's on your mind?"

"Am I that transparent, Jen?"

"Clear as glass. Now, spill it," Jen demanded.

"Cat and I think Tara might be gay."

Jen sat back abruptly in her seat. "Whoa! I didn't see *that* coming! Not that I'm surprised, mind you, but what makes you think Tara is gay?"

"Well…lots of things. She's a major tomboy. For as long as I remember, she's preferred to dress like a boy. It's like pulling teeth to get her into a dress."

"A lot of young girls don't like dresses. That doesn't make them gay."

"True. But there are other clues. She's always been one tough cookie. I can remember when she was only four and Seth was six, she bloodied the nose of a boy at the daycare they went to because he made fun of Seth being in a wheelchair after he came out of his coma. And then there's Kelly…"

"I've heard about Kelly," Jen said.

Billie frowned. "You say that like it's a bad thing," she said.

"Not necessarily a bad thing.  Look, Karissa has said a few things about her, but I think she's just jealous that she doesn't have all of Tara's attention for herself anymore."

"What kind of things has she said?" Billie asked.

"Just that she acts kind of weird."

"Weird?  You're making me nervous here, Jen.  Weird, in what ways?"

"Karissa says she kind of acts like a boyfriend would act.  You know, she holds hands with Tara, and rubs her back sometimes, but then Karissa also says she's seen Kelly do that to other girls as well, so she's either a cheat...or that's just the way she is with everyone."

"Seth made a comment to Tara at dinner last night when we were talking about our vacation.  He said it might be good for her to take a break from Kelly for a while.  Tara was kind of upset that we wouldn't take Kelly on the trip with us."

"Maybe it *would* be good for them to be apart for a while," Jen suggested.

Billie lowered her face into her hands.  "How I wish we could just wave a magic wand and bypass the teenage years. Being the parents of teenagers is not for sissies."

"Don't I know it?" Jen said.

"Cat is really worried about her.  She doesn't want her to be gay."

"Seriously?  How can she say that when she's gay herself? Isn't she being a little hypocritical?" Jen asked.

"Apparently, as a young adult, Cat had some traumatic encounters and negative treatment—primarily in school and in her church.  She doesn't want that for Tara...or for any of the kids for that matter."

Jen nodded.  "I can understand that.  Have you talked to Tara about it?"

"Not yet.  We plan to speak to her while we're on vacation."

"Do you want me to ask Karissa if she's noticed anything?" Jen asked.

Billie sat back and sighed while she cupped her coffee cup between her hands on the table. "As tempting as that is, maybe you shouldn't. Heck, we don't even know yet if Tara leans that way. As I pointed out to Cat last night, Tara may not even know yet. I don't want Tara to think we're talking to her friends behind her back."

Jen reached across the table and wrapped her hands around Billie's. "I understand. But know that I am here for you...and so is Fred. If you need to talk, you know where to find us."

Billie smiled. "We love you, Jen. I hope you realize that."

"Ditto, Big Guy. Ditto."

\*\*\*

Billie grabbed the newspaper from the mailbox on the way into the house after her run. She threw it on the table and then set up a cup of coffee to brew. While she waited, she perused the news but found nothing of interest, so she set the paper aside in favor of the research material she had printed out the previous day. She was specifically interested in the package of information on Yellowstone National Park.

She sat at the table and spread out the information on Yellowstone, organized into piles...one for general campground information, one for park amenities and highlights, and one for activities. One activity item in particular, caught her eye.

"What's this? Hey, cool!" Billie uncovered information on the Junior Ranger program. "Sky will love this!"

"Sky will love what?" asked a voice from the living room doorway.

Billie turned around in time to see Cat enter the kitchen. A rush of heat and overwhelming emotion filled her chest at the sight of her wife. Billie had long believed Cat to be an amazingly beautiful woman...slight in stature, with golden-red hair cut in a pixie style, piercing green eyes, and perfect curves, but the first thing in the morning, when Cat's guard was down and her hair was messy and her eyes still droopy with sleep, was when Billie thought she was the most sexy.

Cat walked directly to where Billie was sitting and planted herself on Billie's lap. Billie wrapped her arms around Cat's supple body and held her close. "Good morning, my love," she said into Cat's neck. "How did you sleep?"

"I've had better nights. What are you looking at?" Cat asked.

"I was just looking over some of this information on Yellowstone." Billie picked up a sheet of paper she thought would particularly interest Cat. "Look. They offer a Junior Ranger Program. Skylar's the perfect age for it. Why don't you read it out-loud while I fix us each a coffee?"

"Okay."

Cat stood and allowed Billie to get up, then sat in the same chair she vacated.

"Two coffees coming up. I'll be right back." Billie kissed Cat's cheek and then went to fetch the coffee.

"Listen to this: '*Yellowstone National Park has a Junior Ranger Program for children ages 5 - 12. Children are introduced to the natural wonders of Yellowstone and their role in preserving the park and the environment for the future. Participants receive an official Yellowstone Junior Ranger vest and patch featuring a stylized bear track. Requirements include attending a Ranger-led program, hiking on a park trail, and completing activities on geology, park wildlife, and fire ecology.*'" Cat read directly from the Internet article. "You're right, Billie, I think Sky will love this."

Billie returned to the table with two cups of coffee. "We'll have to sign her up for it as soon as we get there. It looks like it may be a week-long program," Billie said.

Cat sipped her coffee. "Hmm, this is good. Thank you, love."

"It's kind of hard to screw up coffee pods," Billie joked. "I'm glad you're enjoying it."

"I am. Have you found any details yet on the camping facilities?" Cat asked.

Billie looked at Cat and noticed how tired she looked. "The research can wait. I want my chair back…up with you."

Cat stood and surrendered the seat to Billie, and then reclaimed the space on Billie's lap.

"That's more like it." Billie wrapped both arms around Cat. "How are you feeling this morning?" she asked.

"Tired, but okay," Cat answered. "Thanks for listening last night."

"You know you can talk to me at any time about anything, right?" Billie asked.

Cat nodded and then placed a kiss on the end of Billie's nose. "I know I can. Thank you, my love," she said.

"Why don't you finish your coffee and then go back to bed. I'll keep the kids quiet so you can sleep as long as you want," Billie offered.

"No, I'm up now. I'll be all right, sweetheart—that is, after I put away at least two more cups of coffee. I see by the styrofoam coffee cup that you stopped on your way home from your run," Cat mentioned.

"Yeah, it's become a ritual for Jen and me," Billie replied.

Cat rose from Billie's lap and made herself a second cup of coffee. "How is Miss Jennifer this morning?"

"Jen's fine. We talked a bit about the trip," Billie explained.

"Speaking of which, what does Yellowstone have to offer for campsites?" Cat asked.

Billie picked up the pile containing general campground information. "It says here that there are twelve campgrounds within the boundaries of the park, most of which are on a first come, first serve basis. Apparently a lot of people drive through and camp just for a night or two. The campgrounds are intended mostly for RV's but there are cabins in some of them."

"Maybe we should make reservations before all of the cabins are taken for the week we plan to go," Cat suggested.

"Probably," Billie began, "but I'm not sure the campgrounds are what we are looking for."

Cat retrieved her coffee cup from the brewer and returned to the table to look over Billie's shoulder. "What do you mean?"

"It says here that in addition to the campgrounds, there are frontier type pioneer cabins in an area they call the 'backcountry'. That actually sounds more intriguing than staying in a campground," Billie explained.

Cat placed her hand on Billie's shoulder. "Okay, stop right there. Didn't you say you wanted all the comforts of home on this camping trip? A frontier pioneer cabin doesn't exactly sound like a four-star hotel. I'll bet there are no facilities, no water, no electricity and maybe not even a bathroom," she warned. "By the way, do you want a fresh cup of coffee?" she asked.

"Oh, yes. Thanks, love," Billie handed the styrofoam cup over her shoulder to Cat who took it to the counter for a refill. "Look, Cat. I know I was adamant about camping in luxury, but after reading this material, I'm pretty excited about staying in one of these cabins. Listen to the description: '*Located in remote parts of the park, the cabins are accessible only by foot and horseback. Each cabin is rectangular in the "Rocky Mountain" style with a covered porch. The roofs are cedar shingles, but were originally sod. Floors were originally dirt, but have been replaced with concrete. Cabins are one or two rooms incorporating sleeping, cooking and work areas. Cabins have both wood heat and cooking stoves. Interior furnishings are typically sparse and include bunk beds, bookcases, table, and many have desks.*' Doesn't that sound cool?" Billie asked.

"Only accessible by foot or on horseback?" Cat asked incredulously. "Sounds like total isolation to me. We'll have to rent horses and ride them anywhere we want to go. Maybe it's a good thing that Jen and her family *won't* be joining us," Cat chuckled.

"Total isolation sounds pretty good after what we've been through this summer. Being away from the hordes for some much needed family time may be just what the doctor ordered. So, what do you think?" Billie hoped Cat would be as excited about it as she was.

Cat carried Billie's coffee to the table and set it in front of her. She then rested her upper body on her elbows, directly in front of Billie. "I think you've lost your mind, my love, but I have to admit, it does sound kind of fun. It could be a real learning opportunity for teaching the kids self reliance," she added.

A wide smile split Billie's face as Cat agreed with her plan. "We have a ton of planning to do. We'll need a separate suitcase just for pots and pans, dishes, survival gear and what not. Oh, and we'll all have to pack light. As it is, we may need to drag a litter behind a horse to carry all our luggage and supplies."

Billie jumped to her feet and ran out of the kitchen. She returned within seconds with a pen and paper to begin making her list. "This is going to be so cool!" she exclaimed again as she sat down and totally absorbed herself in planning their back-to-nature trip.

A warm fuzzy feeling filled the pit of Cat's stomach. She was thoroughly enjoying the excitement radiating from her wife. This was going to be one memorable vacation.

# CHAPTER 6

Tara lay across her bed on her back, with her head hanging off the side so that she had an upside-down view of her room—including her friend, Kelly. "You won't believe what my mother has planned for our camping vacation."

"Yeah? What's that?" Kelly pulled her T-shirt off over her head.

Tara's eyes nearly popped out of her face at Kelly's boldness.

"Tara? Tara?" Kelly asked.

"Huh?" Tara stammered as her attention was drawn back to the moment.

"You were saying something about your mom's plan for your camping trip," Kelly reminded her.

"Oh, yeah! Well, for starters, we're going to live like hermits for a week," Tara replied sarcastically. She watched Kelly's shirt hit the floor.

"Sounds like fun. My dad and I have been camping before with nothing but a tent. We had to live off the land for nearly a week. It's amazing how you can survive with the ordinary things you can find in nature when you have to." Kelly began to search through Tara's closet.

Tara sat up quickly in the middle of her bed and crossed her legs in front of her. "You don't understand, Kel. We're talking about my Mom here. Your dad is a Marine. He's had survival training. My mom can't even boil water. Thank God Ma can cook. We went tent camping a few years back and it as horrible. We all got poison ivy. It rained cats and dogs. A bear attacked our campsite and ate all our food, and to top it all off, Seth and Stevie burned their tent down with fireworks. It was the worse camping trip ever."

"Well it still sounds like fun. I wouldn't mind going myself," Kelly said.

"I wish you could go too. I asked my parents if you could come along, but they want this to be just our immediate family," Tara explained.

"Well, I guess that makes sense." Kelly held a sweater in front of her and she admired herself in the mirror. "So, what exactly does living like hermits mean?" she asked.

"Mom has it in her head that it'll be fun to stay in an old pioneer cabin with no electricity or water. We'll have to use oil lamps for light and a wood stove for cooking. There won't even be a bathroom! Can you believe it?" Tara asked.

"I'm sure there'll be an outhouse." Kelly pulled the sweater over her head and modeled it in front of her friend. "Whadda ya think?" she asked.

"It looks better on you than it does on me," Tara replied and then quickly turned the subject back to the family camping trip. "I don't know how I'm going to take a bath with no running water."

"You can bathe in the lake, or maybe there's a well where you can pump water into a big tub. It really does sound like fun, Tara," Kelly offered.

Kelly reached for the hem of the sweater and pulled it off over her head. She placed it neatly back on the hanger before she returned it to the closet and reached for another.

Tara watched her friend disrobe with interest. She was especially intrigued by the way Kelly's tanned abdomen was accentuated when she lifted her arms over her head to remove the sweater. There was very little Tara *didn't* like about Kelly's looks: blue eyes, short, boy-cut, dirty blond hair, athletic build, and a swagger that screamed confidence. She was also quite enthralled with Kelly's nonchalant attitude about undressing in front of her.

Tara cleared her throat. "Anyway, she wants us to live in this cabin with no electricity, no water and no bathroom…and it's so far away from everything that we'll have to ride in and out on horseback. We won't have the internet either, and probably no cell signal, so our phones won't even work. Sometimes I wonder what she's smoking."

Kelly drew another sweater over her head and pulled it down snugly around her waist. "Stop complaining, Tara. I wouldn't mind spending a week in a rustic old cabin. Where's your sense of adventure?"

"I left it at Happy Trails Campground a few years ago."

"How about this one?" Kelly asked. She modeled the sweater back and forth across the room. "I think it's a little tight."

Tara climbed off the bed and approached her friend. She eyed Kelly closely. "You're right. It's way too small. Turn around and let me look at the tag."

Kelly turned round and waited patiently while Tara turned the collar down to see the tag. "Well that explains it. This is Skylar's sweater."

"Really?" Kelly asked. "Well then, maybe I should take it off." Kelly grabbed the hem and struggled to pull the sweater up and over her shoulders.

"Here, let me help," Tara offered. Tara reached for the hem and with Kelly's help, managed to pull it up to her friend's neck.

Just then, the door to Tara's room opened and Cat walked in.

"Tare, is Kelly staying for lunch?" Cat stopped dead in her tracks. There before her were Tara and Kelly, both of whom were removing Kelly's shirt, leaving Kelly bare to the waist except for her lacy white bra.

"Ah...ah...," Cat stammered.

Kelly and Tara looked at each other, and then at Cat before they finally managed to remove the sweater.

"I think this is Sky's," Kelly said. She handed the sweater to Tara, quickly grabbed her own T-shirt and pulled it over her head.

Stunned into silence, Cat just looked at the sweater then back at Tara.

"It was in my closet, Ma. I don't know how it got in there. Kelly was just trying on my things," Tara admitted.

"Lunch?" Cat suddenly remembered why she was there.

"Sure," the two teenage girls replied together. They giggled and blushed when their eyes met.

"Lunch," Cat said again. She backed out of the room and pulled the door closed behind her. Cat stood in the hallway and stared blankly at Tara's door. She barely remembered the conversation inside the room. Her mind simply registered what she had seen. "Billie!" she yelled, and ran toward the stairs to the first story.

Tara and Kelly stood inside the door and stared dumbfounded at each other as they simultaneously realized what Cat thought she saw.

"Oh shit!" Tara said out loud. A shocked expression graced her features.

"Oh shit, indeed." Kelly grinned ear to ear.

***

"Wow! This vacation sounds like fun," Seth shoved the last bite of sandwich into his mouth. "I kind of like the idea of camping in the wilderness...all alone, no crowds, no noise...just peace and quiet."

"You don't mind that we won't have electricity or running water?" Billie asked.

"Heck no! It'll be cool to live like the pioneers did."

"Being in the wilderness probably also means your cell phones will have no signal," Billie pointed out.

Seth frowned, but then shrugged it off. "I won't deny I'll miss my devices, but heck, it's only for a week—right?" Seth looked at his watch.

"Do you have to work this afternoon?"

"Yeah. I gotta be there in about an hour."

"You *did* secure the time off for this trip, right?" Billie asked hopefully.

"Sure did. I can't wait. I'm looking forward to a break from bagging groceries." Seth gulped down the rest of his milk.

"Good. Speaking of groceries, I need to put together a shopping list for our trip." Billie tore a sheet of paper from the memo pad hanging near the phone.

"Sheesh, Mom. Chill! We're not leaving for two weeks yet!"

"It never hurts to be prepared," Billie said in her own defense. "Now let's see...bread, canned soups, jerky..."

"Billie! Oh, my God!" Cat scurried down the stairs, through the living room and into the kitchen. She stopped short when she saw that her wife was not alone.

Billie jumped to her feet. The tone of Cat's voice struck fear in Billie's chest. "What is it Cat?" she asked quickly.

Cat looked back and forth between Billie and Seth as though debating with herself about what to say in front of her son.

Billie looked at Seth. "Scout, could you give us a moment?"

Seth began to rise to his feet, but Cat stopped him. "No, stay right here. You probably know more about this than we do."

Billie took Cat by the shoulders. "Sweetheart, what is it?"

"I just walked into Tara's bedroom to see if the girls wanted lunch, and they were...they were both...I...I mean, Kelly was taking her shirt off and Tara was helping her!" Cat finally managed to say.

Billie and Seth wore twin looks of surprise and they were stunned into silence.

Within a few seconds, Seth recovered, and rose to his feet. "Gotta get to work," he said hurriedly.

"You stay right where you are, young man," Cat pointed at her son, stopping him in his tracks.

Seth obediently returned to his seat and leaned forward, resting his forearms on his thighs.

"Cat, maybe it wasn't what you thought," Billie offered.

"Billie, I *know* what I saw!" Cat turned to her son and placed her hands on her hips. "Okay, spill it."

Seth sat back and threw his hands out to the sides. "Spill what?" he challenged.

"You know *just* what I mean, Seth. That comment you made at dinner a few days ago gave you away," Cat replied.

"Comment?" Seth asked. "What comment?"

"Cat, calm down, let me handle this." Billie pulled out a chair and directed Cat into it and then she turned to Seth. "Scout, the other night when we were discussing where to go on vacation, Tara asked if Kelly could come along, and when Mama objected, you commented to Tara that..." Billie began.

"That it would do her and Kelly good to be apart for a while," Seth finished. "I remember."

"So what exactly did that mean?" Cat demanded roughly.

"It meant that they are together every day and it wouldn't hurt for them to take a break—that's what!" Seth said a little gruffer than he intended.

Billie immediately recognized Seth's attitude as a protective mechanism to counteract Cat's attack. "Okay... that's enough— from both of you. Biting each other's heads off is not going to solve anything."

Billie paced back and forth across the room a couple of times as both Seth and Cat sat back in their seats with their arms crossed and pouting after being scolded. Finally, Billie stopped and addressed her son.

"Seth, because of your comment the other night, Mama and I formed the strong impression that there was something going on between Tara and Kelly, *and* that you knew about it," Billie explained.

"I..." Seth interjected.

"Let me finish." Billie held her hand up to silence her son. "Now, whether there is a relationship between the girls or not, *and* whether you know about it or not, Mama and I have no right to ask you to betray Tara's trust."

"Billie!" Cat whined.

"No, Cat. This is something we need to discuss with Tara." Billie looked toward Seth. "Seth, you'll be late for work if you don't get moving."

"Thanks, Mom," Seth kissed both his mothers on the cheek (albeit a bit apprehensively as he approached Cat) and then headed to the door where he stopped and turned around. "Tara's pretty smart, you know. She won't do anything stupid. Don't worry about her." A moment later, he was gone.

Silence prevailed for the next few seconds. Billie leaned against the counter top by the sink and looked at Cat who still sat at the table. Their gazes locked from across the room and Billie thought she saw a bit of remorse in Cat's eyes.

Cat rose to her feet and approached Billie. She wrapped her arms around Billie's waist and looked directly at her. Billie's arms instinctively enveloped her.

"I'm sorry, Billie," Cat apologized. "You're right. We have no right to ask Seth to betray Tara's trust."

"You're apologizing to the wrong person, my love."

"Yeah, I know. I'll do proper damage control when he comes home tonight. That was really awful of me to act that way, but when I saw the girls like that, I guess I panicked."

Billie placed her hands on Cat's shoulders and gently pushed her back an arm's length away. "What exactly did you see, Cat?" Billie asked.

"Kelly was taking her shirt off and Tara was helping her," Cat replied.

"And...?" Billie asked.

"And, nothing. That was it."

"No kissing, no caressing, no nakedness?" Billie prompted.

"Not unless you count Kelly in her bra as being naked," Cat answered. A frown settled on her brow at Billie's line of questioning.

"But you didn't actually see anything sexual or romantic," Billie persisted.

"Billie, what are you getting at? Did I see them writhing naked in each other's arms? No I didn't, but how do we know it wouldn't have turned out that way if I hadn't come upon the scene when I did?!" Cat replied sharply.

"How do we know it *would* have?" Billie asked softly. "Cat, sweetheart, the truth is, we don't know, and because of that, we can't jump to conclusions. Let me talk to Tara about it, okay?"

Cat locked eyes with Billie for long moments before she relented and nodded her approval. Billie pulled her into a close embrace and kissed the top of her head. The ladies stood in the embrace for several minutes before Billie broke the silence.

"Cat?" she asked softly.

"Hmm," replied Cat.

"You may need to come to terms with the possibility that our daughter is gay. You know we can't expect her to be something she isn't. Do you understand what I'm saying?" Billie asked.

Cat looked at Billie. "I understand," she replied. "But I don't have to like it."

Billie frowned at her.

"I'm sorry, Billie. It's just that she's only fifteen years old. I'm not sure she's old enough to really know her heart."

"Did you know at fifteen, Cat?"

Cat fidgeted. "Yes, but that was different."

"*How* is it different?" Billie persisted.

Cat crossed her arms in defiance. "It just is—that's all!" she said stubbornly.

Billie laughed and wrapped her arms around Cat. "You are so cute when you're cornered,"

"Oh, shut up," Cat playfully slapped Billie on the arm.

"Go easy on her, Cat. We don't know anything for sure. Don't assume guilt before we've uncovered the facts. Okay?"

Billie's comments made Cat grin.

"What's that grin for?" Billie asked.

"Now, who's cute, Madame Lawyer?" Cat teased.

\*\*\*

Later that evening, Seth and Tara shared the couch and a bowl of popcorn in the basement family room while they watched a movie. Their mothers and sister were sleeping soundly two floors above them.

"Tare?" Seth said tentatively part-way through the movie.

"Yeah?"

"I owe you an apology."

Tara frowned at her brother. "For what?"

"That comment I made at dinner a few nights ago when Mom asked us about going on vacation kind of opened a can of worms."

"What do you mean?"

"Well, after Mama walked in on you and Kelly today, she was kind of freaking out about it, and asked me what I meant when I said you and Kelly could use a break from each other. Now they suspect there is something going on between you two. I think she's worried you might get hurt or something."

Tara sat silently for several moments, deep in thought with her hands folded in her lap.

Seth placed his hand on hers and squeezed gently. "Tara, what happened when mom found you and Kelly together this morning?"

Tara looked at her brother with genuine sincerity in her eyes. "Nothing happened between me and Kelly. She was trying on my sweaters while we talked about our camping trip and Mama walked in while I was helping her take off a sweater that was too small for her. She couldn't get it off by herself."

"So nothing happened," Seth reiterated.

"Nothing happened. I have to admit though that part of me wanted something to happen," Tara confessed.

"Yeah?" Seth asked in a nonjudgmental way.

Tara's gaze met Seth's eyes; confusion clearly written on her face. "Seth, sometimes I...I don't know. Sometimes I feel kind of strange around Kelly. Sometimes I wish I was her. She's just so cool. She knows what she wants and she's not afraid to go after it. She's not afraid of anything. I was kind of shocked when she just whipped her shirt off in front of me like it was something she did every day. I was kind of jealous of her when she did that," Tara explained.

"Jealous? What do you mean?" Seth asked.

"Maybe jealous is the wrong word. Maybe envious is better. Yeah, that's it. I was envious. I wish I was confident enough in myself to do something like that," Tara replied.

"You want to go whipping your shirt off in front of people?" Seth asked teasingly.

Tara bumped her brother with her shoulder and grinned. "You know what I mean." Tara fell silent for a few moments. Finally, she spoke again. "Seth, have you ever met someone that makes you feel all hot in your stomach?" Tara asked.

Seth smiled. "Oh, yeah. Last year in school there was this girl in my Algebra class. Man, was she hot! One day she walked by my desk and smiled right at me and I thought I was going to fall into a dead faint right at her feet. My stomach got all hot, I was light headed. Boy, she had me good!" he replied.

Silence fell upon the teenagers for several minutes before Seth asked the next question. "Does Kelly make you feel that way, Tara?"

Tara avoided her brother's eyes. "Sometimes," she said. "But I don't know what it means. I don't know if it's envy, or something else," she admitted. "Sometimes I don't know if I want to be *with* her, or be *like* her. Does that make sense?" she asked her brother.

"Yeah, I guess so," he replied before taking his sister's hand once more. "Tare, you know I'll support you no matter what— right?" he asked.

Tara smiled and then placed her head on her brother's shoulder as she reached for another handful of popcorn.

# CHAPTER 7

The next two weeks passed slowly for Billie. Never before had she looked so forward to a family vacation. Past vacations mostly focused on entertaining the kids…generally at amusement parks. Of course there was also that disastrous trip to Happy Trails Campground. She enjoyed each and every one of them…well, except for Happy Trails, but this time it was different. This time they would be communing with nature. This time they would be dependent on their own survival skills. This time they would be far away from the hustle and bustle of civilization. No phones, no TV, no work—just precious time spent alone with the four people she loved more than anything else in the world.

As the time for the trip grew near, the excitement level in the house increased exponentially. Cat, in her normal anal-retentive way, had lists hanging all over the house…lists for clothing, lists for supplies, lists for last minute details they needed to tend to before leaving. Skylar spent a great deal of time debating over what to bring. She finally pared down a huge pile of books, games, and stuffed animals to a few that would fit into her backpack. Seth, who normally waited until the last minute to pack, was ready to go a whole week in advance. Only Tara was lax in her readiness for the trip.

Tara's initial excitement seemed to wane as the trip grew near. Instead of joining the family in making plans for their week in the wilderness, she spent hours by herself in her room, or in the family room on the phone with Karissa or Kelly. Her distant behavior was not lost on Billie and Cat, who strongly suspected the reason for it. Even Jen noticed a change in the teenager, and she expressed as much over coffee one Saturday morning a week before the trip.

"So what's up with Tara?" Jen wondered out loud.

Cat and Billie exchanged a nervous glance before Billie replied. "What do you mean?"

"Well, she was at my house with Karissa and Kelly yesterday and she just seemed down in the dumps. It wasn't like her. She's never that quiet," Jen observed.

"Quiet, how?" Cat was clearly concerned about her daughter.

"I don't know. She seemed preoccupied, I guess. Distant. She had a faraway look on her face. So, what's up with her? What it is you're not telling me?"

Jen looked back and forth between her friends and waited for a reply that never came.

Jen placed her coffee cup on the table then leaned forward with an expectant look on her face.

Cat sighed deeply and slumped into her chair. Billie rubbed her back

"Does this have anything to do with the possibility that Tara is gay?" Jen asked.

Cat leaned forward and narrowed her eyes at their friend. "How long have you known?" she asked.

"I've suspected it for a while. Billie all but confirmed it during coffee after our walk last weekend."

Cat's gaze darted to Billie. "You discussed this with Jen?"

"It was the morning after you told me. Let's just say that Jen knew something was bothering me, and she forced me to talk. You know that's her super power."

"She's right, Cat. I used my truth lasso on her until she spilled the beans."

Cat grinned. "That was Wonder Woman."

"Wonder Woman, Lexa, Xena…whatever," Jen replied. "The power of persuasion is very powerful if you know how to use it. Now, talk to me, Cat."

Billie rose to her feet. "Hold it right there," she insisted. "This discussion calls for more coffee."

"And cheesecake," Jen added. "Do you have any?"

"In the fridge," Billie replied. "You get the cheesecake and I'll make the coffee."

"Gee, this conversation reminds me of The Golden Girls, ya think?" Jen joked.

Cat sat back and struggled to control her emotions while her wife and friend gathered their refreshments. She stared at her hands crossed and resting on the table in front of her.

Jen retrieved the cheesecake from the refrigerator and three plates and utensils from the cupboards and placed them on the table. She sat down across the table from Cat and covered Cat's hands with her own. "Cat," she said softly. "Sweetie, what is it?"

Cat lifted her eyes to meet her friend's gaze. "Matthew Shepard," was all she said.

Jen's forehead furrowed and then softened as an expression of realization crossed her face. "Oh, Cat. Honey, I totally understand how you feel, but Tara can't live her life looking over her shoulder. None of us can. What happened to Matthew Shepard was unspeakable. It was deplorable, but that doesn't mean it'll happen to Tara. That doesn't mean she shouldn't follow her heart. Tara is a wonderful kid. You two have done one hell of a job with her. You're great moms. She needs to be proud of who, and *what* she is, just as you two are proud to be who *you* are."

By the end of Jen's speech, Cat was in tears, as was Billie, who listened to the whole conversation while she stood in front of the sink with her back to her wife and friend.

Jen squeezed Cat's hands and then looked over her shoulder to Billie. The noticeable rise and fall of her shoulders was a dead giveaway that she was crying. Jen released Cat's hands, pushed herself away from the table and approached Billie. She wrapped herself around the back of her tall friend and placed a kiss between Billie's shoulders.

"Look at me, Big Guy."

Billie turned around.

"Go sit with your wife," Jen insisted, "I'll make the coffee."

Jen cast furtive glances at her friends while she made fresh coffee for all of them and carried them to the table. She placed a cup in front of each of them and then cut slices of cheesecake. After handing out utensils and napkins, she sat opposite Billie and Cat and waited patiently for them to speak.

"Thank you, Jen," Billie saluted Jen with her cup before sipping the rich, dark liquid.

Cat wrapped her hands around her cup before she raised her gaze to her friend. "Jen, how long have you known?" she asked for the second time.

"Well, I don't really *know* for sure," she responded. "It's just a feeling I have about Tara. I think you guys call it 'gay-dar'? I don't have any real proof, but I guess that doesn't answer your question," she added. "Let's see, how long have I suspected?" she pondered out loud to herself. "I'd say for about a year now."

"A year?" Cat exclaimed. "You suspected our daughter was gay for an entire year and you didn't say anything to us?" Cat's voice raised an octave with each word.

Billie reached under the table and placed a hand on Cat's thigh. She squeezed it lightly in an attempt to covertly calm Cat's growing temper.

Cat closed her eyes and quickly composed herself before she addressed her friend again. "Jen, I'm sorry. It's just that I'm really afraid for her. It seems I'm the last one to realize what my own child is up to these days," she apologized.

"Sweetie, we don't *know* that Tara is gay. It's just a feeling, that's all," Jen repeated. "When Billie mentioned it to me over coffee, I was shocked. I didn't say anything to you guys because quite frankly, considering your own situation, I thought it would be obvious to you."

"So, have you seen or heard anything that might reinforce this feeling you have?" Billie asked, before taking another sip of her coffee.

"Nothing concrete. Just her mannerisms and maybe the way she acts around Kelly," Jen offered.

"Kelly?" Cat asked.

"Yeah. Tara and Karissa have always been very close in a best friend kind of way, but she seems to be flirtier and compliant with Kelly...almost henpecked," she remarked.

"Henpecked?" Billie's eyebrows rose high onto her forehead. "You didn't mention that the other morning."

"Maybe that's the wrong word. Maybe I mean gob-smacked. You know...awestruck. Kind of like a lovesick puppy dog. When she's around Kelly, she reminds me of Stevie when he had his first crush. Know what I mean?" Jen asked.

"Now that I think about it, I guess I have seen Tara behave that way. Talk about not seeing the forest through the trees!" Cat scoffed.

"So, have you talked with Tara about it?" Jen inquired.

"No we haven't. In fact, I think we've kind of been in denial about it. We think Seth knows though. But he hasn't offered anything concrete either," Billie replied. "All he told us was to trust her not to do anything stupid."

"Sounds like good advice to me. She's a smart kid, and like I said, the two of you have done a great job instilling values in your children."

"Thanks, Jen," Cat said. "So...change of subject. Tell me about the class you're taking."

A smile split Jen's face, and it became apparent to Cat that Jen was excited about starting her new teaching job in a few weeks.

"The class starts on Monday. It's part class and part certification testing. I'm both excited and nervous at the same time..."

For the next hour Cat and Billie listened attentively to their friend describe her challenging few weeks ahead, in preparation for starting her first employment in more than fifteen years. At the end of that hour, they managed to eat nearly the entire cheesecake as well as drink multiple cups of coffee.

Finally, Jen rose to her feet. "I gotta get going. Fred is beginning to think I've moved in with you two!" she chuckled. Jen rinsed her coffee cup and plate and placed them in the dishwasher. She faced her friends and rubbed her stomach. "I need to figure out how to tell Fred I'm not hungry for dinner. Cheesecake is amazingly yummy, but it sure does sit heavy on the stomach!"

Billie and Cat escorted their friend to the door where she hugged and kissed both women and gave them extra tight squeezes.

"Good luck with Tara," Jen said. "Like I said, she's a good kid. Just be open and honest with her, but most of all, trust her to do what feels right to her."

"I just hope she's mature enough to understand the difference between what feels *good* to her and what feels *right* to her," Cat replied. "Sometimes they are mutually exclusive concepts."

"Wise words indeed," Jen replied. "Promise me you'll call if you need to talk, or if there is anything I can do to help. Oh, and when you *do* talk to her, put yourself in her shoes. Remember what it was like when you realized your parents knew. Okay?" Jen advised.

"My parents never knew. I didn't come out until after they died," Billie replied.

"Well then think about how you felt when you worried about them finding out. Sheesh, do you *always* have to be difficult, Tall One?" Jen quipped back.

"Always!" Billie joked and then hugged her friend again.

"We love you, you know," Cat added as she too hugged her friend once more.

"Ditto, kiddo!" Jen quipped and scooted out the door.

***

"I don't really want to go." Tara looked at the girl lying beside her. The two girls had retired to Tara's room after dinner to spend their last evening together before Tara left for a week-long vacation.

"Why not? It sounds like fun," Kelly replied.

"I don't know. I keep thinking I'll be bored," Tara confessed.

Kelly rolled onto her side to face Tara and propped herself up on her elbow. "Bored? I could think of a million things to do on a camping trip." Kelly tapped Tara's forehead with her finger. "You need to use your imagination, Tara."

Tara locked eyes with her friend, and remained silent as a cavalcade of emotions paraded across her face.

Kelly frowned and placed an open palm on the Tara's face. "Something else is bothering you, Tare. What is the real reason you don't want to go?"

Tara snapped her head out of Kelly's grasp and looked away. She was embarrassed and a bit angry at Kelly's ability to read her thoughts.

Not easily deterred, Kelly lay back and looked at the ceiling. "You know you want to tell me," she prodded.

"No I don't," denied Tara.

Kelly refused to let her friend off the hook. She risked a covert glance at Tara. "Yes you do, and you might as well get it over with, because I'm staying right here until you do." Kelly stubbornly crossed her arms across her chest.

"Somehow I don't think my moms will go along with you spending the night. Especially in my bed," Tara retorted.

"Your moms don't allow sleepovers?" Kelly asked.

"Well, the sleepover part would be okay. It's the 'in my bed' part I don't think they'd be too crazy about. They're already suspicious," Tara explained.

"What do you mean?" Kelly prodded.

"They already think something is going on between us," Tara admitted. "They've asked my brother as much."

Kelly fell silent for several moments, and then turned once more to her friend. "Do you want something to be going on between us, Tara?"

Tara's heart was beating so hard she was convinced Kelly could see her chest rise and fall through her shirt with every beat. A sense of panic began to form in the pit of her stomach as she considered her friend's question. Suddenly feeling trapped and cornered, she began to rise from the bed, only to be stopped by a restraining hand on her arm.

"Tara, don't go. I'm sorry. I shouldn't have asked that," Kelly apologized.

Rather than climb off the bed, Tara sat up and crossed her legs in front of her. She leaned forward and rested her arms on top of her knees and then focused on the bedspread in front of her.

Several minutes passed, during which Kelly was convinced she had ruined her friendship with Tara forever. Finally, when she couldn't take the silence any longer, Kelly rose from the bed and slipped her shoes on. She walked to the door, but stopped and turned around to address her friend. "I'm sorry, Tara," she said.

"Yes," Tara said as the bedroom door swung inward. Kelly froze where she stood.

Kelly turned around. "What did you say?"

Tara looked over her shoulder at Kelly. "I said, yes. I want something to be going on between us," she confessed.

Kelly breathed deeply to control her own wildly beating heart. She stepped back into the bedroom, closed the door and leaned against it for support.

"Do you?" Tara asked.

Kelly's eyes were wide with fear and excitement as she nodded her head.

Tara felt light-headed as her mind absorbed what her heart was feeling. She struggled to put a name to the turbulence that had taken up residence within her stomach at the news that Kelly felt the same way she did. She risked a shy look at Kelly. She realized that she, too, was under the spell of elated confusion. Tara reached out her hand in an invitation for her friend to join her in their silent celebration of attraction.

Shakily, Kelly slowly made her way to the bed where she sat in front of Tara, mirroring her pose and contemplated the same patch of bedspread.

Each girl covertly darted quick glances at the other until their timing coincided and their eyes met, creating a magnetic field so strong, neither could look away.

Feeling bold, Tara reached forward and took Kelly's hand. She held it tightly in her own. Every now and then, excited giggles escaped one girl or the other as their hands provided the physical connection they craved.

After contemplating the bedspread once more, Tara looked at Kelly and grinned. "Now what?" she asked.

Kelly breathed deeply and exhaled. "I don't know. I've never actually done this before," she admitted.

"Neither have I."

"Then I guess we should start out slow. Let's not rush it, okay?" Kelly suggested.

"Okay." Tara couldn't stop herself from grinning. "Now I *really* don't want to go camping."

Kelly frowned. "Tara, you have to go. Your moms are looking forward to this vacation."

Tara squeezed Kelly's hands. "But I don't want to leave you. I don't know if I can make it through a whole week without seeing you," she confessed. "Hell, I won't even be able to call you."

Kelly's heart soared at the knowledge that Tara was willing to give up what sounded like a wonderful vacation just to be with her, but her rational mind told her not to take Tara up on her offer.

"Tara, I want you to go. Just think how happy we'll be when we're together again after a week," Kelly baited.

"But I'll miss you!" Tara whined.

Kelly touched the side of Tara's face. "I'll miss you too, Tare, but I won't exactly be in your moms' good graces if they find out you're not going because of me," she reasoned.

Tara looked defeated. "Yeah, I supposed you're right." Tara looked at their entwined hands. "Promise you won't forget me while I'm gone," she said softly.

Kelly lifted Tara's chin. "How could I forget you, silly? You are on my mind nearly every minute of the day. Heck, I've even dreamed about you!"

"You have?" Tara found it difficult to catch her breath and tears came to her eyes as she struggled to contain her emotions.

"Are you crying?" Kelly teased. She reached forward and wiped a tear away from Tara's eye.

Tara grabbed Kelly's hand. "I can't help myself. I've never felt this way for anyone before. I mean, I love my moms and my siblings, but this is entirely different. What I feel is so intense, sometimes it's hard to breathe."

"I know what you mean. My parents have caught me staring off into space at the dinner table. They've even suggested I talk to the family counselors on base. I can only imagine how they'd freak if I told them I was too preoccupied thinking about you to even eat."

"Seriously? They wanted you to see a military shrink? That's intense!"

"You got that right! I learned pretty quickly to be more focused at dinner. The last thing I need is to pour my heart out to a shrink."

"How long have you been feeling this way?" Tara asked.

"Almost from the beginning," Kelly replied. "I don't know what it is about you. I mean, I really like Karissa, but I don't like her in the same way I like you. You know what I mean?"

Tara nodded. "I do. I feel the same. So now you know why it's so hard for me to be excited about this trip. I mean, today is the first day of *us*, and now we have to be separated for a week. What if you…what if *we* feel differently by the time I get back?"

"If either of us—or both of us—feels differently about *us* by the time you get back, then I guess it wasn't real in the first place. I'm betting that won't happen," Kelly said.

"I just don't want you to forget me." Tara closed her eyes and allowed another tear to escape.

"I'll tell you what…" Kelly reached for the permanent marker on Tara's nightstand. "Why don't we give ourselves something to remember each other by while we're apart?" She turned Tara's hand over, took the cap off the marker and drew two circles, one above the other in a figure '8' on the back of Tara's hand. She then drew a horizontal line through the lower circle.

Tara looked at it in fascination. "What does it mean?" she asked.

"It's an ancient symbol that represents a person's spirit or soul. As long as you carry this symbol with you when we are apart, my spirit will be there to keep you company," Kelly explained.

Tara smiled broadly and then took the marker from Kelly. She took Kelly's hand and drew the identical symbol in the same place Kelly had drawn hers. She put the cap back on the marker and then looked at Kelly. "I promise not to wash this spot the entire week we're gone," she vowed.

Kelly just smiled and looked at her watch. "I gotta go, Tare. I told my mom I'd be home by ten."

Tara immediately felt a sense of loss as her friend rose from the bed. "I'll walk you home," she offered.

"You don't have to do that Tara. I only live a block away," Kelly pointed out.

"I know, but I want to," Tara followed her friend out of the bedroom.

As the girls approached the bottom of the stairs, they noticed that Billie and Cat were in the living room, going over last minute details for their trip.

"Mom, I'm walking Kelly home. I'll be back soon," Tara announced as they walked through the living room.

"Are you packed Tara? We need to be at the airport by eight tomorrow morning," Cat reminded her.

"Almost," Tara confessed. "I'll finish when I get back." She pushed Kelly ahead of her before her parents could delay them any longer.

"Whew! That was close!" Tara exclaimed when they stepped out into the night air. "If you give them a chance, they'll hold us there forever talking our ears off!"

"I like your parents, Tara." Kelly locked arms with Tara.

Tara suddenly felt very grown up and walked a little taller than usual as she escorted her lady home. "They're okay," Tara admitted. "I could certainly do worse."

"Their relationship should make telling them about us easier," Kelly said.

"You would think so, but I got the impression from Seth that they were bummed out at the possibility," Tara replied.

"I wonder why?"

"You know mothers. They worry about everything. I'm sure they just don't want me to get hurt."

Kelly stopped walking and faced Tara. She touched the side of Tara's face. "I would never hurt you, Tara."

Tara smiled. "I know you wouldn't."

Tara took Kelly's hand and they resumed walking.

"What about your parents, Kel? How do you think they'll react?" Tara asked.

Kelly contemplated the question for several long moments before answering. "I really don't know how they'll take it. I've never heard them say anything negative about gay people. In fact, they were pretty supportive of marriage equality when it passed several years ago. And I can remember my Dad being happy when Don't Ask Don't Tell was lifted. He said he didn't care who a fellow soldier slept with as long as he had his back on the battlefield. So I guess they'd be okay with it, but you never know. It's easy to support something when it doesn't directly affect you. I guess we'll just have to wait and see."

Tara nodded and they walked the remaining distance to Kelly's house in silence. They stopped just short of her property.

"I guess we should say goodnight right here. I'd like to tell them about you face to face and not have them find out by catching us in the act," Kelly explained.

"In the act?" Tara questioned.

"You *are* going to kiss me goodnight, aren't you?"

Tara blushed to the roots of her hair. "Ah...yeah, I guess."

Neither girl quite knew how to approach the kiss so they just stood there staring at each other, until finally, they simultaneously moved forward and slowly closed the distance between them until their lips touched, tentatively at first, then with full contact. Several seconds later, they pulled apart, both quite breathless from the experience.

Tara leaned her forehead against Kelly's. "I don't want to leave you," she whispered.

"I know," Kelly whispered back. "It will be okay. We need to trust what we feel."

Tara took a step back, but held tight to Kelly's hands. "I...I guess I'll see you in a week, then," she stammered.

Kelly smiled and hugged Tara closely once more. "In a week." She released her friend and ran the rest of the distance to her front porch. Both waved before Kelly entered her house.

Tara stood there for what felt like an eternity, which was as long as it took to compose herself, and then turned to walk home.

*** 

Billie and Cat put the finishing touches on their list just as Tara returned home. Instead of slothing slowly through the living room as she normally did, Tara bounded in and made a beeline directly to her mothers. She bestowed a kiss and affectionate hug on each of them.

"Gotta finish packing! Goodnight! Love ya!" Tara quipped before she literally ran up the stairs to her room.

Cat and Billie sat dumbfounded by their daughter's uncharacteristic behavior.

"Was that our daughter?" Billie asked Cat.

"It *looked* like Tara," Cat replied.

Once in her room, Tara hurriedly packed her suitcase then twirled herself around in circles before she fell onto her bed. She hugged herself tightly and grinned ear to ear. She lay on her back, and giggled at the mere thought that Kelly felt the same way she did.  She raised her hands high above her head and looked at the symbol Kelly had drawn on the back of her hand.

"This is Kelly's soul.  I own your soul, Kelly…and you own mine," she said out loud.  "We are soul mates."

Tara felt tingly all over…especially on her lips.  The kiss was amazing.  She would never forget it for the rest of her life.

It was a long time before sleep overcame excitement and escorted the teenager into dreamland.

# CHAPTER 8

The Charland house was a bustle of activity the next morning as the family scurried to complete last minute chores before leaving to catch their plane. Finally, packed tightly into the family van, they made their way through the busy streets en route to the airport. A sense of excitement fell over the troupe, evident by the hum of voices inside the car. Billie drove, accompanied by Cat riding shotgun, with Tara and Seth claiming their usual seats in the back of the van, and Skylar enjoying the entire middle seat for herself.

The route to the airport required them to pass directly by Kelly's house, at which point, Tara plastered herself to the window and waved wildly until the house was out of sight. Seth noticed his sister's unusual behavior.

"Was she there?" Seth asked.

Tara snapped around and looked at her brother shyly. "Huh?" she asked.

"Was Kelly there? Did she wave back?" he asked quiet enough to keep the questioning between them.

Tara blushed and looked down at her hands. She was unable to keep the smile from her face. She shot a quick glance in her brother's direction. "Yeah."

Seth watched his sister for a few moments. He instinctively knew something had changed in her relationship with Kelly. "Wanna tell me about it?" he asked softly.

Tara inhaled deeply and looked at Seth. Still smiling, she replied, "We talked last night. She feels it too. We kind of agreed to take it slow. I walked her home and...and," the teenager faltered and once more looked down at her hands.

"And you kissed her?" Seth prompted.

Tara felt her heart skip a beat, and she found it difficult to breathe. She pressed her hand into her chest and nodded in reply while she wiped a tear from the corner of her eye.

"Wow!" Seth said. "That's cool, Tare. I'm happy for you."

"Thanks!" Tara never felt so close to her brother as she did at that moment. "I just hope Mom and Mama feel the same way."

Seth threw his arm around his sister's shoulder and drew her in. "I get the impression Mom is okay with it. Mama is concerned about you getting hurt, but give her time. She'll come around. You'll see."

"I hope you're right Seth." Tara sat upright again and turned to stare out the window.

In the front seat of the van, Billie peered frequently into the rear view mirror and noticed the exchange between her children in the far back seat. She also noticed Tara waving to Kelly as they drove by her house, so she naturally assumed the topic of conversation to be Kelly. She was glad Seth was acting as his sister's advocate, and she instinctively decided not to tell Cat about the exchange. At some point, Tara would talk to them herself. In the meantime, she would try to make Cat understand that Tara's need to be happy far outweighed the probability of danger should her heart lead her in Kelly's direction.

*** 

The flight into Yellowstone Regional Airport was uneventful, although the three-hour layover in Cincinnati, Ohio was difficult for Skylar to bear. Several times during the layover, the pre-teen complained about being bored and pestered her mothers to entertain her. Seth and Tara on the other hand, took advantage of the downtime to catch up on sleep they'd missed from the night before...Seth from staying up too late watching TV and Tara from lying awake in her bed for several hours preoccupied with thoughts of Kelly. Finally, their flight was called and within hours, they landed safely in Cody, Wyoming.

Soon after landing, the Charlands collected their luggage, checked out their rental van, and were on their way to Yellowstone.

"Well, so far, so good," Billie commented to Cat, who was trying to program the GPS with the directions to Yellowstone.

Cat spared a glance at Billie. "What does that mean?" she asked.

"So far so good," Billie repeated. "So far, no disasters, no delays, no screw-ups."

"Don't count your eggs too soon, Billie. We're not there yet," Cat pointed out.

"Don't be a pessimist, Cat. After all, you promised me a disaster-proof vacation, remember?"

"Yeah, yeah, yeah. I remember, but that was before you went all Daniel Boone on us and decided we should stay in a wilderness cabin. I'm still not sure you're going to like that, Billie."

"We'll be fine. What can go wrong?" Billie asked rhetorically.

"What, indeed!"

Surprisingly, within an hour, they arrived at Yellowstone without getting lost along the way.

"Here we are!" Billie announced as she pulled the van through the gates of the national park. She parked the van in front of the office. "Sky, you need to come with me so we can sign you up for the Junior Ranger program. I'll ask the rest of you to be patient while we check in and figure out where we need to go to get horses."

Fifteen minutes later, Billie and Skylar returned and climbed back into the car.

"So, did you get directions to the horse stables?" Cat asked.

"Actually, the guide will be along in a minute. In fact, there he is, driving that golf cart," Billie replied.

Cat leaned over and looked across Billie toward the office. "I see him."

"We need to follow him to the stables." Billie fastened her seat belt and started the engine.

When they arrived at the stables, the family of five piled out of the van and retrieved their luggage from the back hatch while the guide pulled over a small wheeled trailer that would be hitched behind one of the horses.

The guide turned to the group. "My name is Jimmy and I'll be guiding you to your cabin, but first we have a few things to cover." Jimmy turned to the pile of luggage stacked behind the van. "Well, I'll be. I'm guessing all that luggage will not fit in the trailer."

"Is that the largest trailer you have?" Billie asked?

"Yes, Ma'am."

As it turned out, the guilty party was Cat, as the kids and Billie packed a week's clothing in one suitcase each, and personal items in a pack that could be carried on their backs.

"Sorry, Cat, but we need to figure out how to downsize and lose at least one suitcase," Billie said.

For the next twenty minutes, Billie and Cat rearranged their luggage until they managed to eliminate one of Cat's bags which they left in the rental van.

While Billie and Cat worked to reduce the luggage, Jimmy retrieved five horses and tied them to the hitching posts. All five of them were bareback. The saddles were lined up on the top rail of the fence surrounding the corral.

Jimmy motioned for the family to join him at the fence line. "Gather 'round. Before anyone can ride, y'all have to learn how to saddle, unsaddle and care for your horse. It will be your responsibility to take care of these animals, so I will teach you how to do it properly."

Skylar raised her hand.

"Yes, Missy?" Jimmy asked.

"Can my mom help me put the saddle on my horse? I don't think I can reach."

Jimmy chuckled and ruffled Skylar's hair. "I reckon so, but you gotta promise you'll help. Deal?"

Skylar extended her hand, which Jimmy shook gently. "Deal!"

Jimmy assigned a horse to each family member and ran them through the mechanics of saddling, after which, he gave a quick lesson on the basic commands required to control the animals before they set out.

Jimmy stood by and watched as Billie loaded the luggage into the cart.

"Which one of those bags contains your provisions?" the guide asked.

Billie pointed to the largest suitcase. "This one."

"Good. I either need to see what you brought, or if you have a list of provisions, that will do as well. I need to be sure you'll have at least the minimum to spend a week alone with no facilities."

'Billie the Nerd', having done extensive research in preparation for the trip, had packed every essential imaginable, and then some and was readily able to produce the list for inspection.

Finally, they were ready to go. Despite the minor luggage delay, Billie still claimed victory as the vacation, in her opinion, continued to be disaster free.

It soon became apparent that extensive horsemanship experience was unnecessary as the horses were very gentle and intimately familiar with the trail and the routine of delivering campers to the back country.

The trip to the cabin took an entire two hours on horseback. Cat's backside was so sore, she literally finished the last fifteen minutes of the trip standing in the saddle. As she dismounted, she said, "Now I know how Jen felt when her horse got away from her while horseback riding at Happy Trails a few years ago."

Jimmy dismounted and waited for the family to do the same. "Follow me, folks. I'm gonna show you where to corral the horses, but first, we'll go to that small barn over there to unsaddle." The family followed behind Jimmy in a caravan to the small barn barely visible behind the house where he supervised the unsaddling process and then showed them where the feed and water were kept, while discussing the feeding schedule with them.

Before leaving the barn, Jimmy squatted down and drew the layout of the property in the sand on the floor of the barn. "Here is the cabin, and we are here, in the barn behind it. There are several trails leading away from the cabin. Some will take you to excellent hiking trails. This one here leads to the lake, and this one here will bring you to the kayak depot. You can rent single or tandem kayaks there. Most importantly, this trail here is the one that leads back to the main part of the park. There is a paper map with this information mounted on the wall inside the cabin as well."

"I hope we don't get lost," Tara said dryly.

Jimmy tilted his cowboy hat back on his head. "That is a real possibility in the wilderness. For that reason, I recommend you take short trips for the first day or two to get a feel for the area. Your concerns are not unfounded. It's easy to get lost out here. I'm not saying you shouldn't venture out further into the wilderness, but if you do, you might want to bring something to mark the trail in order to find your way back."

"That's good advice, Jimmy. Thank you," Billie replied.

"Just a few more details, then I'll be on my way before dark," Jimmy said. "You are allowed a campfire, but only in the designated fire ring. Never leave the fire unattended, and be sure you saturate it with water before turning in for the night. Things are a mite dry around here at this time of year, so please be careful.

"The firewood is stacked over there by the cabin. The outhouse and water pumps are behind the cabin. Keep in mind, there's no electricity, so you'll have to pump your water by hand. The only other water supply is the rain barrel at the far end of the cabin. It has a spout in it that is connected to the gutters on the roof. I wouldn't recommend drinking that water, but it is adequate for extinguishing your campfires and for bathing. You could also bathe in the nearby pond. You'll find that on the map as well."

Jimmy look at his watch. "Well, folks, I'll need to head back in order to make it before dark."

Billie extended her hand. "Thank you for everything, Jimmy. We're looking forward to spending a relaxing week here."

Jimmy mounted his horse and pushed his hat down onto his head. "I hope you folks have a good week. Oh, and look me up at the end of your vacation. I will be the one seeing to your horses when you return. Have a great week!"

Jimmy rode away and left them standing in the middle of a large pile of luggage on the front porch of the cabin with the sun slowly setting in the western sky.

"Okay," Cat said, enthusiastically. "We'll be out of daylight before we know it, so maybe we should get the luggage inside and unpacked."

"Sounds good to me." Billie grabbed her own suitcase and urged her children to do the same before she pushed the door to the cabin open and stepped inside. Once inside, she struggled to see, as the interior of the small cabin was darkened by curtains drawn over every window. "Cat," she called, "Which suitcase is the lantern in? We can get a little more daylight by drawing back the curtains, but it will be dark soon, so we'll need it once the sun sets."

"I'm not really sure. I think it's in the largest one." Cat dragged her own bags in and dropped them onto the floor. "Wow! It's really dark in here," she observed.

"I'll take care of that in just a minute." Billie felt around inside the largest suitcase for the propane lantern and found it completely by feel. "Here it is. Now if I can find the matches, we'll be in good shape."

"Some campers we are!" exclaimed Tara as she waited impatiently for light before even daring to venture too far into the cabin.

"Hold on." Cat rummaged through her backpack. "Here." She handed the box of stick matches to Billie. "I knew I packed them in here."

Within seconds, the lantern came to life and cast a warm glow over the interior of the cabin. Each member of the family was awestruck as the quaint atmosphere of the dwelling came to life.

"Wow! This is cool!" Seth exclaimed. The room was dominated on one end by a large fireplace, in front of which, a bear rug covered the floor. "It feels just like a hunting lodge!"

Skylar spotted the bunk beds in the corner next to the fireplace. She ran toward them and threw her pack up and over the rail. "I claim the top bunk!"

As it turned out, there were two sets of bunks, one on each side of the fireplace and a double bed at the opposite end of the room. All of the beds were rustic in style with stuffed feather mattresses and handcrafted quilts. The center of the room contained a large wooden table and against the wall opposite the door was a wood stove, used both for cooking and heating the small cabin. Various shelves graced the walls on either side of the stove. As their eyes became used to the subdued light in the room, it was obvious that everything was covered with a thick layer of dust.

Cat looked around. "Well I can see this cabin hasn't been used in a while. All right everyone, before we do anything else, the quilts need to be shaken. Claim your bed and get to work."

Groans were heard all around as the kids dragged their luggage to their respective beds.

"Cat, I think I'll start a campfire so we can at least see what we're doing out there." Billie headed out the door, only to immediately return in a burst of excitement. "Come quick! You've got to see this!" she exclaimed.

Eager to avoid housekeeping chores, the kids immediately dropped their quilts where they stood and ran toward the door.

"Hey!" Cat exclaimed as her offspring deserted her. Since she was unable to stop the stampede toward the door, Cat dropped her quilt onto the bed and followed. She hastened her steps as sounds of wonder and excitement reached her ears.

Finally, the family stood on the front porch, spellbound by the fiery red glow that filled the entire sky before them.

Cat made her way to Billie and stood by her side. Billie's arm instinctively draped around her shoulder and drew her close. "Oh, my God!" Cat whispered softly as a sense of serenity filled her soul. "It's beautiful, Billie."

"It's times like this that I realize how insignificant each of us is compared to the power of nature," Billie replied.

They stood on the porch and watched as the sun slowly dipped over the horizon and dragged the amazing light show with it. Soon their silhouettes were all that was left, backlit by the soft glow of the lantern emanating from the open cabin door.

Feeling overwhelmed, Cat wrapped her arms around Billie's waist and accepted a hug from her wife who kissed her gently on top of the head. "It's too bad the power of nature can't do the dusting for us," Billie said dryly.

"Ah!" Cat exclaimed. "You're right! Okay troops, back to work!"

A chorus of groans followed her into the cabin.

*** 

With a little elbow grease and a lot of complaints, the Charland clan managed to make the small cabin comfortably clean. After they unpacked their personal items and settled in, they gathered around the campfire that Billie had so diligently built in the yard in front of the cabin. Using a makeshift torch for light, Billie and Seth rummaged through the tack shed until they found some rustic benches made from boards and wood stumps, which they dragged out and arranged in a circular fashion around the fire. While Billie and Seth worked to provide seating, Cat, Tara and Skylar used the propane lantern to search the edge of the nearby woods for sticks to toast marshmallows.

Finally, with chores complete, the family sat around the fire and enjoyed s'mores while they excitedly made plans for the upcoming week. With six days ahead of them, they decided to stay close to the cabin for the first day and to take short jaunts to go fishing and exploring. After that, they would include trips to

Old Faithful, Custer's Battlefield, the Devil's Tower and the Grand Teton National Park. Weather permitting, they would also go kayaking and hiking. All of these plans would be worked in around Skylar's Junior Ranger program, which required one full day of organized activities with the park ranger staff, as well as several tasks she had to complete on her own in order to earn her Junior Ranger badge.

Seth focused intently on browning a marshmallow for his second s'more. When it was ready, he sandwiched it between two graham crackers and chocolate. "Perfect!" he said. "Hey, Mom, we don't have a refrigerator, do we?" Seth said.

"No, we don't," Billie confirmed.

"Drats! I could really use a cold soda with this s'more," he complained.

"Sorry about that, Scout. I guess you'll have to drink water. We brought powdered fruit drink mix, if you'd like to make up a pitcher. The water from the well is pretty cold," Billie suggested.

"Water is okay." Seth rose to his feet and looked around. "Anyone else want some?"

A chorus of 'I do's!' rang out from around the campfire.

"I'll give you a hand, sweetie." Cat picked up the lantern and followed her son into the cabin, leaving her three girls sitting around the fire.

"Mom?" Tara asked. "You said the water in the well is really cold?"

"Yes it is. I guess there's a natural spring that runs under the property," Billie responded.

"It's gonna be kind of cold taking a bath in it," Tara complained.

Billie poked at the fire with her stick. "I've been thinking about that myself," she admitted. "We'll either have to suck it up and brave it, or wait until later in the day and bathe in the pond after the sun warms it up."

"And this is supposed to be a *fun* vacation?" Tara replied sarcastically.

"We can go swimming instead of taking a bath?" Skylar asked hopefully.

"You can go swimming *and* take a bath at the same time," Billie clarified.

"Cool!" Skylar replied, followed by a loud yawn.

"You look tired, rugrat. Why don't you have your fruit drink and then climb into bed?" Billie suggested.

"But it's dark in the cabin," Skylar complained.

"I'll tell you what. I'll start a small fire in the fireplace and then you can lie in your bed on the top bunk and make shadow puppets on the ceiling with your fingers. How's that sound?"

"Will you and Mama be in soon?" She yawned once more.

"Very soon." Billie rose and extended a hand to her younger daughter. Wanna help me make the fire?" she asked.

"Sure!"

"I'll be back in a minute or two, Tare. Okay?"

Tara stared into the fire and only nodded her head in acknowledgment.

A slight frown crossed Billie's features in reaction to the teenager's indifference as she first led Skylar to the outhouse, and then into the cabin. Once inside, she took Cat aside and confided in her about Tara's odd behavior.

"She seems pretty preoccupied, Cat," Billie explained.

"Yeah, I noticed that myself. She hasn't really had a very positive attitude since we left home."

Seth stood nearby, well within earshot while he stirred the fruit juice.

"She'll be fine in a day or two," Seth offered.

Cat and Billie looked quickly at their son

"Do you know something we don't know?" Cat asked.

Seth looked at the pitcher and avoided his mothers' eyes while he stirred the contents. "I just know that she'll be fine. You'll see," he added.

Billie looked at Cat. "Maybe I should take this chance to talk to her," she suggested.

"Maybe," Cat replied. She turned to her son. "Seth, do you mind staying inside for a while so Mom can talk to Tara?" she asked.

"No, I guess not," he said.

Billie placed her hand on her son's shoulder. "I was going to start a small fire in the fireplace for Skylar. Would you mind doing that for me, Scout?"

Seth nodded.

"Thanks, honey." Billie grabbed a glass of juice for Tara, and one for herself. She turned toward the door before looking back at her son. "And Seth, don't worry, I'll go easy on her. I just want to be sure she's okay."

Seth just nodded and watched his mother exit the cabin.

\*\*\*

"Here you go, Tara." Billie handed the glass of juice to her daughter.

"Thanks, Mom." Tara watched Billie sit next to her.

Mother and daughter stared at the fire in silence as they sipped their juice.

Long moments passed without a word between them until finally, Billie broke the impasse. "Tara, are you feeling okay?" she asked softly.

Tara replied without looking at her mother. "I'm fine, Mom."

"Are you sure? You seem a little preoccupied." Billie poked at the fire with her stick.

"I'm sure." Tara fell silent once more.

"Mama is worried about you, and to be truthful, I guess I am too, just not in the same way Mama is."

Billie's comment caught the teenager's attention. "What do you mean?" Tara asked.

Billie thought for a moment before she answered. She wanted to say the right thing to avoid alienating the girl. "Well, we've kind of noticed a change in you over the past few months. We'd like to chalk it up to puberty, but I think it's more than that," Billie began.

Tara held up her hand to her mother. "Please don't tell me we're going to have another 'talk'!" she exclaimed. "That discussion about the birds and the bees when I first started my period was really embarrassing!"

Billie chuckled. "No, I won't torture either of us with that again."

"Thank God!" Tara said.

"So, like I was saying, we've noticed a change in you, and we've got a pretty good idea what's causing it."

Tara looked at her mother with unspoken anguish lurking just behind her eyes. She wanted desperately to talk to Billie about the tangle of emotions that were running amok within her chest, but she so didn't know how to start.

Billie cupped Tara's chin in her hand. "Sweetie," she said. "You know you can talk to me about anything, right? You can talk to *both* of us."

Tara nodded. Her eyes began to brim with unshed tears.

"You know we love you unconditionally, and there is never anything you could do to change that, right?" Billie asked.

Once again Tara nodded, only this time, a lone tear escaped and rolled down her cheek.

Billie smiled. "Good," she said. "Now, why don't you talk to me about Kelly."

Tara pulled her chin out of Billie's grasp and looked at the fire. She blinked rapidly as tears cascaded down her cheeks. Billie slid down the bench, closer to Tara and placed a comforting arm around the girl. Tara rested her head on Billie's shoulder and she released the emotion and confusion that she had pent up inside for several days.

For several long moments, Billie waited patiently for Tara to speak. When it became obvious the child was unable to start the conversation, Billie decided to speak for her.

"It's real tough to talk about, huh?" Billie squeezed Tara's shoulder gently.

Tara nodded and wiped the tears from her cheeks with the back of her hand before she cast a pathetic look in her mother's direction. The pain and confusion on Tara's face mirrored what Billie felt in her own heart for the girl.

"Let's see if I can help you out," Billie said. She paused for a moment to gather her thoughts before she began to speak. "Whenever Kelly is with you...whenever you speak to her on the phone...whenever you even *think* about her, this overwhelming anxious feeling fills your gut. You become light-headed. Your breathing becomes labored. Your heart feels like it's beating out of your chest. You find yourself thinking about her day and night. Every little thing reminds you of her. Sometimes you want to *be* her." Billie paused to look at her daughter. "Am I close?"

Tara wiped her eyes again and nodded rapidly, all the while keeping her eyes glued to the fire.

"You miss her, don't you, Tara?" Billie prompted.

Once again, Tara nodded rapidly, only this time, she spared a glance at her mother. "How do you know all this?" she asked.

"Because eleven years ago, your mother walked into my aerobics class and by the time the class was over, I was feeling the same way about her that you are feeling about Kelly right now," Billie explained.

"Does it get any better?" Tara asked hopefully.

Billie smiled and nodded. "Yes, it gets better. I have to admit that I still have moments like that sometimes, but for the most part, the out of control feelings are pretty much gone. Luckily though, your mom still has the power to turn my insides to mush!" Billie laughed.

"I know what you mean." Tara sniffed loudly. "Kelly's turned my world upside down. I can't eat. I can't sleep. Heck, I didn't want to come on this vacation because of her. I wouldn't be here right now if she hadn't made me promise to go. I miss her like crazy," Tara admitted.

"Does she know?" Billie asked.

"Yeah, and funny thing is, she feels the same way," Tara replied and then quickly added, "We've decided to take things slow. We're both kinda freaked out about it."

Billie smiled and nodded her approval at the girls' approach to their new relationship.

Several moments passed as mother and daughter stared at the fire. Finally, Tara broke the silence.

"Are you mad?" she asked.

Billie looked at her daughter and smiled in reassurance. "No, I'm not mad. I am hoping like crazy that you don't end up hurt, but I'm not mad. I can't make a decision like this for you, Tara. Only you can do that. I can only support you and give you the love and guidance you need," she explained.

"Seth said Mama is pretty upset about it."

Billie once again took Tara's chin in hand. "Mama is worried about you, Tara. She's not upset, she's just worried."

"Why?" Tara was clearly confused.

"She's afraid you'll become the next Matthew Shepard. She's scared to death that you'll be ridiculed or worse because of your preferences."

"Doesn't she want me to be happy? I would think *she* of all people, would understand!" Tara exclaimed.

"Oh, she understands, Tara. She understands much more than you know," Billie replied. "She wants you to be happy, Honey. She would give her life for your happiness, but she also knows how nasty the world can be sometimes. She's lived it, and she is terrified that someday you might find out for yourself how bad it can be."

"I don't want to become another Matthew Shepard either, but I can't live my entire life being afraid. I can take care of myself, Mom," Tara said defensively.

"I know you can, sweetheart, but that won't stop Mama—or me for that matter—from worrying about you. You are very special to both of us. We love you dearly and neither of us wants to see you hurt, emotionally or physically. Do you understand?"

Tara held eye contact with her mother for several long moments as she read the truth of Billie's words in her eyes. Finally, Tara laid her head once more on Billie's shoulder as they both watched the fire in silence.

Unknown to mother and daughter, Cat had quietly made her way onto the porch and stood silently in the shadows as she listened to their conversation. As the discussion ended and the fire reduced to embers, Cat closed her eyes and allowed tears of relief to flood her own cheeks. Somehow, hearing the truth had lifted the anxiety that had plagued her soul while the truth had been mere speculation. Knowing the truth and seeing Tara deal with it in a mature manner gave her peace of mind and a resolve to be loving and supportive of her daughter, no matter what.

***

After the conversation by the campfire ended, Cat quietly made her way back inside before Billie or Tara realized she was there. Seth, who sat at the table playing Solitaire by lantern light, looked up in anticipation as he searched for a positive sign on his mother's face. "Everything all right?" he asked.

Cat approached her son and took his face between her hands. "Everything is fine, just like you said it would be," she replied. She kissed him on the forehead.

Seth nodded and smiled as his attention was drawn once more to Tara's entrance.

"Mom, do we have any writing paper?" Tara asked the moment she was inside. "I told Kelly I would keep a journal for her."

"Sure, Honey. That's a great idea. Let me get it for you." Cat rummaged through her backpack and retrieved the writing pad and a pen. She placed it on the table in front of her daughter. "Say hi to Kelly for us, okay?"

Tara sat next to Seth and smiled at her mother. "Sure!" she replied brightly and then began to write.

Cat noticed that Billie had not come into the cabin behind Tara. "Where's Mom?"

"She's putting the fire out. She said she'll be in soon," Tara replied without looking up.

Cat didn't wait for her to come inside. Instead, she slipped out of the cabin into the darkness of the night. She quickly located Billie crouched by the fire where she was stirring the embers into cold ashes. Billie stood as she heard Cat's approach, and turned to take her into her arms.

"Everything will be all right, Cat," she said. "Our daughter will be fine."

"I know she will, Billie. I was there, on the porch. I heard the entire conversation. Thank you for loving her, Billie. She is so lucky to have you in her life," Cat replied sincerely.

"I am the lucky one, Cat," Billie replied. "I am humbled by her wisdom at such an early age. You've done a good job raising her."

"*We* have done a good job, Billie. *Both* of us, and if truth be known, she is much more like you than she is like me," Cat pointed out.

Billie smiled and lowered her head for a kiss. "I love you," she said softly.

"I love you too, Big Guy," Cat answered. "Now douse this fire so we can hit the sheets. I'm beat!"

# CHAPTER 9

Billie rolled over and opened her eyes. There before her, a few inches away, was the woman of her dreams. But something was different. Something was out of sorts. Something was unfamiliar. The faint aroma of campfire registered on her consciousness and her logical mind sought to justify its existence. *Campfire?* she wondered to herself. Billie closed her eyes again and allowed memories of the previous day to replace the cobwebs sleep had left behind.

*Horses. Campfire. Blazing sunset.* Such were the thoughts that crossed Billie's mind as she smiled broadly and then opened her eyes once more; only this time to look into the depths of pastel green looking back at her.

"Good morning," Cat whispered softly.

Billie kissed her wife. "Good morning to you, my love," she replied.

"You smell like a campfire." Cat sniffed Billie's hair. "I love that smell."

Billie grinned. "I was just thinking the same. I guess I should take a bath, huh?"

A mischievous grin crossed Cat's face. "A bath sounds good," she replied. "A bath in the pond. No kids. All alone. Just you and I. And nature. And a bar of soap," she said enticingly.

Billie's eyes opened wide and she thought of just what they could do with that bar of soap.

Billie threw off the covers and swung her legs over the side of the bed. "I'll grab the towels."

Soon, the ladies made their way hand in hand, down the well-worn path to the pond. Billie carried the towels, while Cat carried a bag with toiletries and a change of clothing for each of them.

When they reached the side of the pond, Billie draped the towels over a sturdy bush and then unceremoniously stripped off her clothes. She threw them on the ground next to where Cat placed their bag. Cat was a little more cautious. She looked around carefully before she removed her clothing and added them to the growing pile started by Billie. While Cat undressed, Billie reached into the bag and retrieved their bottle of shampoo and the bar of soap. She offered her hand to Cat and led her into the water.

"Damn, this is cold!" Cat exclaimed. The cool water immediate caused a wave of goose-bumps to parade across Cat's skin, not to mention, the temperature change immediately commanded two very enticing peaks to stand at attention.

"Oh, yeah!" Billie's sight was immediately drawn to a certain part of Cat's anatomy and her eyebrows danced wickedly on her forehead.

Cat noticed where Billie's eyes were directed and she splashed the cold water across Billie's stomach. "Take that!" she said.

Billie gasped for breath. "Why you...I'll tell you what I'll take, you little imp!" Billie replied haltingly and struggled to regain the breath the cold water had taken away. Billie lunged forward, caught Cat around the waist and immediately submerged both of them beneath the surface of the pond. The shampoo bottle and bar of soap flew in separate directions as the two bodies impacted the water.

Cat resurfaced immediately. "Oh! My! God! Billie Jean Charland, that was mean!" She furiously rubbed her hands up and down her arms in an attempt to regain some of the warmth the sudden immersion had chased away.

"C'mere," Billie said. "I'll warm you up."

Cat waded toward Billie. A pout was planted firmly on her face. She walked into the circle of Billie's arms.

Billie tried to hide a smile as she wrapped long arms around Cat and rubbed her hands across her back.

"It's nnooot wwworking." Shivers caused Cat's words to exit her mouth in staccato.

Billie noticed the shampoo and soap floating lazily nearby. She reached for the soap and rubbed the bar between her hands until a rich lather formed. She dropped the bar back into the water and ran her soapy hands up and down Cat's back as Cat moaned out her pleasure.

"God, Billie. That feels good."

Billie turned Cat around so she was facing away from her and then pulled her body close to hers. The layer of soapy lather that now covered Cat's back created a very slippery and stimulating surface between them. Billie ground herself into Cat's back and reached for the floating soap once more. Within moments, she dropped the soap back into the water for a second time and snaked soapy hands around the front of Cat, only to begin a very thorough exploration of her breasts.

Cat rested the back of her head on Billie's shoulder and closed her eyes. "Do you have any idea what you're doing to me?" Shudders wracked Cat's body.

"I know *exactly* what I'm doing to you," Billie whispered into Cat's ear. She continued to grind herself into Cat's back and gently nipped at her neck. She then slid one soapy hand between Cat's legs, while the other held one ripe nipple between soapy fingers. She periodically pinched the tender nub and sent bolts of desire into Cat's core.

"Ah. Billie. Umm," Cat began a rocking motion against Billie's hand.

Billie matched Cat's motion and the two bodies swayed in one rhythm. Within moments, the rhythm increased as Cat neared climax. Billie's ardor rose nearly out of control with every bump and grind. When she felt Cat was nearly at her peak, she slipped her free hand between her own legs and assisted herself to climax as she and Cat plunged into the waves of fulfillment together.

Barely able to stand, Billie turned Cat around and lowered both of them up to their necks into the water. The ladies clung to each other and traded tender kisses and words of love.

By the time they regained their strength, their bodies had acclimated to the cool water and they were able to bathe and then return to the cabin to rouse the children from sleep and start their day with a hearty breakfast.

\*\*\*

"All right everyone. Rise and shine. No sleepyheads on this vacation!" Cat threw open the drapes and allowed sunlight to flood the rustic cabin.

"Aw, Ma! We're on vacation. Let us sleep!" Seth pulled the covers over his head.

"Nope! It's beautiful outside! Mom and I have already taken our baths in the pond, so if you want to clean up before breakfast, you'd better get moving!"

Tara sat up in bed and rubbed her eyes. "Is the water cold?" she asked.

"A little, but you'll get used to it quickly." Cat avoided the sly grin on Billie's face.

Skylar looked over the side of the bunk at her older sister. "Can I go with you, Tare?" she asked.

"Yeah, I guess. Come on." Tara grabbed her backpack and shoved a change of clothes into it.

A few minutes later, toiletries and towels in hand, the girls headed out the door.

"Stay close to shore, girls!" Billie called after them from the porch as they sprinted down the path. She reentered the cabin and noticed Seth was still in bed. "Roll it on out there, Scout. If you hurry, you can bathe in the rain barrel before your sisters come back."

"Nah. I think I'll wait for the girls to come back then I'll go take a swim too." Seth burrowed deeper into his covers to catch a few more minutes of sleep.

"Well, it will have to be a quick swim or you'll miss breakfast," Cat pointed out. "It will be ready at about the same time the girls return."

Always eager to eat, Seth threw off his covers. "On second thought, that rain barrel sounds pretty good to me."

\*\*\*

"Eggs are up," Cat called from her position at the campfire. She picked up the plate of bacon that was warming on the stone fire ring and carried it, and the pan of scrambled eggs to the picnic table where everyone anxiously awaited breakfast. Within moments, the food was dished out and everyone dove in.

"I propose we explore the park's geysers today," Billie suggested. "What do you all think?"

"Will that include Old Faithful?" Seth asked. "The pamphlet says it erupts almost two dozen times a day."

"What is a geezer?" Skylar asked.

"Geyser, Einstein...not geezer," Tara teased.

"Tara, be nice," Cat said. "Sky, a geyser is caused by ground water being heated up by volcanic activity under the ground. When it becomes hot enough, it kind of boils to the surface, and sometimes it comes up pretty violently and shoots water a hundred feet into the air."

"That sounds cool," Skylar said.

"Actually, it's hot. Ha! I crack me up!" Seth joked.

Billie shook her head and tried hard to hide her grin. "Very funny, Seth. So, it sounds like geysers today then." Billie opened the park map and spread it out on the table in front of her. "Let's see, it looks like the closest geyser to us is in Upper Geyser Basin. That's the one with Old Faithful in it."

"Yes!" Seth pumped his fist in the air.

Billie high-five'd her son. "Eat up, crew. The sooner we finish breakfast, the sooner we can explore."

"Take care of your plate when you're finished eating. Don't forget—all trash goes into the rubbish bag. We need to carry out whatever we carried in," Cat reminded the family.

After breakfast, they saddled the horses and set out toward the Upper Geyser Basin. As they approached the Old Faithful area, they dismounted and left their horses at the stable in order to cover on foot, the one hundred and fifty or so hydrothermal wonders that were within one mile of Old Faithful.

As luck would have it, they arrived at Old Faithful just minutes before it was predicted to erupt. The family stood behind the rope barrier and waited in anticipation as a low rumbling began. It grew louder and louder, until suddenly, a small spray of water began to shoot into the air from a mound several hundred yards in front of them. As they patiently waited, the spray grew larger and taller. Before their eyes, Old Faithful awoke from its slumber and spewed warm water high into the air; some of it falling as a fine warm mist on the tourists who clapped and exclaimed loudly at the magnificent display.

Cat stood beside Billie while Old Faithful erupted. As the momentum built, Cat slipped her arm around Billie's waist and Billie wrapped her arm around Cat's shoulder. "It's breathtaking, Billie. Thank you for suggesting this," Cat said.

Billie grinned. "Look at the kids. They are totally mesmerized." Sure enough, all three kids stood as close to the barrier as possible with their gazes locked on the column of water spraying from the geyser. After about five minutes, the height of the spray reduced, and eventually stopped.

"That was freaking awesome!" Seth exclaimed. "Can we see it again?"

"Yes! Can we, Mama?" Skylar added.

"With any luck, it will be due to erupt again on our way back, but right now, there's a lot more to see," Cat replied.

"Tara, what's next on the map?" Billie asked.

Tara pulled the folded map from her back pocket. "It looks like Lower Geyser Basin. It says here there are 'paint pots' there."

"Well, you've got the map, sweetie. Lead on," Billie said.

After a short walk, the family arrived at the boardwalk that led through the paint pots.

"Ewww! Who farted?" Skylar exclaimed.

Cat laughed out loud. "Those aren't farts you smell, love. It's sulfur gas."

"It smells like the bathroom after Seth has been in there for an hour," Tara teased.

"Ha, ha," Seth deadpanned.

"No, Mama is right. It's sulfur gas that is coming out of the ground," Billie added. "See all the mud on both sides of the boardwalk? Some of it looks like it's boiling. That's a sulfur gas bubble breaking the surface."

"The ground farts?" Skylar asked seriously.

"The mud does kind of look like diarrhea," Seth observed.

"You would know," Tara said.

"Ok, time out," Cat said. "We're supposed to be on vacation. Can we take a break from the snippy comments as well for a few days?"

"Yeah, Seth," Tara said.

"You started it," Seth replied.

"Enough!" Billie said sternly. "Like it or not, we are going to enjoy this vacation! You got that?"

"Mom, why does the ground fart?" Skylar asked.

Second only to Old Faithful, the highlight of Midway Geyser Basin was Excelsior Geyser, sporting a crater two hundred by three hundred feet in size, which spews a constant discharge of water—more than four thousand gallons per minute. Also in Midway was Grand Prismatic Springs—a natural hot spring as wide as a football field, and nearly half as deep. Finally, the last basin within walking distance was Lone Star Geyser Basin which required a five-mile round trip hike from the trail just south of Old Faithful.

By the time the family returned to the Old Faithful site, more than half the day had passed.

"All right. We can check the geysers off the list. What did you think?" Billie asked.

"So, all of these geysers are sitting on top of a volcano, right?" Tara asked.

"Right. The hot water needs an outlet because it builds up pressure. Sometimes the outlet is a steam crack, sometimes it's a hot spring or a mud pot, or even a geyser," Billie explained.

"What do you think would happen if the volcano actually erupted?" Tara added.

"We'd all be toast," Seth replied.

"Actually, all of these geological features are the result of pressure valves for the volcano. As long as the geysers erupt, the pressure is released. I don't think there's much chance of an actual volcanic eruption similar to what you might see in say…Hawaii," Cat explained.

"I thought it was cool—except for the fart smell," Skylar said.

Billie ruffled Skylar's hair. "I agree, dumpling."

Cat looked at her watch. "It's only one o'clock. We can either go back to the cabin, or find something else to do. What do you say?"

"I vote we find something else to do," Seth said.

"Me too!" the two girls said at the same time.

"Okay. Cat, come here. I want to get the pamphlets from your back pack," Billie said. She retrieved the pamphlets and handed one to each of the kids. "Mama and I are going to sit over there on that bench while you three agree on what to do next…oh, and make sure Sky gets a vote too, okay?"

"Keep in mind that we need to return here around four for the ride back to the cabin before dark," Cat reminded them.

Billie and Cat walked several feet away and sat on a bench, not far from Old Faithful while the kids put their heads together to discuss the next round of activities.

"What is it about Seth and Tara?" Cat asked.

Billie raised her eyebrows high onto her forehead. "What do you mean?"

"Earlier in the trip, they were like best friends. Now, they've been nit-picking each other all morning."

"Well, it's not often they're forced to spend this much time together without their electronic devices."

"Isn't it funny though that when Seth thought you and I were upset with Tara, he immediately came to her defense, but when it's an even playing field, they rag on each other?" Cat pointed out.

Billie laughed. "I see your point. It might be one of those things…you know…he can pick on her, but he won't allow anyone else to. I wasn't raised with siblings, so I don't have anything to compare it to. What about you and your sisters?"

"We fought like cats and dogs. At least Amy and Bridgit did. Drew was the baby, and too young to get into it with the rest of us. My role was to keep the peace. But now that you mention it, I can remember Amy decking a few kids in the playground at school who were mean to Bridgit or me. I guess it's just a sibling thing."

"It warms my heart that Seth and Tara are as close as biological siblings," Billie said.

"I agree. Overall, they're pretty good kids. Oh—here they come."

The kids ran across the viewing area at the Old Faithful geyser and stopped in front of their parents.

"Do we have a consensus?" Billie asked.

"We do. We want to go to Jackson Hole," Seth said.

Cat tilted her head. "What's in Jackson Hole?"

"A wax museum and it says in this pamphlet that there is an old time opry. That might be cool," Tara added.

"And we're hungry," Skylar said. "Maybe there is a good restaurant there."

Billie laughed out loud. "Leave it to you to let your stomach do your talking for you, Sky!"

"Jackson Hole it is," Cat said. "We'll have to walk over to the stables to get the van. Let's get a move on, kiddos. We need to be back by four."

As it turned out, the family returned to the park with plenty of time to spare as they rode into their campsite about a half hour before sunset, with just enough time to care for and feed the horses before they lost daylight. Having eaten before leaving

Jackson Hole, a light snack around the campfire was enough to satisfy their appetites before retiring for the night.

The three younger Charlands were beat from their day of hiking and exploring and eagerly retired to their beds just before midnight. Cat and Billie chose to sit by the fire as the last of the wood died to glowing embers and made sure the fire was totally extinguished prior to retiring themselves. They sat side by side on their bench as they watched the red-gold flames dance just above the wood.

Billie reached out for Cat's hand and brought it to her lips for a delicate kiss. "Thank you, Cat." Billie smiled into her wife's eyes.

Cat raised her eyebrows in question. "For what?"

"For being here with me. For loving me. For giving me the kind of life I never would have known without you," Billie replied.

Cat frowned and reached forward to tuck a stray lock of hair behind Billie's ear. "Are you all right, love?" she asked.

"Never better. It's just that being here with you and the kids makes me appreciate what we have. We are truly blessed, Cat."

"Yes we are." Cat leaned over to accept a kiss. "Now what do you say we extinguish this fire and turn in. These old bones aren't used to walking and hiking all day. I'm kind of beat," she admitted.

"Old bones? I'm older than you are, dear heart," Billie teased.

"Yeah, but you're in better shape," Cat pointed out.

"That comes from chasing Jen through the park every Sunday!" Billie chuckled. "You should join us. It might do you some good."

"Nah. I like my sleep too much to get up that early. I'll leave chasing Jen to you, okay?"

Billie touched the side of Cat's face. "The only lady *I* want to be chasing is you."

Cat laughed. "Well, that wouldn't be much of a challenge, considering you've already caught me!"

"And I'm never letting you go. After all, who else would guarantee me a disaster-free vacation?" Billie asked.

"Who, indeed?" Cat yawned loudly.

"It *has* been great, Cat. Even having to use an outhouse hasn't been that bad, and I kind of enjoyed bathing in the pond this morning." Billie's eyebrows danced on her forehead.

"You, my love, are insatiable," Cat scolded light heartedly.

"Are you complaining?"

"Me? Complain? Not me. No way. Insatiable is good." Cat effectively backpedaled. Unable to stop herself, she yawned once more.

"Okay, Kitten, go on inside. Get ready for bed. I'll be right in after I soak the fire," Billie replied.

Cat yawned yet a third time as she rose to her feet. "Don't be long, my love," she said softly.

"I won't." Billie watched Cat retreated to the cabin. A feeling a well-being filled her heart at the good fortune love had brought into her life.

# CHAPTER 10

Billie and Cat roused the children out of bed early as not to waste a moment of their vacation oversleeping.

Billie looked around the breakfast table. "What would you kids like to do today?"

"I don't know." Tara yawned. "Maybe kayaking?" she suggested sleepily.

"I was thinking maybe some hiking," Seth offered. "After I wake up, that is."

"I have my Junior Ranger class today, Mom," Skylar reminded her mother. "I think it's at ten."

Billie looked at Cat. Slight worry etched her brow as it became obvious their three children's plans for the day took them in opposite directions. Billie had promised the kids an enjoyable vacation and she didn't want to dash any of their hopes, so she took Cat aside and discussed possible workarounds with her privately.

"I think I have an idea about how we can satisfy everyone's plans, well, maybe anyway. It depends on what *you'd* like to do today," Billie began.

"What *I'd* like to do? What do you mean?" Cat asked.

"Well, I'm thinking that one of us can kayak with Tara, and the other can hike with Seth. Sky's meeting place for the Junior Ranger program isn't that far from the kayak depot, so she can be dropped off and picked up on the way. What do you think?"

"I guess that makes sense," Cat admitted. "What would *you* rather do today, kayak or hike?"

"It doesn't matter to me."

"Okay then. Do you have a coin?" Cat asked.

Billie dug a quarter out of her pocket and handed it over to Cat who immediately flipped it into the air. She caught the coin and slapped it down onto the back of her left hand and covered it with her right.

"Whoever calls it goes kayaking," Cat declared. "You first."

"Heads," Billie called.

Cat removed her right hand from the quarter. "Heads it is! You kayak, I hike. That works for me." Cat grinned, as hiking was her true preference.

"All right then. Let's tell the kids," Billie said.

The kids were more than agreeable with the compromise arrangement. Billie and Tara inherited the job of dropping Skylar off at the Junior Ranger program so they all had to leave almost immediately to get Skylar there by ten after a nearly two-hour horse ride. Before leaving, Cat and Billie worked together to package a quick lunch for their tribe to take to their respective activities. Within minutes, Billie, Tara and Skylar were mounted on horseback and on their way.

"Have fun and be careful! I love you," Cat called to her wife and daughters as they rode away.

***

Cat found room in her backpack for their lunch and zipped it closed. She slung it over her shoulder and stepped onto the porch. "Seth, are you ready?" she called.

"Sure thing, Ma. I saddled our horses. Here, let me help you up." Seth held her mount steady as she swung herself onto the saddle.

"Thanks love."

"Did you grab the survival kit?"

Cat reached into the backpack and pulled out a compact package. "Knife, first aid kit, compass, thermal blanket, mirror, candle, matches, collapsible shovel. Yes, I have it. Not that we'll need it, mind you, but yes, it's in here." She stored it carefully away in the backpack and swung it onto her back once more.

Seth mounted his own horse and grabbed the reins. "At least we have good weather for this," he said.

Cat looked at the sky. "I was thinking that same thing. No sign of rain today and it's supposed to be in the eighties. That's a good thing, for us...and for Mom and Tara. I think we're dressed warmly enough." Cat looked at the shorts, Tees and hiking boots both she and her son were wearing. "I brought hoodies for us if we need them later. Are you ready?"

"Yup! Lead the way," Seth replied.

Within moments, they galloped through the fields toward the trailheads they had marked on the map. When they collected the maps, Cat took the time to discuss the various trails with the park ranger, and learned there were several grades of trails available to them in the park. Prior to setting out that morning, she and Seth agreed to hike the Shoshone Lake Trail; a moderate seventeen-mile round-trip trek that crossed the Continental Divide at Grant's Pass.

About a half-hour into their ride, they reached the edge of the woods where they released their horses into the nearby paddock. Cat wrote their names into the visitor register and then grabbed a trail guide. Moments later, they set out on foot down the well-worn path.

Just inside the line of trees that bordered the pasture, Seth stopped and looked at Cat. "Let me know at any time if you need to stop."

Cat looked at him coyly. "Are you worried I won't be able to keep up with you?"

Seth hip-checked his mother. "Well, you *are* old."

"You little imp. I'll give you old! Let's just see who taps out first."

"You're on!"

"Let's put a wager on this. Whoever calls a rest stop first has to make the bed of the winner for the rest of the vacation," Cat suggested.

Seth extended his hand. "Deal. I generally like to sleep in, so you'll have to stand by until I'm out of bed each morning."

Cat shook his hand. "Pretty sure of yourself, aren't you?"

"Absolutely."

Cat chuckled at the mischievous glint in Seth's eyes. "We'll see about that."

A short distance into the woods, they scoured the sides of the trail for walking sticks and managed to find suitable ones for both of them. The Shoshone Lake Trail had no boardwalks and was rated at a moderate difficulty level. According to the trail guide, moderate trails fluctuated between periods of level walking, inclines of varying slopes, and steep rock climbing. The ever-changing terrain reminded Cat of interval training programs at the gym.

At several points along the trail, Seth stopped and waited for Cat to catch up, and even offered assistance to help her climb the steeper grades. One particular climb was over the tops of large boulders that ascended about a quarter of a mile upward. She found herself thanking God that Seth was with her, as she relied on him several times to assist her over that leg of the hike. By the time they reached the top, she was exhausted.

Cat sat on a nearby boulder. "Okay, I know I'm going to lose the bet, but I've got to stop. These old bones can't take much more without rest!" She was so sore she secretly wished she had won the coin toss and a day of kayaking with Tara.

"Well, you know, we can't all be he-men like me, I guess," Seth flexed his muscles.

"You are certainly your mother's son!" Cat joked.

"Huh?" Seth questioned.

"Never mind. Do me a favor and hand over the backpack, will you, sweetie? I need a drink of water." Cat fished their drinks out of the sack and handed one to Seth.

"Have a seat." Cat patted the rock next to her.

"Don't mind if I do."

"Are you having fun, sweetie?" Cat asked.

"Yeah! This is great," Seth replied. "How about you?"

"This trail is a little tougher than I expected, but it's been great so far," Cat admitted. "I hope your mom and sisters are having a good time."

Seth placed an arm around her shoulder. "I'm sure they are, Ma," he replied. "Thanks for bringing us here. This is really fun."

"I was wondering just how enjoyable this would turn out to be considering the primitive conditions your mother has us living in, but so far it's been okay. Not that I mind. I enjoy primitive camping, but after Happy Trails, I'm surprised Mom was willing to consider camping of *any* kind!" Cat reminisced. A smile graced her features at the memories.

"Actually, I thought Happy Trails was kind of fun...well, except for the poison ivy, that is. Steve and I thought it was pretty cool when the bear devoured our supplies. What I really *could* have lived without, however, was seeing Mom stark naked during the bear attack." Seth grimaced. "A guy seeing his mom naked is *not* cool!"

Cat chuckled. "That certainly was a memorable vacation, wasn't it? I guess I can't blame your mother for not wanting a repeat of *that* nightmare."

"So far, this vacation has been pretty cool. Thanks again for bringing us."

"You're welcome, Scout." Cat rose to her feet and grabbed her walking stick. "So are you up to more hiking, or are you going to let an old lady beat you?"

"I've already won the bet, so I have nothing to lose, but..." Seth stood and bowed at the waist with much fanfare. "Lead on, fair lady."

Cat handed the backpack over to Seth and started once more down the trail.

Seth threw the bag over his shoulders, grabbed his walking stick and followed Cat. A few minutes later, he stopped short. "Ma, did you see that?"

Cat abruptly stopped, turned around and walked back to her son. She looked into the forest in the direction of his gaze. "See what? Is it an animal?"

"No. I thought I saw a flash of light. Over there." Seth pointed to an area about a hundred feet from where they were standing.

"Well, I don't see anything now," Cat said.

Cat and Seth both looked up into the trees for several more minutes without seeing anything unusual.

"Huh. Maybe it was my imagination," Seth admitted.

"Maybe," Cat replied. "In any case, we need to keep moving so we have time to finish the trail and get back to the cabin before dark."

"All right. Let's go." Seth moved one foot forward and then stopped dead for a second time. "There it is again!" he exclaimed.

"I saw it that time," Cat said.

"What was that?" Seth asked.

"I don't know. Maybe heat lightning?" she suggested.

"The lady we talked to at the ranger station yesterday said the weather was supposed to be nice today," Seth replied.

Cat looked at her son. "Don't tell me you're afraid of a little rain," she teased.

"Hey, I might melt! You *know* I'm made of sugar. How else would I be so sweet?" Seth grinned.

"There's no conceit in *this* family, is there? *You've* got it all!" Cat joked.

"It's a tough job, but someone's gotta do it!" Seth laughed and continued to follow his mother down the trail.

***

"Okay, Sky. Tara and I will be back to get you at about four. Do you have your lunch?" Billie checked Skylar's backpack. "Yes, there it is. All right sweetie. Have a great day with the Junior Rangers. We'll see you this afternoon. Okay?"

"Okay, Mom. I gotta go. There's my ranger buddy!" Skylar spotted the new friend she had made when she checked into the Junior Ranger program the day before after their tour of the geysers.

"Have a good time today, love bug. I love you!" Billie called to the girl's retreating back.

Moments later, Billie and Tara were on their horses and heading toward the kayak depot.

"Are you excited, Tare?" Billie asked as they rode along.

"To kayak? Yes, but I still wish Kelly was here. She would have loved to kayak with us."

Billie looked straight ahead as they rode, and fought the feelings of regret that Tara was attempting to plant in her mind...with some degree of success, she acknowledged. "There will be other opportunities to include Kelly in family activities, Tara. This trip is for us."

"I know, but I just miss her so much," Tara whined.

"I can understand that, but it's only for a few days. If a relationship can't survive a few days apart, then it's not much of a relationship."

"I guess so." Tara sulked.

Fifteen minutes later, Billie spotted the depot. "There it is. Oh, and I see the hitching post to the right of the ticket booth."

Billie and Tara hitched their horses and approached the ticket booth, intent on renting two white-water kayaks.

"What do you mean, you're out of singles?" Billie asked the clerk.

"We're out of singles. It's a beautiful day today. Everyone wants to kayak. We have several two-seaters available, but no singles. If you want to wait a while, some singles may come in, but right now, we're all out."

Billie looked at Tara. "What do you think, Tare?"

"I guess it's better than nothing," the teenager replied.

"Okay, then. I guess we'll take a tandem...oh, and we'll need lifejackets and paddles as well."

"Do you want a map?" the clerk asked.

"That would be great," Billie replied. "Is one route better than another? We need to be back around four o'clock."

The clerk opened the map and pointed to the Firehole River. "Take this route here. It has some amazing scenery, and you should be able to get back in time."

"Awesome. Thanks for your help." Billie paid for the kayak rental and collected the map.

The clerk pointed to a building across from the parking lot. "The kayak shed is just over there. You'll find the life jackets and paddles there as well."

Billie and Tara entered the shed and saw two red, tandem kayaks hanging on the wall. They both had fairly large, open cockpits.

"Well, it doesn't look like we'll be doing a lot of rolling in this!" Tara exclaimed in a disappointed tone as she accepted the bright orange life jacket Billie handed to her.

"We still have a few days left of vacation, Tare. We can come back tomorrow or the day after, and with any luck, they'll have a couple of singles. Okay? In the meantime, I'm sure we'll have a good time in this one," Billie said encouragingly.

"Yeah, I guess, but I was looking forward to practicing my rolling skills." Tara threw their back pack into the cockpit.

With Billie on one end and Tara on the other, they lifted the eighteen-foot kayak by the handles and carried it the short distance from the depot to the edge of the river where they carefully slid it into the water. They secured their life jackets tightly and slipped into the seats, with Tara in front and Billie behind, and began to gently paddle away from the shore. Within moments, they fell into a steady pace, gliding freely down the river.

"This is great!" Billie exclaimed. She looked from side to side and enjoyed the feel of nature around her. "Listen, Tara," she said.

They stopped paddling and fell silent as their kayak glided unassisted through the water.

"What am I listening for?" Tara asked. "Did you hear something?"

"Just listen," Billie repeated. "Listen to the sounds of nature."

Tara frowned and she forced herself to listen to the background noise she had ordinarily pushed into her subconscious mind. After a few moments, the sound of nature became a symphony to her ears. Suddenly, she heard the gurgling of water, the whoosh of the wind, chirping birds, chit-chattering crickets and the rustle of dried leaves in the breeze. She turned around in the cockpit and her gaze met Billie's. A look of wonder was evident on her face.

"Wow! I didn't realize how loud it is!" she exclaimed. "I never really heard it before. It's amazing that I could block it all out."

"Cool, huh?" Billie asked.

"*Very* cool!" Tara replied. She turned around and began to paddle once again, but abruptly stopped when she saw a bright flash light up the sky.

"What was that?" Tara looked over her shoulder at Billie.

Billie too was looking at the sky. "I don't know. Maybe heat lightning?" she suggested.

"Is it supposed to rain today?" Tara asked. "It seems too nice to rain."

"I don't think so. The lady at the ranger's office yesterday said it was supposed to be partially sunny and warm. Heck, if it starts to rain, we'll pull over and find shelter until it stops. It might actually cool things down if it *does* rain," Billie speculated.

"It wouldn't hurt my feelings if things cooled down a bit. It's pretty hot out here under the sun," Tara observed.

"Well, let's not worry about it for now. We'll deal with it if, or when it happens, okay?" Billie suggested.

"Sounds like a plan to me!" Tara once more resumed paddling.

For the next hour, mother and daughter paddled in silence. Each enjoyed the solitude of nature as their watercraft stealthily made its way down the meandering river.

# CHAPTER 11

"Jeff, what time have you got?" Jason Richards asked the ranger standing at the opposite side of the observation tower.

Jeff removed the binoculars from his eyes and looked at his watch. "Nearly two o'clock," he answered and then continued to scan the tops of the trees.

"See anything yet?" Jason also scanned the horizon from his side of the tower.

"Nope. Not a thing," Jeff replied.

"Good. Maybe we'll make it through the summer without incident," Jason suggested.

"One can only hope." Jeff lowered his binoculars. "I'm going to make a run to the station for something cold to drink. Can I get you anything?"

"Sure. Bring me back a brewsky."

Jeff raised an eyebrow at Jason.

"Just kidding. A cola would be great. Oh, and maybe a bottle of water too. Thanks, Jeff. I'll hold down the fort while you're gone."

"Okay. I'll be back in a few." Jeff climbed down the three story ladder that led to the observation tower.

From his perch high above the ground, Jason watched his friend and co-worker climb into the Jeep and head down the mountain.

\*\*\*

Cat looked back at her son. "How are you doing, Seth?"

"Fine, Ma. How are *you* doing? Do you need to stop for a while?"

"Well, it probably wouldn't hurt to look at the trail guide." Cat hoped her suggestion came across as believable instead of the ruse it really was to cover up the fact that she did *indeed* need a break.

Finding a level place to stop and rest was not easy. They had been on a relatively steep incline for the past hour. Cat's thighs felt as though they were on fire from the rough climb, and they shook as she forced herself to climb the last few feet to the plateau directly ahead of them.

Seth climbed onto the shelf and sat beside his mother to spread the map across both their laps. "Okay, we've been hiking for about...let's see, four hours now?" Seth looked at his watch. "If my calculations are correct, we should be more than half way through the trail."

"Where exactly are we on this map?" Cat struggled to find their location.

Seth studied the trail guide carefully. "Well, the last marker I can remember seeing was right here." He pointed to a spot that was a significant distance behind them on the map. We should have seen another marker right here." Again, he pointed to a spot about a mile behind where he believed they currently were. "But the marker wasn't there, unless I missed it. Did you see one?" he asked.

"The only marker I've seen is the first one you pointed out," Cat admitted. "Maybe it fell off the tree, or maybe it was vandalized," she suggested. "Or maybe we're lost?" she asked skeptically.

Seth scratched his head. "I hope not. I guess it's possible, but I'm pretty sure we stayed on the trail."

"Well, then maybe we should just forge on ahead. Sooner or later we'll come across another marker," Cat said encouragingly.

"You're probably right," Seth replied. "Are you ready to go, or would you like to rest a little longer?"

"Let's stay a while longer. It's not often I get to spend time with just my son." Cat affectionately rubbed a hand up and down his back.

Seth grinned. "You got that right. There's usually a ton of girls around all the time," he complained. "Sometimes it's tough being the only guy in a household full of girls."

Cat frowned. "Does it bother you to be the only guy, Seth?" she asked.

"Sometimes, but mostly, it's okay. Tara is more like a guy than a girl anyway. Sometimes it's like having a brother," he joked.

Cat agreed and grinned. "Your sister is quite a character, isn't she?"

"Tara is cooler than you know. I like having her for a sister," he admitted. "But don't tell her that! She'll use it against me for weeks!"

"We've been concerned about her, lately. She's been pretty distant with all of us. Knowing about Kelly kind of makes it easier to understand her behavior, but I really wish she'd talk to me more."

"Tara's pretty independent. I wouldn't take it personally. I mean, she talks to Mom."

Cat grabbed her chest. "Ouch! That one hurt! I know she feels more comfortable talking to Mom, but I miss that connection with her. I just want her to know that she can talk to me about anything and I will try very hard not to judge."

"I think she knows that, Ma. It's just that sometimes you form special bonds with one parent over the other. It doesn't mean she loves you any less."

"I know, but...well, I guess I should just be happy that she has Mom...and you, to talk to. It warms my heart to see the bond between the two of you."

"She's a pretty cool sister. I'm glad you and Mom met and we became a family."

Cat cupped the side of Seth's face with her palm. "You're pretty special yourself, Seth," Cat remarked. "It can't be easy growing up in a house full of girls...and being raised by two moms on top of it all!"

"Actually, having two moms has been the best part. I have friends who don't see much of either parent.  It's usually because of work, or because they just don't have time for their kids," Seth said. "I can't remember a time while growing up that you and Mom weren't there. Sure, I didn't have a dad, but then Mom can kick some pretty mean ass when she wants to," he exclaimed.

"Seth Michael Charland! Do you eat with that same dirty mouth?" Cat asked in mock disdain.

Seth threw his head back and laughed. "Ma," he said. "If a dirty mouth was fatal, Grandma Jo would have died of food poisoning years ago!"

Seth's observation sent both of them into peals of laughter as they held their stomachs and chuckled.

Finally, unable to hold it any longer, Cat jumped off her stone perch and crossed her legs. "All that laughing is going to make me wet myself! I've got to pee really badly!" She looked around for a private place to relieve herself.

"Over there, Ma," Seth pointed to an area behind a large rock.

Cat took off like a bat out of hell, as Seth headed in the opposite direction to find a private spot of his own.

Moments later, relieved and refreshed, they met back on the path and collected their belongings.

Cat looked at her watch.  "We should probably get moving. It's already about two o'clock. If we waste too much time, it'll be dark before we get back to the cabin."

"Okay, then. Let's go."

***

"Hey Tare, how about we pull over to the bank and rest a while? I could use a break from the sun," Billie suggested.

"Sure." Tara steered the kayak toward the shore.

Tara scrambled out of the kayak then held it steady for Billie to climb out. Once on shore, Billie pulled the front end of the narrow boat onto the bank and then reached for the backpack behind her seat. She pulled out two bottles of water and offered one to Tara.

"Thanks." Tara eagerly took the water and drank half of the bottle's content before coming up for air.

"Thirsty, huh?" Billie remarked.

"Yeah. I didn't realize how much until now," Tara explained and then fell silent once more.

Billie watched the woman-child for several moments as she appeared preoccupied with something in the distance.

"What 'cha thinking about?" Billie asked.

Tara looked at her mother shyly. "Kelly," she admitted.

"Ah! I see," Billie replied. "It's tough being away from her, huh?"

Tara picked up a stick and doodled in the sand beside her. She nodded her head in reply to Billie's question.

Billie remained quiet and hoped Tara would offer more about her relationship with Kelly.

"Mom, when did you realize you were gay?" Tara asked.

Billie inhaled deeply and carefully contemplated her question. "Well, I guess in some ways I always knew—at least deep down inside. I denied it for a long time, mostly to avoid disappointing my parents," Billie admitted. "I guess I stopped denying it when Seth was born."

"Did you love Seth's father?"

Billie pulled her knees in close and wrapped her arms around them. Before she answered the question, she allowed her gaze to focus on the opposite shore and tried to recall just what she *did* feel for the man who had fathered Seth. Finally, she turned to her daughter.

"In some ways I guess I loved him—or at least I thought it was love." She looked out again over the water. "I met Brian while in college. He was very handsome, and very popular, not to mention quite charming. I wouldn't say I was attracted to him romantically, but he was fun to be with. We spent a lot of time together. We studied in the library, went to football games, and we spent a lot of time going out with mutual friends. Then one weekend, he came home with me and my parents fell in love with him. They thought he walked on water. I don't know how it came to be, but somehow my parents got the impression he was my boyfriend, and they were ecstatic."

Billie paused to drink from her water bottle. She spared a glance at Tara, and saw the teenager was still doodling in the sand but listening intently to her mother's story.

"Anyway," Billie continued. "One thing led to another and Brian proposed to me. I wasn't in love with him, but I married him more to make my parents happy, than for love."

"Did you know when you married him that you were gay?" Tara asked.

Billie stretched long legs out in front of her, crossed them at the ankles and then leaned back on her hands. "I knew I was different, but to actually say I knew why...I don't know. I wasn't physically attracted to Brian when I married him, and even less so after Seth was born, but I didn't put a name to it until near the end of my marriage. By that time, Brian had developed a drinking habit and had become abusive—but then, you don't need to hear the details of that ordeal." She suddenly remembered she was talking to her teenage daughter.

"So when did you realize you were gay?" Tara prompted, relentless in her search for information.

"Persistent little imp, aren't you?" Billie commented.

Tara laughed.

"Okay, let's see. When did I know I was gay?" Billie repeated. "Well, like I said, I knew I was different. When I was in college, I had several female friends I was close to. Not too long after Seth was born, one of them contacted me and we went out for dinner. Over dinner I told her I had married Brian, and she nearly choked on her food and said, 'What were you thinking? Gay girl and straight boy! No way, girlfriend.'" Billie stopped for a moment to gauge Tara's reaction.

"She knew you were gay and you didn't?" Tara asked in disbelief.

"It appears so," Billie replied. "Keep in mind, I was raised an only child, and we pretty much kept to our own, so I didn't have a lot of exposure to the diversity of different cultures. Anyway, she really opened my eyes that night. After that, things fell into place. I was suddenly able to put a name to the way I was feeling and my entire life changed because of it."

"What did Brian do when he found out?" Tara asked.

Billie's eyes narrowed as she recalled the confrontation with Brian when she finally admitted her feelings to him. She could almost still feel the belt across her back. An involuntary shiver passed through her as she shook off the thoughts. She looked at Tara "That is something I would rather not tell you, sweetling. Please understand."

Tara nodded and reached for Billie's hand. She looked directly into Billie's eyes and said, "I'm sorry you had to live through that. I remember what he did to Seth and Mama when he broke into our house. I'm glad you aren't with him anymore."

Billie fought back the tears welling in her eyes. "Thank you, sweetie. If nothing else, you need to learn how to be independent and how *not* to cave into the demands of others. If I'd had the courage to stand up to my parents, I never would have married him. But then, things happen for a reason. If I hadn't married Brian, I wouldn't have had Seth...and I probably would not have met your Mom...or you…and certainly not Skylar. I would gladly live through that all over again to be sitting here on the river bank with you right now."

Tara leaned her head against Billie's arm. "I love you, Mom."

"I love you too, sweetie. I love you like you came from me. I love both you and your sister as much as I love Seth."

Tara nodded and fell silent.

Billie initiated the next question. "So, tell me about you."

Tara looked up. "Me? What would you like to know?"

"Tell me when you knew," Billie asked.

Tara frowned. "I'm not sure I even know *yet*," she replied.

"And, Kelly? How do you feel about her?" Billie prompted.

Now it was Tara's turn to hug her knees close to her chest. She rested her chin on her knees and looked out over the water. "Kelly makes me feel all funny inside," she began. "Sometimes I feel like I'm gonna hurl. Sometimes I feel like I swallowed butterflies, and sometimes my stomach gets all hot. I know I really miss her a lot right now," she admitted.

"Does she ever make you feel uncomfortable?" Billie asked.

Tara rested her cheek on her knees and looked sideways at her mother. "Uncomfortable like, guilty or nasty?" she asked for clarification.

Billie smiled at her daughter's insight. "Yeah, something like that," she replied.

"Not really. I never feel ashamed of what I feel, and I never feel like it's wrong to like her, if that's what you're asking," Tara explained.

"So, have you kissed her?" Billie asked, unable to look her daughter in the eyes.

Tara blushed and looked down at her feet. "Yeah." She giggled.

Billie smiled. "I see."

Several moments of silence passed before Billie reached out to rub Tara's back. "You know Mama and I love you and support you no matter what, right?" she asked.

Once more, Tara nodded without replying.

"We just want you to be happy and safe, Tara. There is so much you need to understand about relationships like ours. So much you need to know to protect yourself," Billie said.

"Mom." Tara looked Billie straight in the eyes and stopped her cold. "I'm not going to do anything stupid. I promise. Kelly and I are not sure about where this is going yet. It might go nowhere, but if it does, we'll be careful. I know there are people in the world who aren't ready for this. Hell, I'm not even sure *I'm* ready for this yet, so we'll take it slow, and we'll wait to see what happens."

Billie smiled. "Just know that we're here for you, okay?"

"I know you are, Mom, and I love you and Mama so much for it."

Billie held her daughter and fought to keep the moisture from her eyes before she broke the embrace and sat back. Billie looked at her watch. "Wow, it's almost two o'clock. Are you ready to head out? We want to be sure we get back to camp before dark."

Tara jumped to her feet and offered a hand to her mother. Within moments they were steadily paddling along.

\*\*\*

Jeff climbed the last few steps into the lookout tower.

"It's about time you got back!" Jason scolded.

"Sorry about that. The boss had me run a few errands before he let me go." He handed Jason a cold soda. "Here, maybe this will cool your britches."

Jason cracked open the can and drank deeply. "Ah, that is good," he said, followed by a very long and loud burp.

"Hey! Good one dude!" Jeff raised his hand to Jason for a high-five. Jeff walked around the perimeter of the look-out tower and over the tree tops for as far as the eye could see. "All quiet?" he asked.

"There's been some heat lightning, but nothing else," Jason replied just as a loud crack of thunder and bright flash of lightning split the sky.

"Holy Shit!" Jeff said. "That came out of nowhere!"

"Dry lightning. That was close." Jason grabbed his binoculars to scan the treetops.

Jeff did the same as the two rangers silently inspected the panoramic view before them.

\*\*\*

Cat and Seth reached a very narrow part of the trail that was littered with loose rock.

114

"Seth, I think we're lost. I can't imagine the park would allow normal hikers on trails like this." Cat held onto the rock face with both hands and shimmied her way down the narrow ledge.

"You may be right, Ma." Seth looked at the trail beyond where his mother was standing. "Keep moving. I can see the trail widen in just a few more yards," he said.

"Good. Seth, please be careful, honey. Okay?"

"I'm all right. I'm more worried about you. Stay close to the rock face and move slowly. The loose rocks on this trail are dangerous."

"You're telling me!" Cat chuckled in an attempt to lighten the mood.

Just then a deafening crack of thunder and bright flash of lightning startled the hikers. Cat was caught totally off guard and she screamed and jumped, and ultimately lost her footing.

"Ma!" Seth screamed when Cat's feet slipped off the edge of the trail. He threw himself to the ground and reached forward in a desperate attempt to catch her. "Ma! Grab on!" he yelled.

"Seth!" Cat scrambled for something to hold on to, only to have the loose rocks slip from her grasp and tumble down on top of her as she plummeted down the slope.

\*\*\*

"Look, Tara. Up ahead. Rapids!" Billie pointed out.

"Cool!" Tara turned the kayak and headed directly for them.

"All right, be sure to steer into them. This isn't a white-water kayak. We'll need to take it easy through here," Billie warned.

"Don't worry, Mom. This will be a snap," Tara said confidently.

Tara approached the rapids and carefully steered the bow of the boat straight into them while at the same time, Billie used her paddle as a rudder to keep the boat straight. Together, they rode the rapids and enjoyed the roller coaster ride of swells and dips along the way.

"Way cool!" Tara shouted as they maneuvered the boat into the roughest part of the stream.

At the very same moment an especially large swell lifted their boat, a deafening crack of thunder and bright flash of lightning startled them. Tara swung around quickly to look at her mother and nearly capsized the boat in the process.

"Whoa, Tara, settle down," Billie warned. "We need to get out of these rapids, honey. Come on, paddle!"

Billie and Tara worked together and managed to paddle the kayak to the closest shore. They quickly climbed out of the boat and pulled it onto the bank.

"What the hell was that?" Tara asked loudly.

"My guess would be thunder and lightning," Billie replied.

Tara looked at the sky. "Wow! That was loud!"

Billie looked up as well. "It still doesn't look like rain," she observed.

"Do you want to head out again?" Tara asked.

"In a while." Billie sat on a nearby rock and wondered where Cat was at that moment.

# CHAPTER 12

"Ma! Oh, God, Ma!" Seth screamed. He climbed down the slope in the direction Cat had fallen. "Ma! Can you hear me?"

*Seth? Seth, where are you? Where am I? Billie. Baby, I'm sorry...* Such were the thoughts that ran through Cat's mind as she lay in a stupor at the bottom of a steep ravine.

Partway down the slope, Seth stopped to locate where Cat had landed. Finally, he spotted her several feet below.

"Ma!" he yelled. "I'm coming. Don't move!"

Cat opened her eyes and looked around. She inventoried her aches and pains to determine the extent of her injuries. *Okay, my left arm hurts like hell. It feels like I have major road rash on my legs and I've got a splitting headache. Otherwise, I'm good!*

Seth finally reached her and he threw himself down beside her. He brushed the bangs from her forehead. "Don't move, Ma. You're gonna be all right."

Cat looked at her son and forced a smile to her face. "Seth, it's not as bad as it looks," she said. "Help me to sit up."

"No! Lay still," he urged.

"Seth, I can't lie here all day. Help me to sit, please." She struggled to lift her upper body from the ground.

"Slow. Take it slow." Seth helped Cat to sit. "How are you feeling?"

"Like I just fell off a cliff." Cat chuckled. She looked into her son's face and saw the raw fear in his eyes. She raised her good arm and patted him on the cheek. "I'll be fine, honey. Really, I will. Like I said, it's not as bad as it looks. Okay, now help me to my feet."

Seth hesitated.

"Look, sweetie. If you don't help me, I'll do it myself. You know I will, so please give me a hand here."

Seth positioned himself behind her and lifted Cat under the arms until she was stood on her own. "Are you okay?" he asked before he released her.

Cat shifted her weight from one foot to the other. Convinced her legs were okay, other than the scratches and bruises sustained during her slide down the rocky slope. She took a few tentative steps and almost fell on her face.

"Ma!" Seth caught her before she fell to the ground.

Cat shook her head to chase off the dizziness she felt when she tried to take a step. "Wow! I felt dizzy for a moment there. Help me to that rock over there, will you, love?"

Seth checked her over once she sat on the rock. "Mama, you've hit your head." He lightly touched the bruise on Cat's forehead. "Maybe you have a concussion."

Cat felt the spot Seth had indicated and winced at the contact. "Oh! Maybe you're right. Is it bleeding?"

"I don't see any blood, but it looks like a nasty bruise. Maybe you should sit for a few minutes before you try to walk again."

Cat nodded and then looked at her son. "Are *you* all right, Seth?" she asked.

Seth rubbed Cat's arm. "I'm not the one who fell off the cliff, Ma. I'm fine."

"Wow, that's tender." Cat moaned. Contact with her left arm suddenly reminded her it was injured.

"What is it?" Seth was concerned that he had apparently hurt his mother.

Cat examined her left forearm and noted the swelling, but no sign of a compound fracture. "I hurt my arm in the fall. Hopefully it's not fractured. Maybe I should splint it just in case."

Seth located two relatively flat pieces of wood nearby. "We also need to find a stream to wash the blood away."

"Blood?" Cat watched Seth attached the wood to her forearm with strips of his T-shirt.

"Yeah. It looks like you've scraped your legs up pretty bad."

"What do you think that bang was?" Cat asked.

"It sounded like thunder to me," Seth replied. "It startled the life out of me. I wasn't expecting to hear thunder on such a sunny day!"

"Did I see a flash of lightning, or was I imagining things?" Cat asked.

"I saw it too. I only hope it didn't strike somewhere." Seth checked out his makeshift splint. "Okay, the splint is secure." Seth stood and looked around. He pointed at the slope Cat had tumbled down. "Well, we're not going back up that way. It looks like we'll have to make our way through the woods. Do you think you're up to it?"

"Considering the alternative, I guess I don't have much choice. Let's start by finding that stream you were talking about," Cat suggested.

"All right. Wait right here. I need to get our bag. It's still up there."

Cat sat on the rock with her heart in her throat and watched her son scale the cliff. He returned again a few moments later with their backpack in tow.

"Maybe I should have taken rock climbing lessons from you before we headed out!" Cat joked when Seth rejoined her at the bottom of the ravine.

Seth smiled at his mother's attempt to lighten the mood. He helped her to her feet and held her with his arm around her waist for several moments until he was satisfied she had regained her balance. "Here, hold on to my arm," he offered and they slowly made their way into the forest.

***

"So, how old are your kids now?" Jeff asked.

Jason continued to scan the treetops. "Carrie is eight, Jonathan is six," he replied.

"So they're both in school this year?" Jeff inquired.

"Yup! Susan is thrilled to be returning to work full time now that the kids are going back to school. Next month, Carrie starts third grade and Jon will be in first. He's really excited to be going to school all day instead of half-day kindergarten," Jason explained.

"They must really be getting big..." Jeff stopped talking when he saw Jason waive his hand.

"Jeff! Get your binoculars. Look! Over there." Jason pointed without removing the binoculars from his face. "Can you see it?" he asked.

Jeff aimed his binoculars in the direction Jason indicated and scanned the area carefully. "I see it!" Jeff said. "Damn! It looks bad." He snatched the two-way radio from his hip.

"Home base 201, this is ranger tower 570. Smoke spotted in the area of Shoshone and Lewis Lakes. Repeat. Smoke spotted in the area of Shoshone and Lewis Lakes," Jeff said into the two-way radio.

"Holy Shit!" Jason exclaimed. "There's more. Look."

Jeff returned to his binoculars and scanned a larger area, noting, as Jason did, that several fires had ignited in the area that covered approximately a quarter of their lookout view.

"Good Lord! The lightning must have caused sparks to jump from tree to tree!" Jeff once more relayed the new information into the two-way radio.

"This is not good! This is not good! We're in drought. The park will go up like a tinder box if we can't stop it in time." Jason and Jeff quickly made their way down the ladder to the Jeep waiting below.

*** 

"Do you smell that, Mom?" Tara glanced over her shoulder as she continued to paddle.

"Smell what?" Billie replied.

"Smoke. It smells like a campfire," Tara elaborated.

"Well, maybe someone is camping nearby," Billie suggested.

The odor grew stronger further downstream.

"I'm not so sure that's a campfire, Mom." A hint of worry colored her voice.

The small river they were paddling through appeared to be in a valley between two hills. On both sides of the river, the land sloped upward and disappeared over a ridge. The slopes leading to the river were dotted with dense vegetation and trees, all the way to the shoreline.

Billie narrowed her eyes and looked around. "I don't see any fire," she remarked. "I don't see any smoke either."

Tara fell silent once more and continued to paddle. An eerie silence surrounded them as they glided through the water.

"Listen, Mom. There's no sound."

Billie and Tara both stopped paddling and allowed the kayak to glide on its own. Billie took in her surroundings and allowed her mind to focus on the moment. Tara was right. There was very little to be heard. No birds, no insects. Even the water was still. The silence was deafening.

"Let's move closer to land," Billie suggested.

They maneuvered the kayak closer to the shoreline. Billie scanned the shore as they drifted by. There was still no sign of life. No movement. No sound.

"This is creepy, Mom."

"Something is wrong," Billie whispered softly as she strained to listen.

For the next few minutes, they drifted slowly downstream, entering a very narrow part of the river. Tall trees lined both sides, meeting overhead in a dense canopy of leaves that drooped low over the water. The canopy effectively blocked most of the sunlight and cast the small river channel into shadow.

"Mom, this is scaring me," Tara admitted.

"It's creeping me out too, honey."

"It feels like something out of a horror movie."

"That thought crossed my mind as well," Billie admitted.

"Why is there no sound?"

"I don't know, love. It's almost as if something has scared all the wildlife away," Billie said.

They continued to drift as the movement of the water increased in speed.

"We must have hit an undercurrent," Billie observed. Little effort was required from their paddles to keep the kayak moving at a steady pace.

Tara was totally spooked by the eerie nature of the dense, dark canopy and kept her eyes glued to the shoreline as they glided by.

"I half expect cannibals wearing only loincloths and body paint to jump out at any moment and pierce our boat with arrows," Tara said.

Billie grinned. "Are their noses pierced with chicken bones?" she joked.

Suddenly, a rumbling was heard in the distance.

"What's that?" Tara exclaimed nervously.

"Shh. Stop paddling and listen," Billie urged.

The rumbling grew louder.

"Something is rushing toward us," Billie whispered.

\*\*\*

Senior Ranger, Rick Ellis, stood bent over a wrinkled map of the park that was spread out over the hood of his Jeep. He pointed to specific locations as a group of rangers peered over his shoulder.

"Johnson, you take your crew to the Kepler Cascade region. Davis, you've got the west side of Shoshone Lake. Burton, you and your men head for the north part of Lewis Lake, and Erikson, take a crew into the Shoshone Geyser Basin. The first order of business is look for hikers, campers and anyone else you may run across. These areas must be evacuated immediately. Any questions?" He looked around at the men.

When no responses came, he dismissed the men and rolled up the map.

"Looks bad, doesn't it, Captain?" asked his assistant, Ranger Angela Bradshaw.

"I haven't seen one ignite and spread as fast as this since the fires that nearly destroyed the park in 1988," Ellis explained. "I'm hoping the hotshots and smokejumpers can contain it to a region around Old Faithful. If we can do that, we may be able to save the park."

Angela walked back to the ranger station with him. "It seems to be spreading fast," she observed.

"It's been a pretty dry summer, Angie. This year we didn't get the heavy rains we normally see in July. The underbrush is dry and the fuel load is high. The higher the fuel load, the faster it will ignite and burn. The more intensely it burns, the faster it will spread, and because it is so dry, the fuel is consumed much faster and the fire is harder to contain."

"Jason says the lightning struck in an area with a lot of small, loose underbrush," Angela commented.

"Yes. Unfortunately, smaller, flashy fuels like dry grass, pine needles, dry leaves, twigs and other dead brush, burn faster than large logs or stumps. The smaller stuff burns up quicker and allows the fire to move forward faster. What's even worse, is that the heat generated by the fire, dries out the fuel in front of it, so when the fire finally reaches it, it's easier to ignite. Fires like this take on a life of their own, and even generate their own weather system. It's a no-win situation," Ranger Ellis explained.

A news crew was waiting for them when Rick and Angela reached the ranger station.

"Captain, what is the latest status of the fire?" A reporter shoved a microphone into Rick's face while a camera man pointed his lens at Ellis.

"At last report, the fire was moving Southwest at a speed of about fourteen miles per hour," he said.

"Are there any reports of tourists trapped in the affected areas?" the reporter asked.

"We have just sent out crews to search the areas. This is a very dangerous job as they must enter areas already consumed by the wildfires. We expect to know more later this evening," Rick replied.

"Ranger Ellis, how did this fire start? Was it the carelessness of a camper, or a discarded cigarette?"

"We have every reason to believe the fire started by natural causes. There were several incidences of dry lightning earlier this afternoon. That is the most probable cause of the ignition."

"How long does the National Park Service believe it will be before this fire is brought under control?" a reported asked.

Rick ran his hand through his hair. He was a bit impatient with the persistent questioning. He knew the public would be seeing this later that evening, and since public support was important to the Park Service, he fought back his irritation and answered the question. "A fire such as this could burn for weeks, and smolder for many months afterwards. As far as *when* it will be brought under control…well only time and Mother Nature will tell," he explained.

"Mother Nature?" the reported prompted. "As in rain?"

"Rain, wind, evening temperatures. All of these are factors in how hot and how long a fire burns. We will do our best to extinguish it through human means, but we truly rely on Mother Nature to help us out," he finished.

"Rick, there's a call for you from base," Angela called from the doorway of the ranger station.

Rick politely excused himself as the reporter wrapped up the interview. "That was Senior Ranger Rick Ellis reporting on the Park Service's progress toward extinguishing the wildfire currently raging through the Southwest portion of Yellowstone National Park. This is Monica Crocker, signing off."

\*\*\*

The rumbling grew louder as it approached the kayak that slowly drifted down a narrow stretch of river. The canopy of trees overhead created a darkness that seemed to grow darker as the moments passed.

"Mom, maybe we should turn around and go back," Tara suggested.

"I think we're closer to the end of this route than the beginning of it, Tare. Maybe we just need to start paddling our way through this. Something serious is happening here and I for one would like to get far away from it."

"I'm with you, Mom. Let's go."

Billie and Tara dipped their paddles into the water and began to stroke, all the while, scanning the shoreline on both sides and the slopes beyond for the source of the eerie atmosphere that surrounded them.

The air became unbearably dry and warm and the rumbling sound increased significantly in volume and intensity. Billie stared off beyond the shoreline into the dense forest behind it. Suddenly the source of the sound, smell and warmth became very clear. What was also clear, was the fact that they were in immediate danger.

"Oh, my God! Wildfire!" Billie shouted. Flames suddenly became apparent on the ridge above the shoreline.

"Mom!" Tara shouted. "Mom! What should we do?"

Billie looked around frantically. She knew they had just moments to react. "Tara! Roll the boat! Roll the boat!" She shouted as loud as she could in order to be heard above the ever-increasing rumble. Billie grabbed the edges of the cockpit and shifted her weight sharply to the left. "Tara! Work with me on this!" she shouted.

Tara followed her mother's cue and shifted her weight in the same direction as Billie. Soon the kayak tilted sharply to its side and capsized, sending both of them into the water. The paddles, which were connected to the kayak by long bungee cords whipped dangerously around and nearly struck Tara in the head before they settled on the surface of the water.

Billie and Tara both surfaced behind the kayak. Billie looked over the boat to the shoreline and realized the fire was not going to stop at the water's edge. Instead, it used the canopy of trees that were bent gracefully low over the river to reach the other side.

The fire was within feet of reaching them when Billie grabbed Tara and pulled her under the water, only to resurface again under the capsized kayak, inside the cockpit where they had a pocket of air to sustain them for a while.

"Tara?  Sweetie, are you okay?"

"I'm scared, Mom."

"I am too, love.  I am too.  Just promise me you'll hang on."

"I will."

Mother and daughter clung to the inverted seats in total darkness inside the cockpit and relied on their lifejackets to keep their heads above water as their bodies remained protected by the river. Both were terrified into silence as they listened to roaring flames pass overhead.  The air inside their shelter became warm as the fire licked at the bottom of the capsized boat. All they could do was cling to the inside of the cockpit and pray that the danger would pass quickly.

Winds caused by the fierce fire, along with moderately strong water currents, continued to move their capsized boat downstream as the fire raged above them. Wind patterns and heat caused by the fire generated fire whirls, similar in shape and behavior to tornados. One such whirl hurled a flaming log into the air.  It landed on the bottom of the overturned kayak with a loud thud and then bounced off and landed in the water nearby.

Startled by the loud banging on top of their shelter, Tara screamed as the weight of the log pushed the kayak deeper into the water, totally submerging the underwater occupants.

"Tara, honey.  Are you all right?!" Billie asked when they both re-emerged inside the inverted cockpit.

Tara struggled to regain her breath after the unexpected dunking. "What was that?"

"I don't know, but thank God we were *under* the boat instead of inside it. Whatever that was might have killed us!" Billie observed.

"Mom?" Tara whispered tearfully.

Billie reached around until she found her daughter. "What is it, Tara?" she asked softly.

"I'm scared," she replied.

"Me too, honey. Me too. Shh. Don't speak. Conserve our air. It will pass soon." Billie fell silent once more and prayed to any God who would listen to spare their lives and the lives of her loved ones. *God only knows if Cat and Seth are safe. Skylar is with experienced rangers, so surely she would have been evacuated by now.*

Billie could only hope and pray her family would come out of this intact.

# CHAPTER 13

"That was Senior Ranger Rick Ellis reporting on the Park Service's progress toward extinguishing the wildfire currently raging through the Southwest portion of Yellowstone National Park. This is Monica Crocker, signing off."

"Oh, my God!" Kelly caught the tail end of the newscast and jumped to her feet when she heard where the wildfires were. She grabbed the remote control and furiously clicked through the channels until she found a similar report.

"It is unknown at this time if there are any tourists trapped in the midst of the blaze," the reporter said. "The blaze seems to be centered just southwest of Old Faithful in the Shoshone Lake area. Stay tuned for more news at six."

Kelly sat stunned. *Where did Tara say they were going?* she asked herself. *She mentioned 'Old Faithful', didn't she? Oh, my God! Tara. Please be safe... please.* After a few more moments of stunned immobility, Kelly grabbed the phone and called Karissa's number.

"Hello," an adult female voice answered.

"Mrs. Swenson? This is Kelly," the teenager said.

"Oh, hi Kelly! Hold on and I'll get Karissa for you," Jen said.

"No! No, it's you I want to talk to," Kelly explained.

"Me? What can I do for you, Kelly?" Jen asked.

"Mrs. Swenson, did the Charlands say they were staying inside Yellowstone?"

Jen immediately became suspicious. "Kelly, is everything all right? Have you heard from Tara?"

"No, I haven't. I was actually hoping you've heard from them."

"No. I haven't spoken with them since they left three days ago," Jen replied. "Kelly, you're scaring me. Are you trying to tell me something?"

"Mrs. Swenson, I just saw a news report on TV about a wildfire in Yellowstone. I think it's right near where they're staying," Kelly said quickly.

"Jesus, Mary and Joseph!" Jen cursed. "What more will those women have to endure? Kelly, what channel was it on?"

"It's actually on several channels, but I first saw it on channel three."

"Okay. I've got it. Thanks for calling, sweetie. Oh, and if you need someone to lean on until we know more, feel free to come over and spend some time with Karissa and me, okay?"

"I appreciate that, Mrs. Swenson. Tell Karissa I'll be over in a few minutes."

"All right then. Goodbye."

Jen hung up the phone with more force than she intended. "God damned, mother raping bastard, son of a bitch!" she screamed at no one in particular. She shook her fist to the ceiling. "Why must you always do shit like this to them?"

Jen's tirade caused Fred to rush into the kitchen from the living room. "Is everything all right?" he asked.

"The Charlands are in trouble again. It appears they're in the middle of a goddamned wildfire!" she shrieked.

\*\*\*

Movement through the forest was slow and difficult. Cat's entire body ached as a result of her fall down the slope and it was only made worse with every step. She tried hard to hide her discomfort from Seth, but failed miserably. She thanked the Gods above that he forced her to take breaks every half hour.

"Seth, we'll never make it back to the cabin before dark at this rate," Cat complained. "Hell, we won't even make it out of the forest before dark."

"Mom, I'd rather spend the night in the forest than not make it back at all...and that's exactly what will happen if you fall and injure yourself again," Seth reasoned.

Cat limped beside her son. "If we don't show up before dark, your mother will call out the National Guard."

"That's exactly what she'll do, but I'll risk her wrath before I risk your safety again. Here, give me your hand." Seth helped Cat over a large log.

Cat stopped and looked up at her tall son. She touched the side of his face with her open palm. "When did you turn into a man?" she asked. "It seems like yesterday that you were just our little boy."

Seth grinned and took Cat's hand to lead her safely through the forest. A few hundred yards further and he stopped dead in his tracks.

"What is it, Seth?" Cat asked.

Seth looked into the tree tops and sniffed the air. "I smell smoke," he said.

Cat looked around and also tested the air. "You're right. It's probably a camp fire. That means straight ahead there might be someone who'd be able to give us directions out of this place," Cat said hopefully.

"Maybe. Come on." Seth took Cat's hand once more and led her in the direction of the campfire odor.

After another one hundred feet, they still had not encountered the help they were looking for.

"This is not good," Seth said.

"Is it my imagination, or is the smell of smoke getting stronger?" Cat asked.

"I wish it *was* your imagination. Do your eyes burn like mine do?" Seth asked.

Cat stopped and yanked Seth's arm. "Tell me you're not implying what I think you're implying."

"I wish I could tell you everything is fine, Ma, but I have a sneaking suspicion that things are about to get a lot worse. Come sit on this log over here and let's look at the map."

Seth led Cat to a fallen log to sit and he spread the map out on the ground between them. He studied the map for several moments and then folded it up and stuffed it unceremoniously into their back pack. "I give up," he said. "We are hopelessly lost."

"I kind of suspected that before I fell off the trail a while back," Cat admitted. "So, what do we do now?"

"I have to admit that the smell of smoke has me worried, Ma. That flash of lightning we saw at the top of the cliff could have hit nearby, and it could have started a fire."

"I don't *see* any fire," Cat said.

Seth looked into the canopy of trees above their heads and saw the branches at the very top sway. "There is a breeze. It's possible the fire is still a distance away and we're smelling smoke that has travelled on the wind."

Cat stood and grabbed her walking stick. "I don't think it's smart to just sit here and let the fire move toward us," she said.

"I agree. I guess we should keep walking until we find signs of life." Seth climbed to his feet. He looked around once more for a suitable exit from their clearing. As he turned around, the smell of campfire hit him full in the face with such force, he took two steps backward. "What the hell..."

Cat grabbed his arm. "What's that sound?" Cat began to cough. "Damn! The smell of smoke is making it difficult to breathe."

"I hear it too. It sounds like a roar." Seth tore off a piece of his shirt and poured some water on it from his water bottle. He gave it to Cat. "Here, hold this over your mouth and nose. It will help to filter out the smoke."

The roar increased in volume and it was suddenly accompanied by loud crackling and popping noises.

Just then, the sound of a low flying helicopter began in the distance. Cat and Seth looked up as the sound grew louder. Suddenly, the helicopter became visible.

"What is that larger container hanging below the helicopter?" Cat asked.

Seth's eye grew large as all of his suspicions were confirmed. "Oh, shit! Oh, shit!" he exclaimed.

"Seth! What is it?" Cat asked.

Seth threw his backpack to the ground and immediately dropped to his knees to rummage through it. He quickly found the collapsible shovel they had packed and he began to furiously dig at the earth. "Ma! Quick! Dig a hole. Quick!" He shouted.

Without hesitation, Cat threw herself down next to her son and began digging as quickly as her injured arm would allow. Luckily, the turf was relatively soft and free of tree roots as a shallow indentation quickly cleared beneath their efforts.

"Seth, tell me we're digging this hole for a good reason," Cat rasped as she struggled with only one hand to clear as much soil from the hole as possible.

"Wildfire!" Seth shouted as he continued to work.

Cat suddenly climbed to her feet. "Wildfire?" She frantically scanned the trees once more.

"Ma! We don't have a lot of time. It's moving toward us pretty quickly!" Seth continued to dig. "Listen to the roar. It's getting louder! Dig!"

Cat grabbed at her son's arm. "Seth! We need to run. Come on. We need to get out of here!" she screamed.

Seth jumped to his feet and grabbed Cat by both arms. "There is no way we are going to outrun a wildfire—especially with you injured. Do you understand?" he shouted into her face.

"So what do you propose we do?" Cat asked hysterically.

Seth pointed to the hole behind them. "We need to get into that hole and cover ourselves with dirt," he said firmly.

Cat's eyes flew open. "Are you telling me that I just helped dig our grave?" she screamed.

"We don't have any other choice! Don't you see? We can't outrun it. There is nowhere to hide. Nowhere! Look around!"

Cat looked around frantically as the roar of the fire increased exponentially. "Seth, what makes you think hiding in a hole will save us from the fire?"

"Ma, please just get in the hole."

Suddenly a strong gust of wind bombarded them with a wave of heat so intense, it took their breaths away.

"Oh, for crying out loud!" Seth had no patience with Cat's indecisiveness.

Seth grabbed Cat's good arm and dragged her into the hole and quickly pushed the mound of dirt next to the hole on top of her. He then climbed in beside her and pulled the remaining dirt over himself.

"Close your eyes, Mom. I've got to cover our heads." Seth shouted above the roar of the oncoming fire as he dragged a small pile of soil over Cat's head and then another pile over himself before wriggling his free arm beneath the surface of the earth.

For what seemed like an eternity, mother and son lay entombed beneath the earth as a raging inferno danced merrily above them.

Terrified beyond reason and convinced she and Seth would die where they lay; the only thoughts that ran through Cat's mind were those of her family. *Please keep them safe,* she prayed. *Billie... Tara... Sky... Seth, I love you.*

***

Jen sat perched on the edge of the couch with her gaze glued to the television. "Oh, my God! Please let them be okay," she muttered out loud.

Fred walked up behind her when he entered the living room. After Jen hung up the phone with Kelly, he went upstairs to tell Steve and Karissa what was going on and to keep the Charland family in their thoughts. Then he returned to the living room to lend moral support while they waited for word of their friends. He looked over her shoulder at the television. "Wow! That's some wildfire!"

Jen looked back at Fred. Tears ran freely down her face. "If they're in the middle of that, they'll never survive."

Within moments, Steve and Karissa joined them in the living room and all four of them sat on the couch glued to the disaster unfolding on the screen. They were so caught up in the televised report that they almost missed the soft knock at the door.

"That's probably Kelly," Jen said.

Karissa immediately jumped to her feet. "I'll get it." She ran to the front door, flung it open and took Kelly into her arms. Both girls cried and clung to each other.

"I'm so scared," Kelly said.

Karissa nodded. "Me too."

Jen approached the girls and wrapped her arms around both of them. "Come sit on the couch, and please don't give up hope. If anyone can survive this, they can."

Jen gave up her space on the couch and walked around the back of it to stand behind Fred.

Jen squeezed his shoulder. "I can't stand here and do nothing. I'm going to try to reach the park ranger's office. Maybe they can tell us something. Then I should probably call Cat's parents."

"I think you need to wait to call anyone until after we know whether or not they're even in danger, Jen," Fred said.

Without looking away from the television, Jen nodded. "I will however, still call the ranger's office."

# CHAPTER 14

"Mom, I can't breathe," Tara whispered. "We're running out of air."

Similar thoughts ran through Billie's mind as she and her daughter clung to the seats in the cockpit of the capsized kayak. Before making a decision, Billie listened carefully to the muted sounds above them. Gone was the intense roaring of the fire. Gone was the crackling and popping of burning wood. Gone was the sound of trees falling nearby.

"Tara," Billie said. "When I count to three, reach up and push on the floor of the cockpit. We need to lift it up high enough for me to get under it and turn it over."

"Okay," Tara replied into the darkness. She allowed her life jacket to keep her buoyant as her hands made contact with her target. "I'm ready," Tara whispered.

"All right. One. Two. Three. Push!"

The bow of the kayak rose above the surface of the water by a couple of inches, which allowed Billie to reach under and gain leverage against the capsized deck of the boat. She planted her hands against the foredeck and pushed it a little higher and then instructed Tara to swim out from beneath the kayak and to roll it upright from the side. Within moments, the kayak was upright again and the ladies held onto the bow and stern while they floated along downstream beside the boat.

Billie and Tara were totally immobilized by what they saw once their eyes adjusted to the muted light. For long moments, neither could speak. Finally, the silence was broken.

"Mom, it looks like a scene from a war movie," Tara exclaimed.

"This must be what hell looks like," Billie mused.

They continued to float downstream while holding on to the boat. Their eyes burned from the residual smoke and ash that filled the air. Everywhere they looked, the landscape was blackened and charred. Many areas were still afire with small blazes. The low hanging smoke cast a dark pallor over everything in sight and caused them intervals of uncontrollable coughing. The only sound they heard was a roar in the distance as the wall of fire continued to move forward.

"We need to get to shore," Billie said. "We can't just continue to drift like this."

"Maybe we should let go of the kayak and swim to shore," Tara suggested.

"No. We're going to need the kayak to find our way out of here," Billie said. "Let's try to drag it to shore behind us."

With Billie on one side and Tara on the other, each held onto the kayak with one hand and stroked with the other while kicking their feet. They struggled like this for quite some time, to no avail. The current was just too strong and they made no progress. The only thing they accomplished was exhaustion.

"This is no use!" Tara shouted as she struggled against the current.

"All right. Stop swimming. Rest for a while. Maybe we can use the current to our advantage further on downstream and steer it to shore." Billie stopped struggling and simply held onto the boat while resting.

"It's getting dark, Mom. We're not going to make it back to the cabin on time," Tara said.

"I know. I'm worried about that too, but I'm more worried about how Mama will react if we aren't there. She'll probably call out the National Guard to look for us," Billie joked.

"Sky is gonna be really mad at us for not picking her up on time, you know," Tara pointed out.

"Oh, my God! I forgot all about picking Sky up at four o'clock!" Billie exclaimed.

"Well, it's not like we forgot on purpose, Mom. Sheesh!" Tara exclaimed. Exasperation clearly filled her voice.

"Hopefully Mama will realize we're late and go to collect her for us," Billie hoped.

Tara looked at her mother. An expression of fear suddenly clouded her features. "Mom! What if Mama and Seth are caught in this too?"

Billie's head snapped around to look at her daughter. Fearful realization fell like a mask over her features as she absorbed Tara's comment. Tears filled her eyes and she felt totally overwhelmed and vulnerable. She fought the tears off in a show of strength for her daughter's sake.

"Let's pray to God they aren't in danger," Billie replied. "We can't lose hope that we'll all survive this Tara. Mama and Seth are smart. If they *have* been caught up in this mess, they'll figure out how to survive it. I know they will. And Skylar...well, if Mama hasn't picked her up on time, at least she's with adults who will surely take care of her until we can get there. What time is it now, Tara?" Billie asked.

Tara looked at her watch. "Thank God it's water resistant. It's almost six," she answered.

Billie frowned. "Really? It's awfully dark for only six o'clock." Billie wondered if the residual smoke was contributing to the darkness.

"Maybe we should try getting in the boat, Mom. We might move faster downstream if we're inside the boat instead of dragging behind it."

"Okay. I'll hold it and you climb in." Billie grabbed the bow to stabilize the kayak and Tara struggled to climb into the cockpit.

"Your turn, Mom. I'm going to hang over the other side of the kayak to try to counteract your weight."

Tara weighed significantly less than Billie and try as she might, her side of the kayak rose high into the air as Billie climbed in. The small boat nearly capsized for the second time.

"Phew! That was close!" Billie righted herself in the cockpit, and looked around for the paddles. Luckily, they were still attached to the bungees and floated nearby. She reeled them in and handed one to Tara. They were slightly melted and charred by the fire, but still useable.

"We're going to have to paddle pretty hard to fight against this current." Billie dug one end of the paddle into the water and pushed with all her might.

Together, Tara and Billie worked to move the kayak to within ten feet of the shore, when the front of the boat hit a partially submerged rock. The kayak careened off the rock and floated back into the mainstream of the current.

"God damn it!" Billie shouted and they found themselves once more fighting against the increasingly rapid current.

With fading daylight and fading hope, Billie and Tara continued to fight against the impossible current until totally exhausted and they paused to rest.

"Mom, I can't do this any longer. My shoulders are killing me," Tara complained.

"I know, sweetie. I know." Billie looked around at their dire situation and struggled to remain hopeful that they would make it out alive. Not being religious-minded, Billie turned her prayers to her mother and father, who had passed away several years earlier. *Mom and Dad...if you can hear me, please see what you can do to help us out here. You must have connections with the Big Guy. Hell, make a deal with the devil if you have to. Just give us a chance to survive this. At least save Tara. She's just a child and has her whole life ahead of her.*

"What are we going to do, Mom? We can't just drift along in this kayak all night. We need to somehow get it to shore."

"I know, Tara. I know. I'm not a miracle worker here. Cut me a break."

Billie immediately regretted her short tone with her daughter as Tara retreated to the far end of the kayak to sulk.

Billie sighed heavily. "I'm sorry, Tara. I didn't mean to speak to you like that. It's just that I feel so powerless here. I'm supposed to be the mom and the protector. Some protector I am."

"It's okay, Mom. I understand."

They fell silent once more and continued to drift along.

Billie's head perked up suddenly.

"What is it, Mom?"

"Shh." Billie listened intently to the sounds of nature around them.

"What is it, Mom?" Tara questioned again, in barely a whisper. Fear of the unknown weighed heavily in her voice.

Billie frowned as she strained to see what lay ahead of them downstream. Her vision cleared as the current rapidly moved them closer.

"Oh, my God! Tara! Brace yourself. We're going over the falls!" Billie screamed as the kayak dropped from sight.

***

Cat lay as still as she could while the deafening roar seem to linger just a little too long above her head. The raging fire moved quickly, sucking the oxygen from the air and from everything in its path. Such was the case for the small alcove Seth and Cat had dug for themselves. As the fire raged overhead, the pair lay as still as possible so as not to disturb the layer of soil on top of them, however the intense heat from the fire caused the moist soil to quickly dry, and then to become hot as small granules of sand burned their exposed skin. Breathing became difficult as their oxygen supply was rapidly depleted by the vortex of fire above them.

Seth and Cat held their breath for as long as was humanly possible. When it came down to a choice of breath or unconsciousness, Cat chose the former by suddenly sitting erect and gasping for air. A split second later, Seth followed her lead.

Luckily for mother and son, the wall of fire had moved fast enough to pass over them quickly, so little danger lingered from the fire alone. However, the same could not be said of the smoke. Their first instinct was to breathe deeply as they escaped their sandy grave. Unfortunately, the air they greedily inhaled was smoke-laden and caused them to cough uncontrollably.

The first thing Seth did was reach out for Cat. "Are you okay, Ma?"

Cat continued to cough, with one hand over her mouth. She held her other hand out to her son, and nodded. "Seth, how did you know to do that? You've saved our lives."

Seth coughed. "Boy Scouts. It was part of our wilderness training." Seth climbed from the hole and crawled on hands and knees to where he had left their back pack—or at least what was left of it. The fire had quickly burned away the nylon material as well as the hoodie sweatshirts and everything else flamable inside it. Luckily for them, the knife was still intact, as was the bottle of water, albeit a bit melted and deformed by the fire. Seth picked up the knife and used it to cut off two pieces of his T-shirt which he doused with some of the water and quickly returned to Cat. He handed the wet rag to her. "Put this over your mouth, Ma. It will filter the smoke."

Cat complied and inhaled deeply through the dampened material. Within moments, their coughing subsided.

"How are you doing?" Seth asked as soon as he could talk.

Cat continued to hold the rag to her face. "I'll be okay. How about you?" she returned.

"I'm good." He offered his hand to Cat. "Here, let me help you up."

Once Cat was on her feet, Seth brushed the cooled granules of sand from her skin that was polka-dotted with several hundred small red burn marks left behind. After repeating the process on himself, he retrieved what was left of the water.

"Drink some of this," he instructed. "It's probably warm, but wet."

Cat drank sparingly with the knowledge that they had just this one bottle of water between them. She handed the water back to Seth. "You need to drink some as well."

Seth took a small drink while he surveyed their situation. "We've got to find our way out of here."

Cat looked at her watch and marveled that it was still operational. "Seth, it's past six o'clock. We'll never get out of here before dark. We're not even sure where we are, and any markers we might have had are now burned-out. We need to look for something that might provide shelter for the night."

Seth nodded. "I agree, but look around, Ma. There's nothing left. Nothing safe, that is. There are small fires all around us."

Cat looked around at the burned-out terrain. The heat coming from the still-burning trees and brush was intense and uncomfortable against skin that was already tender from the burning sand that had covered them in their makeshift shelter. Although the immediate danger had passed when the raging wall of fire sped through, the air was still toxic and heavy with smoke. Cat felt totally overwhelmed. All she could do was wrap her arms around herself and cry.

Seth took his mother into his arms and held her close. "Mama, we'll make it out of here. I promise," he said softly.

"Seth, I'm worried about your mother and sisters. We have no idea where Mom and Tara are. I hope to God they aren't caught in this too," she said shakily.

"I know, Ma. I've been thinking about that myself. At least we know Skylar is safe."

Cat nodded and a shudder ran through her slight frame.

"Don't give up on them," Seth whispered. "Mom and Tara are pretty tough."

Cat stepped out of the circle of Seth's arms and looked around. She wiped the tears from her face, and in the process, smeared the dirt and grime left behind by the smoke and soil. "We need to get back to civilization so we can find them, Seth."

"I know Ma, but like you said, we'll never make it out before dark, and don't even suggest we travel at night. It will be too dangerous. We don't need you falling off another cliff in the dark."

Cat nodded. "Okay. So let's find somewhere to spend the night." Cat took her son's arm and they slowly made their way through the burning rubble.

\*\*\*

Billie and Tara clung to the cockpit of the kayak with all their might as the small craft plunged over the falls. Billie's immediate thought, was that they would both be killed by the impact at the bottom of the drop. However, the waterfall turned out to cascade down the mountainside in steps, which meant multiple falls of shorter distances. What she did not anticipate though, was the scattering of boulders throughout each stretch of the falls.

Their kayak bounced off the rocks like it was inside a pinball machine. Each impact threw them around the inside of the cockpit like rag dolls. It was a miracle that they managed to remain inside the boat, and that the boat didn't capsize as they made their perilous journey down each leg of the falls.

They were not so lucky when they reached the bottom. The last leg was nearly a vertical drop of about thirty feet. The trip down the falls had inflicted serious damage to their bodies from being thrown back and forth against the sides of the cockpit, so when the kayak took its final plunge, neither was able to hold on and they were ultimately catapulted from the boat and into the cold water of the falls.

Billie was frantic with fear. As long as they were in the kayak, she felt some measure of control and some measure of security, since Tara was within her grasp. As they plummeted down the final leg of the waterfall, she lost contact with her daughter as she watched her disappear under the foamy white spray at the bottom of the falls.

"Tara! Tara!" Billie screamed, knowing her voice alone could not save the child. She tried thrusting her body forward to plunge into the water after her, but the current and whirlpools at the bottom of the falls had other plans.

Billie suddenly found herself surrounded by white bubbly water as she was pulled under the surface and dragged along by the current. For what seemed like an eternity, Billie was submerged. While she fought for air, she had to emotionally deal with the reality that she had lost her daughter. Finally, the buoyant qualities of her life jacket brought her to the surface of the water where she flailed around and gasped for air.

Billie rubbed the water from her eyes and frantically scanned the area. "Tara! Tara! Where are you? "Tara!" Billie continued to scream for many minutes, to no avail. Tara was nowhere to be seen. "Nooooooo!" Billie screamed loudly as the current continued to drag her downstream.

# CHAPTER 15

"Damn it! What's taking so long?" Jen held the receiver to her ear. She had called the Yellowstone National Park Service nearly fifteen minutes earlier and was on hold for most of that time.

Kelly and Karissa paced back and forth from opposite ends of Jen's kitchen while they waited for news of their friend. Steve sat at the table clenching his hands in an effort to contain his anxiety. His leg nervously bounced up and down. Fred stood against the counter with his legs crossed at the ankles. He sipped a cup of coffee. A heavy tension fell upon all occupants of the room.

Finally, someone answered her hold. "Yes. Yes, my name is Jennifer Swenson," she began. "I saw the news report on television about the wildfires in Yellowstone and I'm calling to check on whether all of the tourists in the park are accounted for. We have some friends who are visiting there this week and we haven't heard from them."

All movement stopped as soon as Jen began to speak. Every eye in the room was on her as they waited expectantly for news.

A deep frown creased Jen's forehead. "What do you mean you don't have any accountability for tourists at the park? They registered to stay in one of your cabins. Don't tell me you don't have a record of that!" she stated firmly. "W...Wait! Damn it!" Jen shouted into the phone. "They've put me on hold again!" she said incredulously.

Kelly looked at Jen. The intense fear she was feeling was evident on her face. "Tara's in trouble. I can feel it," she said softly.

Jen extended her hand to the teenager who willingly took it. "We don't know that, Kelly. Don't give up on them yet."

Jen's attention was suddenly drawn back to the phone. "Yes. Okay. Their names are Billie and Cat...I mean Caitlain Charland, and their children, Seth, Tara and Skylar. I believe they are staying in one of the cabins in the backcountry," Jen spoke into the phone. "Yes, I'll hold," she added. "Like I have any choice!" she complained to her family.

Jen looked at her watch. "It's about eight o'clock there right now," Jen observed.

"Ah, hello? Yes. Skylar? Yes, she is their youngest child. She's about ten years old," Jen said into the phone. "I see." Jen looked at her family with intense concern on her face. "No, it's not like them to be late for anything. If they haven't picked her up yet, it's probably because they can't. What's that?" Jen asked. A few moments later she added, "Jesus! I assume you have someone looking for them?" Jen asked hopefully. "Good. Look, these people are like family to us. Is there any way you can contact us when they are found?" she asked. "Thank you, and please, if there is anything we can do to help, just ask and we'll be on a plane immediately. What's that? Yes. Yes, I can do that. I will be there as soon as I can. Is there any way I can talk to her?" Jen asked.

Several moments passed before Jen's attention was drawn back to the phone.

"Aunt Jen?" a small shaky voice said.

"Sky? Skylar, honey, are you all right?" Jen asked.

"Mom forgot to come get me. I'm scared," Skylar began to cry.

"Sweetie, I'm sure Mom didn't forget you. She must have been delayed somehow. Honey, do you want me to come wait for Mom and Mama with you?" Jen asked.

"Can you?" Sky replied shakily.

"I sure can. I'll take the next plane out, sweetie. I'll get there as fast as I can, okay?" Jen replied.

"Okay. Please hurry," Skylar urged.

"I will, sweetie. I will. You need to be brave, love. Okay? Now can you put the nice ranger back on the phone, Sky?" Jen asked.

"Look, the girl is there with both her mothers, and older brother and sister. Have *none* of them shown up to claim her?" Jen asked when the ranger returned to the phone. "Well then something is wrong. There is no way in hell any of them would abandon this child. Please do everything you can to find them, okay? All right. I'll be there as soon as I can. I assume Skylar will be well taken care of tonight?" she asked. "Good, and thank you. I'll see you tomorrow." Jen hung up the phone.

Jen looked at four expectant pair of eyes. "Billie was supposed to pick Skylar up from the Junior Ranger program four hours ago and she hasn't shown. She's also late returning a kayak she rented."

Kelly and Karissa clung to each other while Steve just dropped his head into his hands.

"What do they think has happened, Jen?" Fred asked.

"They don't know, Fred. It's not like Billie to be late picking up her kids. There is absolutely no way she or Cat would forget Skylar. And there's the missing kayak. Fred, I am really scared," Jen admitted. "I can't help but think the wildfires have something to do with their disappearance."

"You need to get on a plane as soon as possible to be with Skylar until they find the others," Fred insisted. "I will stay here with the kids."

Jen flew into her husband's arms and began to cry. "I'm so scared," Jen cried.

Fred held her close and rubbed her back. "I know, sweetheart. I'm scared too. But like you said to Kelly, don't give up on them. They've been through worse."

\*\*\*

By eight o'clock that evening, Senior Ranger Rick Ellis and his assistant, Ranger Angela Bradshaw stood around a large conference table along with several members of the Emergency Wildfire Rescue team.

Rick Ellis looked around the table at the stoic faces of the rescue workers. "We have reason to believe there are people still missing in the wildfire area. Specifically, three groups. They include the four-member Robertson family who registered a hike at Douglas Knob, two members of the Charland family who reportedly rented a kayak at the lower Firehole River depot this morning and have yet to return the kayak...or to collect the horses they left there, and two more members of the Charland family who registered a day hike on the Shoshone Lake Trail. We also found their horses in the corral by the trailhead. The Charland family disappearance is further supported by the fact that the youngest daughter was dropped off at the Junior Ranger program this morning and was due to be collected at four p.m. That never happened. She is currently staying with Angela here, until a family friend arrives to claim her tomorrow," Rick explained.

"So far the fire has consumed the greatest part of the Southwestern corner of the park. Luckily, it is heading away from the Old Faithful area, but it has already destroyed thousands of acres between the Shoshone Geyser Basin and the Continental Divide, including the southern part of Firehole River area and Grant's Pass that runs through it," Rick Ellis pointed to the map spread out before them. "This is where we believe several members of the Charland family were headed earlier today. Douglas Knob is just slightly to the southwest of Shoshone Lake, but it's also currently consumed by fire. This is where the Robertson family was headed."

Rick Ellis began to walk around the room as he spoke.

"Relative to the wildfire's progress, as you know, this has been an especially dry year, with little to no rain during a normally rainy June and July. Rain so far this August has also been scarce. Drought conditions have lead to extremely favorable conditions for this fire to spread quickly. Add to that the fact that wind is assisting the fire by adding oxygen to it, and I guess I don't have to explain to you how difficult it will be to fight, and how difficult these rescues might be. We need to be especially wary of the wind causing vortex tilts that might cause forward bursts. As you know, forward bursts can cause fire to shoot out a hundred meters or more at a speed of up to one hundred miles per hour. This particular fire is generating winds that are ten times stronger than ambient wind, so be on the lookout for random areas of spotting caused by the wind, and changes in wind direction. During a rescue effort, strong and variable winds can quickly turn a relatively safe situation into a deadly one.

"Now, as you know, warmer temperatures allow for fuels to ignite and burn faster, adding to the rate at which wildfires spread. Because of this, most of the search and rescue work will be done later in the day and through the night and early morning before the temperatures become uncomfortably hot. If the people who are missing are still alive—and let's pray to God they are—they will tend to stay put at night since they don't know the trails and terrain as well as we do. This should make finding them less difficult as they will not be moving targets. Any questions so far?" Rick stopped pacing and looked at each rescue worker.

"Okay. One more thing…as you know, the terrain in the wildfire area is a mixture of hills and valleys. I don't need to remind you that the steeper the slope, the faster the fire will spread uphill, partially because ambient wind usually blows uphill, and partially because heat and smoke rise, drying out the fuel in front of it further up the hill. For this reason, be especially careful when ascending the slopes. Our goal is to find these people and get them out of there as soon as possible, all without endangering ourselves in the process. You will not be out there to fight the fire. This is a rescue mission, and let's hope to God it doesn't turn from rescue to recovery. Leave the firefighting to the hotshots and smoke-jumpers."

Rick Ellis stopped at the head of the table and placed his hands on it. "One more chance for questions before we get started," he said.

"Do we have a description of the missing people?" one of the rescue workers asked.

"What we know is that the Robertson family is a mother, father, son and daughter. No other information is available about their race or ages. One of the two Charland groups is a mother and daughter, with the daughter being around fifteen years old, and the other group is a mother and a seventeen year old son. Both mothers are in their late 30's. We believe they are Caucasians. Any more questions?" He waited a few moments before continuing. "Okay then, see Angela about your assignments. If you find any of the missing persons, immediately report back to the base. Good luck and Godspeed to all of you."

Several minutes later, with assignments given, the rescue workers headed out on their missions. Rick turned to Angela and saw the concern on her face.

"Keep your fingers crossed that something good comes out of this search," he said.

"I'm really concerned about the girl, Skylar," Angela replied. "I would hate to be the one to tell her that her family has been lost to the fire."

"Well, with any luck, we won't have to do that," Ranger Ellis replied. "Where is she now?" he asked.

"She's in my cabin watching a movie. I told her I'd be back soon, so I guess I'd better get over there," Angela replied.

"Someone is coming for her tomorrow, right?" he asked.

"Yes. A family friend is flying in tomorrow morning. She called just a few minutes before this meeting to say her plane lands in Cody around six a.m.," Angela explained.

"Well, if we *do* have to give the child bad news, then at least she'll have someone to help her through it," he commented.

*** 

Jen put a small carry-on suitcase on the bed and began randomly throwing clothes into it. Fred sat on the bed and watched her make several trips between the clothes dresser and the suitcase. Her movements were frantic and jerky.

"Jen, sweetie. They're going to be all right," Fred said.

Jen sent an angry look his way. "You don't know that, Fred. None of us knows that. They are stuck in a wildfire for Christ's sake! If it's even half as bad as it looked on the news, I can't imagine how they'd survive it."

Fred rose from the bed and approached Jen. He reached out to rub her back.

"No! Don't touch me," she snapped.

"Jen..."

Jen turned sharply toward him. "Why, Fred? Why does shit happen to them? Is it some type of punishment for being who and what they are? What kind of benevolent God would do this to such good people?"

"I wish I had an answer for you, but I don't," Fred admitted.

Jen ran a hand through her hair and then sat on the bed. She lowered her face into her hands and began to cry.

Fred sat beside her and wrapped his arms around her. "They are strong, Jen. If anyone can survive something like this, it's Billie and Cat. Please don't give up hope."

"I'm sorry I snapped at you, Fred. You didn't deserve that."

"No, I didn't, but I understand and feel your frustration. Don't give it another thought, love."

"I have to call Cat's parents," Jen said.

"Do you have their number?"

"Yes. Cat gave it to me as an emergency contact if I needed it. How I wish I didn't need it now."

Fred nodded. "Let me help you pack first, then you can call."

Jen dialed the elder O'Grady's home number and waited for someone to answer. "Come on, Doc. Answer the phone," she muttered.

After several rings, the phone mail picked up. Ida O'Grady's voice cheerfully greeted her. "Hi! This is Doc and Ida O'Grady. We're out of the country for the next several weeks. If you need to reach us, call our daughter, Cat at..."

"Oh, great!" Jen exclaimed. "They're not home. In fact, they aren't even in the country. Now what do I do?"

"Do you have phone numbers for any of Cat's sisters?" Fred asked.

"Unfortunately, no."

"Then I guess there's nothing you *can* do, Jen. Cat will just have to call them herself when she can get to a phone."

Jen looked into her husband's eyes. "Always the optimist, Fred. That is one of the reasons I love you so."

***

Cat and Seth pushed onward through the burned-out forest in an attempt to cover as much ground as possible, and to look for a place to set up camp for the night before it became too dark and too dangerous to continue. Progress was slow and the prospect of finding shelter was slim, as nearly every inch of forest had been burned out and was still smoldering. The density of smoke in the air was so high, it was nearly impossible to take a deep breath without coughing. With her mind in doctor-mode, Cat was concerned that continued exposure to the poor air quality would cause respiratory problems.

The forest creaked and groaned around them as they struggled through the debris. Tall trees that were once so regal and strong swayed perilously to and fro as the winds stressed their weakened trunks.

Seth looked upward at an especially loud creak. "Mom, this is really creepy. It looks like a haunted forest," he said.

"You're right. I can almost imagine the trees coming to life like those in The Wizard of Oz when Dorothy picked their apples. Remember that?" she asked.

Seth chuckled. "Let's just hope the flying monkeys don't come after us!"

"I always hated those monkeys," Cat said.

Seth looked at her with surprise on his face. "That show was around when *you* were little?" he asked incredulously.

Cat laughed. "Oh, yeah. Black and white TV. Outhouses, no running water, and 'The Wizard of Oz'. Them were the good ole days," Cat said in her imitation grandma voice. "Geesh, Seth! The

Wizard of Oz was filmed in 1939! How old do you think I am anyway?" she asked.

"Oops!" Seth said. "You sure look good for your age," he added. Seth scooted several feet away to avoid the swat on the arm Cat sent his way.

Just then, a strong gust of wind shook the weakened trees. Cat and Seth froze where they stood. A very loud cracking sound filled the air and caused them both to look into the treetops above them. On the verge of dusk, it was nearly impossible for them to see what caused such a loud noise until it was too late.

"Ma! Watch out!" Seth lunged toward his mother, but not in time to pull her from the path of a large branch that had broken and fallen from the treetops.

With a sickening thud, the branch grazed Cat's shoulder. It knocked her over and trapped her right foot beneath it. Momentarily stunned, Cat laid there in shock, but not really in any pain. She was totally confused about what had just happened.

Seth circled the fallen branch to find her trapped beneath it. "Oh, my God! Oh, my God!" he exclaimed. He brushed the hair from her face. "Ma! Mama, talk to me," he demanded.

"W...what happened?" Cat was still dazed from the blow.

"You're trapped under a tree. Lie still. I'll try to push it off you," he said.

Seth surveyed the situation. He estimated the branch to be at least two feet in diameter and at least twenty feet long and he knew he had his work cut out for him. Seth placed his back against the limb, braced his feet in the dirt and pushed with all his might. "Ahh!" he screamed as the limb remained where it was. He rested for a moment and then tried a second time. "Ahh!" Again, the limb refused to move.

By this time, the shock had worn off and awareness filled Cat's senses, along with intense pain that invaded her trapped appendage. Cat did her best to hide her discomfort from Seth as he pushed futilely against the log.

Seth finally realized it was not within his power to move the log on his own. He sank to the ground with his back against it and held his head in his hands. "What am I going to do?" he whispered to himself. "It's getting too dark to see. What am I going to do?"

"So much for finding shelter, huh?" Cat joked to cover the pain.

Seth looked at his mother and then at the sky. Cat was right. Darkness was descending quickly. He had to somehow free her from this trap and then find something to protect them from the elements while they waited for daylight.

"Seth, give me the knife. There's a small branch digging into my leg. Maybe I can cut it back enough to break it off."

Seth handed the knife to Cat and then climbed to his feet. While Cat notched the branch, he looked around for something he could use for a lever. He found a fairly large stick which he dragged over to where Cat was trapped.

"Let me see how you're doing," Seth said. He inspected her progress. "If I bend the branch back where you've notched it, I might be able to break it off." Seth grabbed the branch and pushed back until an audible snap was heard. "There. It worked. Nice job, Mom. Now if I can wedge this stick under the log, I might be able to roll it off your foot."

Seth wedged the stick as far under the log as possible. He then rolled another medium sized log up to it to use as a fulcrum. He pushed down on the stick as hard as he could and successfully moved the log a fraction of an inch before the stick he was using snapped in half. The log rolled back into place and Seth fell onto his face on the forest floor.

Unknown to Seth, the rocking motion of the log as it fell back into position had caused excruciating pain as she felt the bones in the foot snap. Waves of pain spread up Cat's leg from her injured foot. She closed her eyes tightly to trap the tears from escaping. "Seth. That's enough. It won't move. You'll just end up hurting yourself," she choked out.

Seth fell to his knees at his Cat's side. "Ma, we can't leave you like this." Tears welled in his eyes. He began to dig furiously at the ground under Cat's leg. "Damn it!" he cursed. "I left the shovel beside the other hole we dug." He continued to dig in the hopes that he could make the hole deep enough to slide her leg out from beneath it.

Seth managed to clear the area beneath Cat's calf, but as he moved closer to the ankle that was trapped beneath the tree, he hit a very hard object. "What the hell?" he exclaimed.

"What is it, Seth?" Cat asked.

"I don't know. I think I've hit something." Seth continued to clear the loose dirt from the hole, and in the process, exposed what appeared to be a large object. "Shit! It's a rock. Your ankle is trapped between the tree and a rock. I wonder how big it is." He continued to clear soil away from the rock by following the edges of it. The hole became larger and larger until Seth sat back on his heels. "It's no use. The rock is too big." He looked at his mother. "I'm sorry, Ma."

"It's not your fault, Scout. Do me a favor and fill the hole back in. It kind of hurts more with my calf suspended over the hole. Please fill it so I can rest my calf on the ground."

Cat took deep breaths to calm herself and held her leg as still as possible until Seth filled in the hole. Slowly, she rested her calf on the ground and as she did so, she realized the pain that had been radiating from her trapped foot was easing. Medically, she knew this was due to the lack of circulation. She also knew that if the log wasn't removed soon, she stood a good chance of losing her limb. All of these thoughts were overshadowed by the fact that they were losing daylight.

"Seth, we don't have much choice right now. The sun is almost set. We need some type of shelter," Cat pointed out.

Seth knelt on the ground beside Cat and wiped the tears from his face. He then looked around until he spotted an area of trees and low-lying brush that had been partially spared by the fire. "I'll be right back," he said. Seth climbed to his feet and made his way to the brush. Sometime later, he returned with several large branches that still contained leaves, and arranged them over and around Cat. "There. That should protect you if it rains tonight," Seth remarked.

"Get under here with me, Seth. I need someone to keep me company."

Despite random areas of still-burning brush, a slight chill began to settle over the forest.

Seth wriggled in next to Cat and placed his arm around her. "I will find someone to help us at first daylight, Ma. I promise," he whispered to her.

"I know you will, sweetie," Cat replied.

"Does it hurt?" Seth asked.

"It did at first, but now it's kind of numb," Cat answered honestly.

Seth was silent for a few moments as he digested Cat's reply. "That's not good, is it?" he asked.

Cat was silent for a long time.

"Ma?"

"No, Seth. That's not good."

\*\*\*

The current was so strong at the base of the waterfall that Billie could not fight against it. White water tossed her around and pulled her under the surface several times only to release its grip as her life jacket returned her repeatedly to the surface. In a particularly rough part of the rapids, she was ricocheted back and forth between several small boulders until the current finally tossed her head first into a larger one and knocked her unconscious.

\*\*\*

Darkness descended over the river as day gave way to night. Only the night owls were witness to a figure as it floated by. The water was a curious shade of pink around it. A patch of bright orange held the figure's head above the water. Several miles downstream, it floated into an alcove, and through the motion of the water lapping gently against the shore, it was deposited partially on the sandy river bank and partially in the water, where it lay quiet and still, wedged against a tree that had fallen on the shore.

*\*\**

The sound of gurgling water was deafening to Billie's ears. She lay in a totally relaxed state, seemingly suspended in air. *What is that sound? Where am I?* she questioned as she floated aimlessly. *What has happened to me? Why does my head hurt?*

A sudden coldness began to creep into her limbs. *I'm freezing,* she thought to herself. *Why am I cold? Has Cat stolen the blankets again?* Billie reached over to retrieve the stolen blankets and found herself capsized. She was face-down and struggled to breathe.

"Pfff...sppp....what?" Billie sputtered until reality crashed in on her. When she reached across herself to retrieve her imaginary blankets, she inadvertently rolled in the water and submerged her face. She instantly brought herself back to consciousness and realized she was floating face down in the cold river water.

Billie flailed frantically in the water until she managed to right herself so that her head and upper body were floating above the water, suspended by the life jacket she still wore. She looked around in the near pitch darkness and suddenly remembered she was not alone when she took the plunge down the waterfall.

"Tara! Tara!" Billie shouted into the darkness. The only sound that returned was the muted hooting of the night owls. "Tara..." she whispered once more and then broke down into uncontrollable sobbing.

After several moments, Billie gained control over her emotions and took stock of her own predicament. *I've got to find Tara,* she told herself. *But it's so dark. I'll never find her in this darkness.*

Billie strained through the darkness to see the subtle outline of a river bank nearby. She successfully fought her way against a very gentle current and reached shore. She crawled out of the water and climbed to her feet. Immediately, she stumbled forward on weakened limbs and fell back to her knees. Billie realized she would get nowhere in her present state. She was so cold, she shook uncontrollably. "I've got to warm up," she muttered. She climbed to her feet once more and stumbled to the edge of the forest where she found a moderate sized tree bough that she was able to burrow under. She pulled her knees into her chest and wrapped her arms around them.

"Tara, where are you," she whispered into the darkness. "I'm so sorry, love." Billie closed her eyes and welcomed the escape from the nightmare that was her reality as she drifted into unconsciousness.

# CHAPTER 16

Seth was awakened suddenly by a movement at his side. When he opened his eyes, he was barely able to make out Cat's silhouette in the dim light of the dawn. She was sitting up and tying something around her leg.

He sat up and pushed their makeshift shelter to the side. "Ma, what are you doing?" he asked.

"I've got to get free of this tree, Seth. I can't stand being trapped here a minute longer." Cat was near hysterics.

Seth watched her wrap strips of torn clothing around her calf, just above where her foot was lodged under the log. He struggled to understand what she was trying to accomplish. "Ma, what exactly are you doing there?" he asked again.

Cat spared a look at her son. "I'm making a tourniquet."

Seth was startled by the crazed look in her eyes. "A tourniquet?" he repeated. "Why do you need a tourniquet?"

Cat looked at Seth with a frown on her face. "Surely, you know what tourniquets are used for," she said.

"Of course I know. It used to stop bleeding when someone has a severe wound."

"Exactly."

"But you're not bleeding," Seth point out.

"I will be when we amputate my foot."

Seth jumped to his feet. "What the hell are you talking about? Are you out of your freaking mind?" he screamed.

"I can't think of another way to free my foot from under this tree. Can you?"

"You are not cutting your foot off, Ma. That's insane!"

"I choose to believe it's smart. The longer it remains trapped under this tree, the less likely it will be that I'll ever be able to use it again anyway. So I choose to take care of it now rather than later."

"You can't be serious." Seth was sick to his stomach at the very thought of what Cat planned to do.

"It's quite simple, Seth," Cat explained. "Once these strips are wrapped around my leg, we slip a stick under them and twist it to tighten the strips. After a while, the circulation stops flowing to the limb below it. Then we can amputate."

"There is no freaking way you are going to amputate your foot, Ma!" he explained loudly. "No freaking way!"

Cat looked at her leg and then back at her son. "You're right. There is no way *I* am going to amputate it…at least not on my own. I will most likely need some help."

Seth squatted down in front of Cat. "What exactly are you saying?"

"You have to help me, Seth. You'll have to cut through the skin then snap the ankle bone," she reasoned.

Seth stood and grabbed both sides of his head. "I can't believe you're saying this."

"You have to help me with this, Seth."

"What part of no don't you understand, Ma? No! I won't do it! I can't! I can't do it. I won't."

"Then I guess I'll have to do it myself," Cat said. Cat tied the last knot and then reached for the stick she had found nearby. She slipped it beneath the strips of cloth and was able to twist it two full turns before the pain became so intense, she had to stop. "Ahh!" Cat cried out, but she held the knot tight. Tears rolled down her face and the excruciating pain almost caused her to pass out.

"Ma, stop. Please stop," Seth begged.

Cat held tight to the stick and did not allow the two full turns to become unraveled as she fought through the pain.

Seth looked around frantically until he found a suitable place to deposit the contents of his stomach. When it was over, he sat back on his knees and wiped his mouth while he regained his breath. Finally, he climbed to his feet and turned back toward his mother. What he saw chilled the blood coursing through his veins.

"Ma! No!" Seth lunged forward and grabbed the jackknife Cat held precariously close to the skin below the tourniquet. In his haste, he grabbed the knife by the blade and slit his palm open in the process. Seth threw the knife as far into the forest as he could before turning to address his mother once more.

"What is wrong with you!" he shouted. "What are you thinking? Damn it, Ma! You could bleed to death out here."

Clarity suddenly filled Cat's eyes at the sight of the blood covering Seth's hand. "Seth, you're bleeding!" she exclaimed.

Seth looked at the steady flow of blood that dripped from his injured hand. "Oh, for crying out loud!" He ripped yet another piece of his T-shirt off and wrapped it around his hand. "It must have happened when I grabbed the knife."

"Come here, let me look at it." Cat released the hold she had on the tourniquet.

Waves of relief coursed through Seth's veins when he saw the tourniquet unravel. He knelt down and extended his hand forward for Cat to examine.

Seth winced when Cat poked and prodded the wound.

"It's pretty deep, Seth," she said. "It really needs stitches. I'll re-wrap it, but you'll need to keep your fist clenched to keep the pressure on it, and we'll have to replace the bandage shortly. This one is already pretty soaked in blood."

"Okay, Mama."

Cat lay back down after tending to Seth's hand. Sitting upright for too long caused discomfort in her lower back.

Seth knelt beside his mother and watched her face as she lay there. It was obvious to him that the circulation was beginning to return to her leg after the tourniquet had loosened. The creases in her forehead and her clenched jaw were evidence of the tremendous pain she was in. He chided himself for not being able to carry out his mother's wishes, but given the same choice, he would stand by his decision. He was convinced there was still hope of rescue. He only hoped he could convince Cat of that.

\*\*\*

Billie's return to consciousness was both slow and confusing. *Oh, my God. I'm so cold. Why does my head hurt? What happened?*

Her eyeballs fluttered behind closed lids and she struggled to stay conscious. She could feel her awareness come and go. Somewhere in the distance, her mind registered something wet lapping against her cheek, but her body was unable to react to shoo the offensive gesture away. Several moments later, the lapping continued and she finally forced her eyes open. Only through the grace of God was she able to remain still, for right beside her, running its wet, rough tongue across her face, was a black bear.

Billie forced herself to remain still and silent; not that she had a choice, since the sight of the bear paralyzed her into inaction. She knew if she made any sudden movements, she would quickly become the bear's breakfast. Her body tensed and ached as the bear sniffed its way down the length of her form. It stopped to lick something off her leg. For several long minutes she laid there as still as a statue, until finally, the bear slowly lumbered away.

Billie closed her eyes and allowed tears of relief to escape her lids. She could hear a slight rustling in the distance, and she instinctively knew the bear was still in the area. For several more moments she continued to lie still until the rustling sound faded and finally stopped. She lifted her head and looked around. The bear was nowhere to be seen.

Billie crawled out from beneath her make-shift tree-bough blanket and struggled to sit. She surveyed her surroundings through the dim morning light. She was sitting on the edge of a river bank. *How did I get here?* Billie ran her hands through her hair and encountered a tender spot on the side of her head. *Obviously, I've hit my head on something. That explains the headache. The question is...how?*

Billie leaned back against a fallen tree and focused on the events of the past several hours and the events that had brought her to this place. Slowly, the memories returned. The wildfire. The capsized kayak. The waterfalls. Tara.

Billie quickly climbed to her feet and looked around in a panic. "Tara! Oh my God! I've got to find Tara!" she said out loud. She forced herself to relive their descent over the falls and recalled the last vision of her daughter as she disappeared under the spray of white water at the base of the falls.

Billie sat down on the fallen tree and lowered her head into her hands. *What if she's dead? I'll never forgive myself for not protecting her. We should have turned around at that first flash of lightning. How will I tell Cat?*

"Think, Billie. Think," she said out loud. She looked around at her surroundings. Everything was blurry and she was seeing double. *Must be the head injury*, she reasoned. She looked around again and tried to focus. *I can't just sit here. If the current pushed me down river, it must have done the same for Tara. She weighs much less than I do, so she would have been carried further. I need to find her. Dead or alive, I need to find her.*

Billie found a makeshift walking stick to support her aching body. Before setting out, she took off her waterlogged life jacket and left it on the downed tree. She took two steps away and then turned back to look at the life jacket. *Of course! Tara was wearing a jacket. Mine stayed on during the fall. Hopefully hers did too.*

Billie began to walk along the river bank and continuously scanned both banks for anything bright orange. *Tara, sweetheart, I'm coming. If you are nearby, please give me a sign.* Billie moved as fast along the bank as her battered body would permit. *Cat, I am so sorry. I've lost Tara. I've lost our baby. If anyone is listening, please let me find our daughter alive.*

\*\*\*

"Jennifer Swenson." Jen gave her name and picture ID to the rental car clerk at the Yellowstone Regional Airport.

It was only six a.m. when Jen landed in Cody, Wyoming. She picked up her rental car, and once inside, she spread the map out on the seat beside her and studied it carefully for the shortest and simplest route to the park. She was not very good at directions, and even worse at reading a map, so what should have been an hour ride, took two and a half hours and three wrong turns.

Finally, at nearly eight-thirty a.m., she pulled up to the ranger station near The Old Faithful Inn. As soon had she made it out of the car, she was nearly tackled by ten year old Skylar.

"Aunt Jen! Aunt Jen!" Skylar threw herself into Jen's arms and began to cry.

Jen wrapped her arms around the little girl and held her close. She placed soft kisses on the side of her face. "Shh. It will be all right, Sky. You'll see," she whispered.

Skylar clung to her. "Aunt Jen, I'm scared." Skylar's body trembled with fear.

"I know, sweetie. I'm scared too," Jen admitted.

"Mom didn't come back for me. Mama is gone too!" Skylar was barely able to speak. Her sentences were interrupted several times by gasps for breath and sobs wracking her small frame.

"You need to calm down, Sky. It won't do Mom and Mama any good if you make yourself sick," Jen reasoned with the child. "I'm here now. I won't leave until they find Mom and Mama. I promise. Okay?"

Skylar nodded and made and attempt to calm herself as Jen brushed the yellow-gold bangs from the child's face.

Just then, a movement caught the corner of Jen's eye as she saw a female ranger approach them.

"Hi, I'm Angela Bradshaw. I've been looking after Skylar." Angela extended her hand in greeting.

"Jennifer Swenson. You can call me Jen." Jen retrieved her driver's license and offered it for identification. "Thank you for taking care of her," Jen added.

Angela looked at the license and then handed it back. "She's been great. No problem at all," Angela replied.

"Do you have any word of them yet?" Jen asked.

Angela looked nervously at Skylar and then sent a covert message to Jen that she didn't want to speak in front of the child.

Jen looked at Skylar and immediately understood. "Skylar, honey, why don't you climb into the car? I'm going to get us a room at the Old Faithful Inn until Mom and Mama return. I just want to say goodbye to Angela. Okay?"

Skylar obediently did as she was told and effectively put herself outside of hearing range of the adults' conversation.

"So what are you *not* telling me?" Jen asked pointedly.

"Well, we don't know much yet. The four Charland members haven't been seen since yesterday morning. The only thing concrete that we do have is the kayak Billie rented. It was found by firefighters, but unfortunately neither Billie, nor her daughter, Tara was in it. That actually might be a good thing, considering how battered it was," Angela replied.

"Battered?" Jen asked.

"It has several dents and holes in it as though it had been smashed against rocks," Angela described.

Jen closed her eyes and rubbed her temples. "Look," she said wearily. "Skylar and I will be staying at the Old Faithful Inn. Please call me the instant you know anything...anything at all. Okay?" she asked.

"I will. I promise."

\*\*\*

"Roger, tend to the brush over there," Michael Elliot instructed one of the twenty hotshots under his command. "The rest of you, gather the loose kindling lying around and pile it together in that clearing. We need to build a firebreak around this area before the wildfire reaches it. If we can burn the fuel under controlled conditions ahead of the fire getting here, there will be nothing for it to burn, and nowhere for it to go but out. Please work quickly, the wildfire isn't far behind us," he said and then pitched in to gather loose brush.

The team of hotshots worked fast and efficiently until the immediate area was cleared of flammable brush, logs and tree limbs. Then, as the team stood around the tall pile of loosely stacked wood, armed with axes, picks and shovels to stop any fire that might wander from the burning pile, Michael set fire to it. Within minutes the pile was ablaze, burning quickly. Within an hour, it had burned down to embers.

"John, Randy, Steve... take the containers and fill them in the river. We need to completely soak these embers before moving on," Michael instructed the men.

John, Randy and Steve each grabbed two empty five gallon jugs from the nearby stack of equipment and headed a few yards away to the river edge.

"Man! This is one of the worse wildfires I've ever had to fight," Randy exclaimed as he led the crew of men to the river.

John, the oldest member of the crew, chuckled. "That's because you were just a child during the last really big fire in 1988," he said. "That was by far the worst fire we've had in the park's history. This one is small in comparison."

"Yeah, well, this one is bad enough, John. I would sure hate to be trapped in it," Randy replied.

"I've been on a few rescue missions...some successful, and some not. It's a pretty gruesome way to die," Steve interjected.

"There's the river," John said. "Spread out along the water's edge and fill your buckets."

John walked toward a downed tree and put one of his two buckets down next to it. He filled the first bucket and then carried it up the bank to put it down. He braced himself on the tree when he lowered the full bucket to the ground. This movement caused him to lean partially over the tree. "Holy shit!" he exclaimed, and he immediately grabbed his radio.

"John to base. We need a med-evac. Repeat, we need a med-evac."

Randy ran to John's side. "What is it?" he asked.

John pointed to the other side of the tree and then turned his attention back to his radio.

Randy quickly climbed over the tree. There on the ground, tucked nearly under the tree, was the body of a young girl, still wearing her life jacket. She was lying half in the water, half on the bank. Randy reached her quickly and dropped to his knees beside her. He turned her over and felt for a pulse, but had trouble locating one. By this time, John had joined him.

"Randy, give me a hand pulling her out of the water. Steve, run back to the crew and tell the chief to send Ethan and tell him to bring the first aid kit. I called for a med-evac, but it will be a while before they get here."

Randy and John pulled the young girl from the water. As they dragged her up the bank, her legs emerged from the cold water, exposing a severe looking compound fracture in her right thigh. The bone was quite literally protruding from the skin and the lower part of her leg dangled; attached only by skin, muscles and tendons. The damaged limb dragged on the ground, leaving dark blood stains in its wake. Friction from being dragged forced the tennis shoe on the damaged foot to fall off.

"Oh, my God!" Randy lowered her shoulders quickly to the ground and ran into the trees to vomit.

"Get your sorry ass back here!" John yelled. He looked back to the girl and realized she was bleeding profusely from the wound. He took his belt off and dropped to his knees beside her. Acting quickly, he wrapped the belt around her thigh above the fracture and cinched it tight in a make-shift tourniquet, but not until a large pool of blood covered the ground on both sides of her leg. By this time, Randy returned to assist him. "Get her life jacket off her. We need to see if there are other injuries," John instructed.

Randy struggled with the zipper and finally cut the jacket off with his jack knife and threw it aside.

"Poor kid. Look at her. It's obvious that she endured a pretty rough ride down the river. She's all banged up."

"I wonder if she was in that kayak we found earlier," Randy said.

"That's possible. I saw you check her pulse. Is she alive?" John asked.

"I couldn't find one, but then, she's actively bleeding, so she must be!" Randy replied before his attention was diverted to a loud rustling noise approaching them. "Ethan! Over here!" he called to the one paramedic they had on their crew.

Ethan emerged from the dense brush at the side of the river, followed by the entire hotshot crew. Michael Elliot was the last one to arrive on the scene.

"All right, guys. Back to work. Three of you grab the pails and go soak the fire. The rest of you help spread out the embers until they are all cold. Got it?" Michael commanded.

The crew did as ordered as Michael approached John and Ethan who were still tending to the girl. "What do we have here?" he asked.

"I spotted her as we were going after water," John explained.

Michael took one look at the girl and tried hard to control his emotions. The girl reminded him of his daughter who looked to be about her age. "Damn!" he whispered under his breath.

Ethan checked her vitals and then pulled bandages and cold packs from his medic bag to pack around her leg wound. "That was quick thinking with your belt, John," Ethan said.

I didn't see any blood in the water, but when we pulled her out, it started to bleed," John explained. "The only thing I could think of to use as a tourniquet was my belt."

"Really cold water or ice can be used to stem the flow of blood in an injury. It would make sense the bleeding would start again after she was out of the water. I just hope she wasn't in the water long enough for hypothermia to set in," Ethan explained.

Ethan checked for a pulse on her carotid artery. "Her pulse is faint, but steady. He did a quick check of her other leg and both arms, but found no further external evidence of fractures. He then lifted her shirt to just above her navel. "Holy, shit. This young lady is in serious trouble," he added.

Michael looked over at Ethan's shoulder and saw the dark purple bruising on her mid-section.

Ethan looked up at him. "Internal injuries. She also appears to have a head injury. We need to get her out of here and to a hospital as soon as possible."

\*\*\*

"Ma, I am going to look for help. I can't take all this waiting." Seth paced pack and forth. Cat had been writhing in pain for the past hour and he just couldn't sit and wait anymore for someone to find them.

"No, Seth. What if something happens to you?" Cat asked.

Seth stopped. "If I don't go, something *will* happen to you. You'll die here!" he exclaimed angrily.

"Don't be ridiculous," Cat replied. "I'm not injured enough to die."

"Well then it's killing me! Do you understand? I can't stand to sit here and watch you in so much pain. I won't sit and do nothing any longer. I am going whether you like it or not!" he shouted.

"Seth! Seth! Come back here this minute! Seth!" Cat screamed as she watched her son walk away.

\*\*\*

"Tara! Tara!" Billie called hoarsely. She continued to make her way along the river bank. Her throat was raw from calling Tara's name so many times.

At one point during her search, she saw a helicopter fly overhead. She assumed it was a search mission, and she waved her arms frantically to get their attention, but to no avail. It flew by without any indication they had seen her, so she had no choice but to resume her search.

Billie's head ached from the blow she had taken against the rock while caught in the rapids. Several times she had to stop and sit to regain her orientation and balance, and to prevent herself from losing consciousness as she walked. It was during one such break that she spotted something orange on the opposite bank. "Tara?" she whispered.

Billie's eyes were as wide as saucers and she trained her vision on the orange spot across the river. She leaned heavily on her walking stick and limped to the edge of the water where she carefully took several steps into the depths. Tears blurred her vision and hope filled her heart that she had found her daughter.

Several feet into the water, she suddenly lost her footing and fell victim once more to the undertow. Luckily, she was crossing at a particularly shallow part of the river and was able to regain her footing by firmly planting the end of her walking stick into the muddy river bottom and using it as an anchor against the current.

"Tara, baby. Mom's coming," she called out and she once more moved forward toward the opposite bank.

After what seemed like an eternity, Billie successfully reached the opposite shore, however the effort sapped what little strength she had. Confusion overwhelmed her and the dizziness returned. She stumbled toward a large rock, sat down and lowered her head into her hands. For several long moments, she fought the urge to give up; to just allow herself to fall into the realm of unconsciousness.

*Oh, God! Oh, God!* she chanted to herself. She fought hard to stay alert. *I can't lose it now. Tara needs me.*

"Tara!" she said out loud. She suddenly remembered why she crossed the river. Billie pushed the confusion and dizziness aside and quickly scanned the area for the orange object she had spotted from the other shore. Within seconds, she located it. It was a mere twenty feet away. Worried that she wouldn't be able to walk without falling down, Billie lowered herself to the ground and crawled to the life jacket. She picked it up and recognized it as similar to the one Tara was wearing.

She examined the jacket closely. *Is this Tara's jacket? Why is it torn? Why is there blood on it? Where is Tara?*

The questions running through her head only served to overwhelm and confuse her more. The lawyer in Billie took over and she consciously looked at a wider view of the area for clues, and hopefully, for answers. Her eyes slowly scanned the area between the water's edge and where she sat. A bigger picture began to emerge. The river appeared much deeper here than where she crossed it. Billie could visibly see drag marks leading from the edge of the river onto the river bank. Reddish-brown streaks could be seen on the trail. The same reddish-brown stains covered a much larger area close to where she found the life jacket.

*Is that blood? Is Tara hurt?* She looked around once more. "What's that?" she asked out loud when she spotted a new object. She crawled over to it. Recognition dawned as she drew near. It was a tennis shoe. Tara's tennis shoe…and it was covered in blood.

"No!" Billie screamed and grabbed her head to ward off the intense pain that invaded her skull. "Tara!" she repeated over and over and she rocked herself back and forth.

"Grr." A sudden sound from nearby drew Billie's attention. Her eyes were wild with fright as her mind registered the meaning of the sound. There before her, a mere ten yards away, was a black bear. Billie knew she was as good as dead if she panicked. She slowly reached behind her until she located her walking stick, then with dexterity she didn't know she possessed in the condition she was in, she quickly jumped to her feet and launched herself into the river where the current took over and carried her downstream and literally out of the jaws of danger.

\*\*\*

Jen paced back and forth across the floor of her suite and nervously chewed her fingernails. Skylar quietly watched cartoons on the couch nearby. She was filled with intense worry as she waited for word about her best friends, who had yet to surface from the wildfires. It was now close to noon, and still no word.

Suddenly, the phone rang.

"Billie? Cat?" Jen said anxiously into the receiver.

Jen listened intently to the voice on the other end. Disappointment clouded her features when she realized the caller was not who she had hoped. "Yes?" she said. "Oh, my God! Yes. Yes, I'll be right there. Wait! I need someone to stay with Skylar," Jen added. "Okay. Good. I'll wait until you get here. All right. Bye."

Jen hung up the phone and turned her attention to the child on the couch who looked up at her with hope in her eyes. Jen approached Skylar and knelt before her. She tucked a stray lock of hair behind Skylar's ear.

"Did they find Mom or Mama?" Skylar asked hopefully.

"No sweetie. Not yet, but they will. I promise." Jen knew her promise would be fulfilled, and hoped that when there *were* found, it was alive and not dead.

"Who was that on the phone?" Skylar asked.

"That was the Ranger station. They need me to go there and give them a better description of your moms and your brother and sister. Angela is on her way over here to spend some time with you while I'm gone. Okay?" Jen explained.

"I wanna go too!" Skylar whined.

"No, sweetie, I'm afraid you can't. It's pretty crazy out there because of the wildfires, and we think it's a better idea for you to stay here with Angela."

Skylar frowned and threw herself back on the couch. She folded her arms across her chest in protest.

A knock on the door drew Jen's attention away from the pouting child.

"That will be Angela," Jen said. She kissed Skylar on the head. "I'll be back soon, honey. Okay?"

Jen's stomach was in her throat on her way to the Ranger station. A Jeep was waiting to take her to the park infirmary. Ten minutes later, she stood in a brightly lit room and looked down at Tara's battered body lying on the table as Ethan worked to stabilize her.

She covered her mouth with her hand and fought the tears that coursed down her cheeks. She walked to the edge of the table and touched Tara's face. "Tara, sweetie. It's Aunt Jen."

Tara's eyelids fluttered, but did not open.

Jen looked at the paramedic. "Will she be okay?"

"I wish I could say yes, but I just don't know. She has some serious injuries. By the way, my name is Ethan." He shook her hand.

"Was she alone when you found her?" Jen asked.

"Yes, she was."

Jen's attention was suddenly drawn to the sound of a two-way radio behind her.

"Med-evac 1 to base. ETA two minutes."

Rick Ellis took Jen's arm. "The med-evac helicopter is nearly here. She'll be air lifted to West Park Hospital in Cody. Will you be able to go with her?"

"I...I can't. Her sister, Skylar, needs me to be with her," Jen said.

Rick nodded. "Well, that may be for the best. I'm sure visitors will be limited anyway."

Just then, the doors to the infirmary swung open and two EMTs rushed in, pushing a stretcher in front of them.

"She's right here, fellas," Ethan said. He stepped aside and allowed them to transfer Tara to the stretcher, directly on the backboard she's been carried out of the forest on. Soon, they were gone.

Ethan approached Jen and squeezed her arm. He reached into his pocket for a small notepad. "Write your cell phone number here. I'll pass it along to the hospital in the event her conditions changes."

Jen wrote her phone number down and handed it back to Ethan. "Thank you."

"She'll need your prayers," Ethan said. "She's one sick young lady."

Jen just nodded and watched him leave the room.

# CHAPTER 17

"Help! Help! Can anyone hear me?" Seth yelled loudly and then walked a few more yards. "Help!" he repeated.

Seth had been walking for about an hour, tying pieces of his T-shirt to burned-out trees along the way to assist him in finding his way back to Cat. After using torn pieces of his shirt for an air mask, to treat his and Cat's wounds and for trail markers, he was down to one small piece of cloth. He tied the last piece to a small sapling and continued his trek. He took mental notes to memorize the contours of the land and the direction of the sun as he moved along. At periodic intervals along the way, he stacked rocks or pieces of burned-out logs into small piles in the hope he could find them again to lead a rescue effort back to Cat.

Before long, Seth was tired and totally disoriented. He looked at his watch and noticed it was nearly noon. He knew the sun would be at its hottest within a couple of hours, and he realized the sun and the heat would only lead to dehydration for both him and Cat. Driven by a new sense of urgency, Seth continued to hike through the burned-out forest, looking for any signs of help.

\*\*\*

Billie allowed the river's currents to carry her downstream and deposit her in a shallow lagoon. With no resistance from the water, she was able to easily make it to shore, where she dragged herself onto a rock and reevaluated her situation.

Numb from her injuries and emotional trauma, she sat, disoriented and confused. Several scenarios ran through her head relative to Tara's disappearance. Her first thought was that Tara had drowned. That thought alone tore at her heart, but that scenario didn't make sense to her because of the life jacket. It looked like it was either cut or torn from her body. It was still zipped, so she didn't appear to have lost it during her trip down the river. The next possibility was that she had floated ashore and walked into the forest. With the amount of blood on the ground where Billie found the life jacket, she seriously doubted that Tara was capable of hiking out of the woods. Her biggest hope was that someone had found her, but then, she didn't see any footprints among all that blood on the beach. Her final thought was that Tara had fallen victim to the bear Billie encountered at the place she had found the life jacket.

Given the blood at the site, the drag marks at the river's edge and the torn and bloody condition of the life jacket, Billie's disoriented mind settled on the last possibility. How else could such a large blood stain have occurred? How else could the life jacket have been torn? How else could Tara have disappeared without a trace? Billie was convinced it was the bear. The bear that had been growling at her for invading its feeding grounds. Tara had encountered the bear, and the bear had emerged victorious.

Billie was distraught with grief. She slid to the ground from the rock she sat on, and weakened by her head injury and emotional state, she fell into unconsciousness.

***

The midday sun was directly overhead and the intensity of heat it cast was nearly unbearable. Combined with the throbbing in Cat's foot still trapped below the tree limb, Cat was miserable. She eyed the pile of branches from the makeshift shelter that Seth had thrown off them that morning. She tried desperately to reach the branch, intending to use it to shield herself from the sun. She strained to reach as far as possible, but her fingertips fell just short of their destination.

"Ah!" Cat screamed in frustration. She strained to reach once more, only to pull a muscle in her side in the process.

Cat curled into a ball to protect her injured side and began to weep and pray. "God, please don't let me die here. Please!" She summoned her remaining strength to try reaching the branch again.

"If I could just reach an inch further," she growled while stretching her arm forward as far as she could. Still, her fingers fell just short of her target. "God damn it!" she screamed and in anger as she lunged her body forward in one final effort to reach the branch.

Everything seemed to move in slow motion as Cat finally reached the branch, but in the process snapped the tibia in the leg lodged under the tree. Waves of searing pain radiated up her leg and into her hip and she fought to retain the contents of her stomach, to no avail. She retched for several moments before she finally regained control and raised herself into a sitting position.

"Oh, my God!" Cat grabbed her injured leg with both hands and tried her best to stabilize the break in order to minimize the pain. "Seth, where are you? Please come back. Please!" She looked around desperately for any sign of her son.

Cat located two small branches within her reach to use as a splint. She inhaled deeply and then used her trapped foot as an anchor point in order to shift her body to manually align the two halves of her leg bone. She screamed loudly against the pain throughout the process, and stopped only after the alignment was complete. Then, she placed the branches on both sides of her leg and tied them tightly around the limb using strips of cloth she had ripped from her T-shirt.

By the time she finished splinting her leg, Cat's hair, face and neck were drenched in sweat. She felt light headed and physically weak and she forced herself to lie down and to remain as still as possible to avoid jarring her broken leg.

Cat lay there helpless, parched and dehydrated. Her mind started to wander. *Billie, did I tell you I loved you before we parted yesterday? I can't remember! I love you so much. I'm so sorry! Please don't let me die. There is so much I want to do. My kids need me. Billie, take care of the kids. I'm so sorry. I'm...*

Finally, the pain was too much to bear and Cat's defenses shut down as she drifted into unconsciousness.

\*\*\*

"Hey! Hey! Over here!" Seth waved his arms frantically above his head. "Over here!"

"Stay where you are!" one firefighter called out to Seth. "We'll come to you."

For what seemed like an eternity, Seth stood and watched four firefighters make their way toward him from the top of a burned-out knoll. "Hurry!" he shouted. "My mom needs help!"

It took a full fifteen minutes for the firefighters to reach him. The first thing they did was to provide him with drinking water and then to look him over carefully for injuries. Considering his bare-chested, soot-covered appearance, they insisted on a quick physical examination.

Seth brushed off their attempts to examine him and insisted that aside from the cut on his palm and the smoky air he had inhaled, he was fine. "Look! I'm fine. It's my mom that needs help. She's stuck under a fallen tree limb," he explained quickly.

"Whoa. Slow down there," one of the firefighters instructed. "First, we need to know who you are," he stated.

"Seth Charland. I was hiking with my mom, Cat...I mean Caitlain, when the wildfires trapped us. We were looking for a way out of the forest when a strong gust of wind knocked a burned-out limb from the treetops. It hit my mom and trapped her leg beneath it," he explained.

"How long ago was this?" the firefighter asked.

"Sometime yesterday. Yesterday afternoon, I think," Seth replied impatiently. "She's still trapped. We need to find her," he insisted.

"Was she alive when you last saw her?"

"Well of course she was alive!" Seth shouted.

"All right. Calm down," the firefighter said soothingly. "Do you think you can find your way back to where you left her?"

Seth nodded enthusiastically. "Yes. I marked the trail. Follow me."

***

Rick Ellis made his way over several large boulders, using his walking stick as leverage. He stopped many times to recapture his breath. Having worked in an administrative capacity at the park for the past several years, he'd had little opportunity to hike and as a result, was no longer in top physical condition. Nevertheless, after the hotshots had discovered the Charland girl earlier that morning, Ranger Ellis felt a personal drive to assist in the search for the rest of her family.

Rick led his crew to the base of the waterfall that Billie and Tara had fallen over the previous day. He turned to face the men. "Since the girl was found a couple of miles downstream, we can only assume she and her mother traveled this part of the river. I need half of you to cross the river and search the other side and the other half of you to remain on this side. We will move slowly downstream. Search the water, river banks and short distance into the forest on both sides. The woman we are looking for is tall, with long, dark hair. Any questions?"

One man raised his hand. "Do you believe she may still be alive?" he asked.

Rick ran his hand through his hair. "Well, considering the condition the girl was in, we should be prepared for anything, but let's hope for the best," he replied. "Any more questions?" He looked around once more at silent faces. "Okay then. Let's go."

***

Seth led the team of firefighters into the forest in the direction from which he had come. He stopped every few yards to locate the markers he had built after running out of material from his T-shirt. Nearly an hour and a half later, they came across the last cloth marker he had left.

"Look! Over there," Seth pointed. "I left that marker about an hour after I started out for help. We're about half way there!"

The firefighters looked at each other and nodded. From the looks on their faces, it was obvious they were impressed with the forethought this young man had put into his search for help.

The firefighters were barely able to keep up with Seth as he ran from marker to marker. They called for several rest breaks as they were struggling to run through the forest in full gear. Finally, after another hour, they approached the clearing where Cat lay trapped under the tree.

"There! There she is!" Seth ran directly to Cat and threw himself onto the ground beside her. He expected to find his mother in the same condition she was in when he left, so he was shocked to find her unconscious and unresponsive. "Ma! Ma!" She shook her, but was unable to rouse her. "Ma! Wake up!" he insisted.

Seth felt a hand on his shoulder. "Hold up, son," the firefighter instructed. "Let me take a look at her."

Seth climbed to his feet and stood behind the firefighter. He looked over the man's shoulder as he tended to Cat. The other three men surveyed the site and discussed how to remove the tree from her leg.

"I need water here!" The firefighter shouted. A member of his team brought a bottle over to him. He pulled the spout on top of the bottle and drizzled water over Cat's face.

Seconds later, Cat began to moan and toss her head slowly from side to side.

"Ma!" Seth began before being silenced by the man tending to her.

"Caitlain," the man said. He softly tapped the side of her face. "Caitlain, can you hear me?" he asked.

Cat struggled to open her eyes. "Seth?" she said softly.

"I'm here Mama. I've brought help," her son replied.

"Caitlain, I need to you lie still. You've succumbed to dehydration. I'm going to lift your head and give you some water, a little at a time, okay?"

Cat drank sparingly before the firefighter gently laid her head back down. "What's your name?" she asked hoarsely.

"Jack. Jack Kilburn," he replied.

"Thank you, Jack," Cat said.

"You're welcome." He looked down at her leg. "Caitlain."

"Cat. Please, call me Cat," she interrupted.

Jack grinned. "Okay. Cat, my crew is trying to figure out how to remove the tree limb from your leg without causing further discomfort or damage. Hang in there for a few more moments, okay?" he asked.

"Well, I guess my plans for running to the store just flew out the window!" Cat tried hard to smile through the pain.

"Yep, the store can wait," Jack quipped back. "I'll be back in a moment." He went to consult with his crew.

Seth moved into the spot that Jack had just vacated and held his mother's hand.

Cat looked into her son's face and smiled through the tears that filled her eyes. "Thank you, honey. I am so proud of you," she said.

Seth just nodded, unable to speak through the emotion that had constricted his throat. He looked her over and noticed the new splint on her leg. "Ma, what happened to your leg?"

"I tried to reach a branch to put over me for shade and I snapped my tibia."

"I...I'm sorry. I should have thought to protect you from the sun before I went for help. I'm so sorry," he said sadly.

Cat grabbed Seth's hand. "Do *not* blame yourself, Seth. Neither of us thought ahead. Please don't blame yourself."

Just then, Jack returned. "Okay," he said. We've radioed our location to the station and they will have an ambulance standing by as soon as we carry you out of the forest. We're going to try to throw a rope over that tree limb up there and then tie the other end to the log. Once that has been done, all of us will pull on the end of the rope. Seth, when we get the log high enough to set her free, we need you to grasp her under the arms and pull her out. Then we'll release the log. Cat, you'll need to brace yourself. This will probably be pretty painful," he warned.

"It can't be much worse than it has already been," Cat replied. "Let's do this."

***

Jen picked up the phone and called the Ranger station for what seemed to be the hundredth time looking for news of her friends.  As with the prior ninety-nine times, she hung up disappointed.

She returned the phone to its cradle and turned to Skylar. "Nothing yet, sweetie."

The hope on Skylar's face when Jen hung up the phone quickly faded, and she sunk dejectedly into the couch.

It broke Jen's heart that she couldn't provide more hope to the child. *No news is good news,* she said to herself. *Who the hell made up that saying? No news is good news? Hell no! No news is NO NEWS! Geesh, what do I look like, an idiot?*

Suddenly the phone rang and Jen jumped out of her skin. "Jesus Christ!" she exclaimed as she reached for the phone. "Hello?"

Jen's knees suddenly weakened and she reached forward to brace herself against the wall. "Oh, my God," she whispered into the phone. "Yes, please. Call me as soon as they get here. Thank you.  Thank you so much!" she hung up the phone.

Jen turned to Skylar and opened her arms to the child.  She ran into them without hesitation. "They found Mama and Seth," Jen said in a voice made shaky by emotion. "They're going to be okay!"

Skylar hugged Jen tight around the neck. "When are they coming back?" she asked.

"Soon, sweetie.  Soon."

***

Rick Ellis and his men combed both sides of the river bank for two miles before coming across the location where Tara had been discovered. So far, the search had yielded nothing. Rick called a break and the men rested for a bit. Before moving on, they scanned the area, looking for clues that might assist them in finding Billie.

"Wow, there seems to be a lot of blood here," one of the men remarked.

"The girl had some pretty serious injuries," another replied.

"What are those marks? It looks like an animal has been here," a third man observed.

"I wouldn't be surprised. With human blood on the ground, it might attract some of the larger park animals," Rick replied.

"I hope whatever animal made these marks doesn't find our victim before we do!" one of the crew remarked.

"Well, let's hope we find her first," Rick rose to his feet. "Okay guys. Break is over. Let's get moving." His team spurred into action.

The crew split in half once more to scan both sides of the river and the men began to move forward in a relatively straight line. An hour later, they had covered two more miles when the river opened into a calm, shallow lagoon.

They continued their search until one of the men on the opposite shore shouted out, "There! I see something over there!"

Rick looked in the direction the man was pointing and saw something that didn't quite fit with the surrounding environment.

Soon, everyone in the crew pinpointed the target and a stampede of feet ran in that direction.

"We found her! We found her!" one of the crew members exclaimed as they descended on the body laying partially obscured by a large rock.

"Give me some room," Rick made his way to the front of the crowd. "Ethan, come with me!" The paramedic that attended to Tara moved in behind him.

Ethan broke through the crowed and knelt beside the body and immediately began taking vital signs while Rick Ellis searched her pockets for some sort of identification. Finding a slim billfold in her back pocket, he opened it.

"Billie Jean Charland," he read from her license. "We've found her."

A cheer rose up from the crowd of rescue workers as they celebrated their find.

"Ethan?" Rick asked softly as he watched the paramedic work.

"She's alive, Rick. Her pulse is strong, but judging by the lump on her head, she no doubt has a concussion. She also has similar bruises on her body that the girl had. They must have taken one hell of a ride down the river," he commented.

Just then, Billie began to stir.

"Billie? Billie, I'm Rick Ellis, and this guy beside you is Ethan. We're here to take you out of this hell," he explained.

Billie opened her eyes and stared in confusion at the men poised above her.

"Billie, can you hear me?" Ethan asked.

Billie turned her head toward the voice. "Tara?" was all she could say.

"Let's not worry about that right now, Billie. We need to get you out of here," Rick said.

Billie's eyes grew wide and she struggled to sit. "The bear. Tara. She's gone. The bear..." she repeated, near hysterics.

"Calm down, Billie. You're going to be all right. Jeff, bring the stretcher!" Ethan called over his shoulder.

With efficiency born of experience, the rescue workers strapped Billie onto the portable stretcher and they headed out of the forest.

***

"Okay, ready? One, two, three!" Jack counted as he and his men tugged on the rope that was slung over the tree.

Seth was poised behind Cat, with his hands under her arms, ready to pull her out as soon as her leg was free.

182

The men grunted loudly while they pulled on the rope. Loud creaks came from above as the limb which bore the weight of the fallen log cried under the load.

Cat laid on her back with her eyes closed and fought against the pain in her foot as the log began to shift.

Jack and his crew managed to take three or four steps backward before the log was high enough to free Cat.

"Okay, Seth. Pull her out!" Jack yelled.

Seth quickly lifted his mother from beneath her arms and pulled her several feet away. Cat screamed out in pain as her injured leg bounced along the ground while Seth pulled.

"She's free!" Seth yelled and signaled to the firefighters that it was okay to release the log.

"Okay, guys, slowly move back." Jack and his team stepped forward three paces and lowered the log to the ground before releasing the rope.

"Phew!" Jack exclaimed. He walked toward Seth and Cat. "That was harder than I thought it would be!"

"Jack! Watch out!" One of the men in the crew suddenly screamed as a deafening crack exploded above them.

"Wha...?" Jack looked up just in time to see the limb they had used for leverage come crashing down on top of him.

"Jack! Jack!" Seth watched the limb make violent contact with their rescuer.

Cat looked on in horror.

Within seconds, Seth and Jack's entire crew were pushing on the limb, trying desperately to move it.

"Come on! Move!" shouted Seth. Angry frustration clearly filled his voice.

From Cat's vantage point, she could see the lifeless body of Jack trapped under the limb. She pulled her professional mask over her features and called out for them to stop as she struggled to crawl over to Jack.

The firefighters looked at her questioningly and continued to push.

"It's okay.  She's a doctor!" Seth said frantically.  Immediately all activity halted.

Cat reached under the log and felt Jack's carotid artery.  Several moments later, Cat bowed her head and cried.

# CHAPTER 18

"We have to find my daughter." Billie struggled to release herself from the straps that bound her to the backboard.

"Ms. Charland, please stop struggling. We have no idea what type of internal injuries you may have. You'll do yourself more harm than good if you continue to fight us," Ethan scolded.

"I'll do *you* more harm than good if you don't unhook me!" Billie shot them the most intimidating look she could muster with a head injury.

Rick Ellis fought to hide the grin that was slowly making its way onto his face as Billie continued to give his chief medic a hard time.

"And what the hell is so funny?" Billie asked sharply, noticing Rick's expression.

Rick's face reddened with embarrassment. He cleared his throat. "My apologies, ma'am."

"Look," Billie said. "My daughter is probably lying out there somewhere, injured…or worse! Now untie these goddamned straps and stop this Jeep. I need to find her," Billie insisted.

Rick placed a calming hand on her shoulder. "Ms. Charland, we found your daughter this morning."

"What? You found her and you didn't tell me? Damn it! I've been out of my mind with worry! Where is she?" Billie demanded.

"She was airlifted to West Park Hospital in Cody," Rick explained calmly.

Billie's eyes were as wide as saucers. "Hospital? How badly is she hurt?" Billie asked as tears filled her eyes.

"I'm not a doctor, ma'am," Rick replied.

Billie quickly turned her attention to Ethan. "Were you there when they found her?" she asked.

Ethan avoided eye contact with Billie. "Yes, ma'am, I was," he replied.

"Look at me!" Billie demanded loudly.

Ethan did as he was told and allowed Billie to see the pain in his eyes.

Billie blinked to rid her eyes of the tears that had welled there. "You're a medic. Tell me. How bad is she?" Billie asked.

Ethan looked away once more.

"Please," Billie whispered. Desperation filled her voice and eyes.

Ethan cleared his throat and looked once more at Billie. "She was in pretty bad shape when we found her, ma'am," he replied.

Billie closed her eyes and allowed more tears to spill down her cheeks as she lost the battle to hold her emotions in check. *Tara,* she anguished, *my baby. I'm so sorry! Cat! I lost her. I couldn't protect her. Tara, I'm so sorry!*

***

Jen and Skylar were waiting in the infirmary when the Jeep carrying Seth and Cat arrived. Seth jumped from the open-topped Jeep as it rolled to a stop and met Jen half way. He held her back from seeing Cat.

"Seth! What are you doing? Let me go," Jen tried to get past the tall young man.

"Aunt Jen, wait. Let me take Skylar. Mama looks pretty bad right now and I don't want to scare her," Seth whispered into Jen's ear.

Jen finally took a step back and looked at the young man before her. She gasped as she took in his appearance. Seth was covered in black soot from head to toe. He was shirtless and bore several scratches on his chest and back, caused by tree branches, as he searched for the help that led the rescuers back to Cat. "Oh, my God, Seth! Look at you!" she exclaimed.

"This is nothing. Just a little dirt, is all. I'm fine. Mama, on the other hand is on her way to the hospital. She's a little banged up," he explained. "Why don't you go see her before they load her into the helicopter? I'll stay here with Sky," Seth offered.

Jen nodded and left the child with her brother. She made her way toward Cat who was still lying on a stretcher placed across the back of the open Jeep.

Seth watched Jen walk away and then knelt in front of his sister and took her hand. "Hey, Munchkin," he said.

Skylar was crying. "Seth, is Mama gonna be okay?" she sobbed.

"Mama will be fine. The firemen are going to take her to the hospital to check her out. She's got a hurt leg and arm, but she's going to be okay. You've got to be brave for her. We all do. All right?" he asked.

"Where's Mommy and Tara?" the child cried.

Seth's brow knit into a frown. "They're not back yet?" he commented, more to himself than to the child.

"I don't know," Skylar sobbed. "Seth, I'm scared," she admitted.

Seth tried hard to push his fears into the background as he dealt with his little sister. "I know, Sky. I'm kind of scared too."

***

"Cat!" Jen called as she drew closer to the Jeep. "Cat!" she called again. She started to run and stopped only when she reached her friend's side.

"Jen!" Cat cried hoarsely.

Jen leaned over Cat and held her close for several long moments. Her body shook with emotion. Finally, she stepped back. "Look at you, damn it!" Jen scolded. "Why the hell can't you live a *normal* life? Are you *trying* to put me in the loony bin?" she asked angrily.

Cat was too wrought with emotion to reply. Instead, her uninjured hand made its way to her mouth while she tried to stifle violent sobs.

Seeing Cat in this state was more than Jen could bear. She held her close and shared her fear and pain. "Don't you ever do this to me again, do you hear me? I couldn't bear losing you or Billie. I love you both so much!" Jen cried.

"Billie!" Cat suddenly exclaimed. "Where is she? And Tara? Oh, my God! Where are they?" she demanded.

Jen's face contorted with pain as she contemplated how to answer Cat's questions.

"Jen! Where are they?" Cat asked once more in desperation.

Jen touched the side of Cat's face and struggled to find the right words.

Cat violently pushed her friend's hand away. "No, Jen! Tell me! Where in hell *are* they? Tell me *now*!" she demanded angrily.

Jen took Cat's hand. "Sweetie, they haven't found Billie yet," she began, "and Tara…well, Tara has been flown to a hospital in Cody," she replied.

Cat struggled to sit up. "Jen, help me get off this stretcher," she said.

"Cat, no! You're injured. Stay where you are." Jen physically pushed her back down onto the stretcher.

The paramedic that was on the rescue crew saw Jen struggle with his patient and he immediately intervened. "Whoa there, Caitlain. You need to stay put. We're about to transport you to the helipad to fly you out of here." He tightened her restraints.

"Where are you taking me?" Cat demanded.

"To West Park Hospital in Cody."

"Is that where you took my daughter?" Cat asked desperately.

"Your daughter?" the paramedic asked.

"Yes. Earlier today. Tara Charland. She's about fifteen," Jen volunteered.

Recognition dawned on the paramedic's face before it clouded over again with concern. "Yes, I remember her." He checked his paperwork over. "All right then." He looked at Cat with his professional mask pulled over his features. "Let's go."

Jen clung tightly to Cat's hand as she watched the paramedic jump into the driver's seat of the Jeep. "Cat, hang in there. They'll find Billie soon. I know they will," she tried to assure her friend. "I will take care of Seth and Skylar until you're well."

Cat's eyes filled with tears as her worst fears came crashing down around her. Too choked up with emotion and fear, all she could do was nod as the Jeep began to drive away.

Jen was forced to release her friend's hand. She waved furiously and whispered 'I love you' as the distance between her and her friend rapidly increased.

\*\*\*

Skylar and Jen waited for Seth as the doctor on call cleaned and stitched the wound in his palm. An hour later, a freshly showered Seth greeted them in the waiting room just as the front door swung open admitting four litter bearers carrying a still-combative Billie.

"Mom!" Seth shouted. He met them half way across the room.

"Mommy!" Skylar jumped up from her seat next to Jen and ran toward her mother.

"Hold on there, guys," Rick Ellis said. "Let us put her down in one of the examination rooms first."

Both children halted their rapid advance and dutifully followed them into the same room Seth was in when his hand was stitched.

"Billie, I'm going to make the arrangements to airlift you to the hospital. I'll be right back," Rick left his men to settle Billie in.

Seth and Skylar threw themselves at Billie as soon as the firefighters worked the backboard from under Billie and left her resting on the table.

Billie immediately surrendered herself to her children. She held them close and gave up all attempts to hold back her tears. "I love you guys," she cried.

Jen leaned against the doorframe and watched the heart-wrenching scene before her.

Billie finally sensed her presence.  She reached a soot-covered hand out to her.

Jen was at her side in an instant and clutched for dear life to her friend.  She had to fight hard to hold back the seemingly endless stream of tears that had taken up residence on her face the moment her plane had touched down the previous day.

"Jen," Billie croaked.  She was too choked up to speak. "Cat, Tara," she whispered.

"Cat's going to be fine," Jen replied shakily. "They just took her by helicopter to the hospital."

"And, Tara?"

"They took her to the hospital this morning. I won't lie to you, Billie.  She's in pretty bad shape." Jen broke down into uncontrollable tears. She lowered her head to Billie's chest and felt her friend's arms circle around to hold her as they shared their pain.

Seth stood by and held his little sister in his arms while he fought back tears of his own.

***

"Her name is Tara Charland," Cat informed the EMT's as they wheeled her stretcher into the emergency room. "Please. I need to know how she is," Cat begged. "They brought her in by air this morning."

"I'll get a nurse for you.  Maybe she'll be able to tell you more. We kind of lose track of them after we bring them in," one of the paramedics offered.  They left Cat alone in one of the examination rooms.

Cat laid there for what seemed like hours before someone finally attended to her. "Thank God!" she exclaimed as an ER doctor looked in on her.

"Who do we have here?  Let's see…Caitlain Charland." He read her information from the paperwork attached to a clipboard. He looked up and failed miserably to hide the surprise on his face when he saw the condition Cat was in from her night in the burned-out forest. "Whoa!" he exclaimed. "It looks like *you've* had better days!"

Cat raised herself onto her good elbow and looked at the doctor's name tag. "Look, Dr. Quinten, my daughter was flown in this morning. Her name is Tara Charland. She's only fifteen. Please, I need to know how she is," Cat implored.

Dr. Quinten pressed Cat back onto the bed and then sat down on the edge of it. He took a small pad of paper from his coat pocket and scribbled Tara's name on it. "Was she caught in the wildfires too?" he asked.

Cat nodded her head vigorously, too choked up to speak.

Dr. Quinten patted the back of Cat's good hand. "I'll see what I can find out. Don't go anywhere. I'll be right back." He walked into the hall to flag down a passing nurse.

Cat watched as he handed the paper with Tara's name on it to the nurse, who nodded and then walked away. Dr. Quinten then returned to Cat's side and looked at the papers on the clipboard once more.

"Okay, Caitlain. It says here you have a broken leg, a crushed right foot, and possibly a fractured arm," he began.

"I'm pretty sure that the radius fracture is non-displaced and the tibia fracture is angulated. I did my best to realign the angulated fracture while still trapped under the tree, but it still hurts like hell, so it may only be partially aligned. As far as the foot is concerned, it is probably comminuted. The tree hit me hard, and pretty much crushed the hell out of my foot," Cat explained.

Dr. Quinten's eyebrows jumped high into his hairline as he listened to her diagnosis. He picked up her chart once more and thumbed through the pages. He smiled when he found what he was looking for. "I thought as much!" he exclaimed after reading the word 'doctor' under 'occupation'.

"So, Dr. Charland," he said. "Considering your background, you probably know what's coming. We'll have to take x-rays and then properly realign the angulated fracture as soon as possible before it starts to knit together the way it is. I don't have to tell you it won't be pleasant, and, if your foot is truly comminuted, it will probably mean surgery. But this is all speculation until we see the x-rays. I'll order them right away." He scribbled instructions on her chart. "I'll also order a chest x-ray to determine any damage from smoke inhalation," he added.

As Dr. Quinten turned to leave the room, he nearly ran headlong into the nurse he had sent on a fact-finding mission about Tara a few minutes earlier. He thanked her for the folder she handed to him and then returned to sit on the edge of Cat's bed to read its contents.

Cat watched his face closely as he read. "Dr. Quinten?" she questioned nervously.

Dr. Quinten spared a look at Cat before he returned his attention to the information in the folder. After what seemed like an eternity, he closed the folder and looked Cat square in the face. "Well," he said. "The good news is that she's alive."

Cat let out a gasp and fought to hold in tears as she listened for the rest of the news. "And?" She prompted the doctor to finish.

"And the bad news is that she's just barely holding her own. I won't lie to you, Caitlin. She's in rough shape. She has internal injuries, compound fractures, excess fluid in her lungs and a concussion. She's in intensive care right now," he explained.

"Internal injuries? What kind?" Cat asked.

Dr. Quinten looked at Tara's chart again. "It says here that she has experienced a head trauma, and she has blood around her heart and lungs…probably from a blunt force trauma. She has widespread hematomas on her abdomen, which usually indicates damage to her liver or spleen. She has already undergone ultrasounds and CT scans to try to isolate the source of the bleeding, and she is on IV fluids and blood transfusions to keep her blood pressure stable. They are waiting for the results of the tests."

"My poor baby. What could have happened to her to cause such injuries?" Cat cried.

"We may have to wait for her to tell us about that—unless someone else was with her, that is."

"What are her chances of survival?"

Dr. Quinten shook his head. "I couldn't even venture to guess at this point. We're doing everything we can for her. It will ultimately come down to her will power and how well she responds to treatment. Her attending physician has put her into a medically induced coma to allow all of her body's resources to be directed to surviving. She may need surgery if the bleeding doesn't stop on its own. It will be touch and go for the next few days. Luckily, she's young. She has that in her favor."

Cat laid flat on her back and closed her eyes. Tears spilled out over her cheeks. "My baby," she cried softly. "Billie, I need you," she added.

"Is Billie your husband?" Dr. Quinten asked.

Cat looked at the doctor and shook her head no. "Billie is my wife. She was with Tara when the wildfires began. She hasn't been found yet," Cat explained.

Dr. Quinten reached for Cat's hand and squeezed it gently. "Look, let's set your broken leg, then I'll run to ICU myself to check on Tara, okay?" he offered.

Cat whispered a pathetic 'thank you' as she watched Dr. Quinten leave the room.

***

The helicopter arrived with Billie just as Cat was being wheeled from x-ray to the cast room.

"I need to see them now!" Billie demanded as she was wheeled into an examination room. She lost her temper when the attending EMT ignored her demands. "Damn it! My wife and child are somewhere in this hospital and if you don't tell me where they are, I'll find out for myself!" She tried to sit up as she spoke.

"Calm down, Ms. Charland," one of the EMT's pushed her back onto the gurney.

"I'll calm down as soon I know where my wife and daughter are!" she exclaimed. "Now get me someone who knows what the hell is going on around here. You got that?" she demanded.

"All right! All right! I'll get someone. Just calm down, okay?" the EMT left her alone in the room.

Not five minutes later, Billie heard a piercing scream followed by agonizing sobs from elsewhere within the emergency room area. Her blood suddenly ran cold as she recognized Cat's voice. Having been left unattended, she was quickly on her feet and headed toward the source of the screams.

It wasn't everyday that a soot-covered six-foot Amazon crashed through the emergency room, so no one was prepared to stop Billie when she quickly located the cast room. There, a trembling and sobbing Cat was painfully enduring a fine realignment of the broken bones in her leg. Upon seeing her, Cat threw her arms open and cried out to her. "Billie! Oh, my God! Billie!"

Within seconds, Billie crossed the room and wrapped herself around Cat. The two ladies held each other close and sobbed uncontrollably as Dr. Quentin patiently looked on.

"Cat! I thought…Cat. I'm so sorry," Billie cried. "I love you so much!"

Cat stroked Billie's hair and placed several kisses on the side of her face. "Billie! Sweetheart. I love you too!" she declared haltingly through her tears.

Billie caught Cat's face between her hands and tried hard to focus as her vision blurred in and out. "Cat…Tara! I…I lost her. The kayak went over the falls. We fell over the falls. The rocks…God, Cat…I…," Billie struggled to explain as she swayed back and forth.

"Billie, she's here. She's alive." Cat suddenly realized Billie was on the verge of collapse. "Dr. Quinten!" she yelled.

"Stretcher in here, STAT!" the doc yelled into the hall as he rushed to catch Billie before she fell to the floor.

# CHAPTER 19

Billie opened her eyes and tried to lift her head from the pillow. A sharp pain immediately shot through her temples. She moaned and closed her eyes again until the pain passed. She lifted her right hand to rub her temple and realized she had something around her wrist. She opened her eyes again into mere slits to see that the offending object was a hospital band. "What the hell?" she said out loud. She lifted her left hand to reach for the band and realized she had an IV inserted in that arm. "What the fuck is going on here?"

Billie pressed the back of her head into the pillow and focused on a spot on the ceiling. She struggled to recall what could have happened to land her in the hospital with an IV stuck in her arm. After a few minutes, it all came back to her...kayaking down the river, rolling the kayak to protect them from the fire...dropping over the edge of the waterfall...losing Tara.

Tears began to fall from Billie's eyes and reality came crashing in on her. She reached for the call button and waited for a nurse to appear. She didn't have long to wait.

A nurse entered the room. "It's about time you woke up," she said. "You've been out for about thirty-six hours. How do you feel?"

"I need to see my wife and daughter," Billie replied.

The nurse frowned. "I'm sorry, but no one has been here to visit you."

"No. They're patients here. Caitlain and Tara Charland. I need to see them, and I need to see them now!"

The nurse was saved from Billie's wrath by Dr. Quinten, who chose that opportune moment to enter the room. He picked up her chart on his way in. "Billie! It's good to see you awake."

"And you are...?" Billie asked.

"Dr. Quinten.  I was Cat's attending physician in the emergency room two days ago.  We've actually met, but you weren't exactly in the right frame of mind to remember."  Dr. Quinten extended his hand to Billie.

Billie shook his hand.  "I need to see Cat...and Tara."

"I can arrange for you to see Cat, but Tara is in the ICU with limited visitation.  In fact, she's being prepped for surgery this morning, so it will be a day or two before anyone will be allowed to see her."

"She's having surgery?  For what?" Billie demanded.  Panic tinged her voice.

"Internal injuries.  The surgery is an exploratory laparotomy to determine and stop the source of the bleeding."  Dr. Quinten watched a veil of fear cross Billie's features.  He sat on the edge of her bed and touched her arm.  "I am going to arrange for you to share a room with Cat.  At a time like this, I think it would be good for you to have each other to lean on."

Billie could barely see through the veil of tears.  "How is Cat?"

"Cat is going to be fine.  She'll be confined to bed for a while to allow her leg to set...and it looks like she'll need surgery on her foot, but she should make a full recovery."  Dr. Quinten stood.  "I'll go put the move-order in, and then I'll check in on both of you later this afternoon.  I should know more about Tara's condition by then as well."

Billie watched Dr. Quinten leave the room and once he was gone, she broke down into tears as she absorbed the situation they were all in.

*** 

An orderly pushed the door to Cat's room open and backed into the room, dragging a hospital bed on wheels.

"What's happening here?" Cat asked.

"You're getting a roommate," the orderly said. He left the bed partway in the doorway while he physically moved her bed toward the window.

"Ah, why wasn't I told about this? This is supposed to be a private room."

"Sorry, ma'am. Doctor's orders," the orderly said.

"What doctor?"

"Quinten."

"Dr. Quinten ordered this?"

"Yes, ma'am." The orderly pulled the bed completely into the room and wheeled it into place beside Cat's bed. "That should do it. Your roommate will be in shortly. They are just processing her move-order paperwork."

The orderly left before Cat could ask any more questions.

Cat pressed her call button, intent on getting to the bottom of this new wrinkle. A few moments later, the door opened and Cat poised herself for a confrontation. Instead, she was greeted by a nurse pushing her new roommate into the room in a wheelchair.

The nurse grinned from ear to ear. "Cat, meet Billie. Billie, meet Cat...your new roommate."

Cat's eyes flew open wide. "Billie!" she cried.

The nurse pushed Billie over to Cat's bedside and locked the wheels. "You got this, girlfriend?" she asked Billie.

"I got this," Billie replied without breaking eye contact with Cat. A moment later, they were alone and Billie got out of the chair and sat on the side of Cat's bed. She opened her arms and took Cat into them. They clung to each other and cried for several minutes before Cat lay back against her pillows.

"Are you really going to be my roommate?" Cat asked. She clung to Billie's hand.

"For the next day, at least. The doc said I should be able to get out of here by tomorrow." Billie touched the side of Cat's face. "I have missed you so much. I love you Cat."

"I love you too."

Billie's face suddenly became serious. "Cat, talk to me about Tara."

Cat looked down at her hands. "She has internal bleeding, Billie. They hoped it would stop by itself, but it doesn't look like that's happening."

Billie lowered her chin to her chest and began to cry. "Cat, it's all my fault. I wasn't able to protect her. I lost her, Cat. I lost her. I'm so sorry."

Cat touched Billie's hand. "Billie, what happened?""

Billie tilted her head back and closed her eyes. Tears squeezed out from beneath her lids and rolled down her face. "We were kayaking down this beautiful river when all of the sudden, things got real quiet and we could smell smoke. The fire moved so fast, we didn't have time to outrun it, so we flipped the kayak over and hid under it, inside the cockpit. It was awful, Cat. We could hear the fire roar over us as it jumped from tree to tree. At one point, the fire was so close; it actually warmed the air inside our hideout until it was difficult to breathe. Finally it passed and we flipped the boat back over and climbed inside. It was so dark and smoky."

Billie began to sob. "Cat, we couldn't see. When we realized how close we were to the waterfall, it was too late. We rode the kayak down the falls and bounced off the rocks like we were in a pinball machine. It was a miracle that we actually stayed inside the kayak…until we reached the bottom. That's when we lost the kayak…and when I lost Tara. She just disappeared under the foamy water. I remember floating uncontrollably down the rapids. The last thing I remember was this huge rock directly in front of me. Apparently, my head made contact with the rock and I was knocked out."

Cat gently touched the bruise on the side of Billie's face from her tumultuous ride down the river.

"The next thing I knew, I woke up on the shore and Tara was nowhere to be found." Uncontrollable sobs wracked Billie's body. "I lost her, Cat. I lost her. I'm so sorry."

Cat sat up again and wrapped her arms around Billie. "Shh. Billie, don't beat yourself up. It wasn't your fault. All we can do now is pray she recovers. She's still with us love. Don't give up on her."

Billie pulled away and looked at Cat. "Dr. Quinten said she's having surgery today."

Cat nodded and wiped tears from her own eyes. "She's a very sick little girl, Billie. She has a head injury and compound fracture on her right thigh, but they are most worried about internal injuries right now. She's bleeding on the inside and they don't know from where. That's why she needs surgery."

"I need to see her," Billie said.

"I do too, love, but unfortunately, I won't be getting out of this bed for a few days yet. You'll have to go for both of us."

"Knock, knock," Dr. Quinten said from the doorway. "May I come in?"

"Yes, please," Cat said.

Dr. Quinten sat on Billie's bed.

"How are you feeling, Cat?"

"My leg hurts like hell, but otherwise, I'm good. I'm more concerned about Tara than I am about myself," she replied.

"That's understandable, so let's address that elephant in the room. As you both know now, Tara is being prepped for an exploratory laparotomy to determine the source of the bleeding. Once they get in there, as long as there is no significant damage to her internal organs, they should be able to seal off the blood vessels that are causing the bleed, and then her body will take over the healing from there."

"As long as there's no significant damage to her internal organs," Billie repeated. "What if they *do* find damage?"

"Damage to most organs in the abdomen will heal. If the bleed is coming from her heart, that will be a bit more delicate. They'll know the source pretty quickly once they open her up. Now, assuming the bleeding can be brought under control, we still need to deal with the head injury."

Cat squeezed Billie's hand.

"I know all about brain injuries, Doc. I had one myself a few years ago. Hopefully Tara's injury is not as severe as mine was," Billie said.

"Did you have an accident?" Dr. Quinten asked.

"Gunshot wound," Billie replied.

"Oh, wow! I suspect Tara's injury will *not* be as traumatic as yours. So, as I was saying, today's surgery will be a turning point. Her chances of survival will increase significantly if the source of the bleed can be located and repaired, but even with that eventuality, her recovery will be long and arduous, and her level of impairment, if any, will need to be assessed."

"I know Cat can't get out of bed, but can I see her?" Billie asked.

Dr. Quinten looked at his watch. "She goes into surgery in about an hour and then she'll be in recovery for several hours afterward. We will be releasing you tomorrow, Billie. Why don't we plan visitation to begin after your release? She will be pretty much out of it at least until midday tomorrow anyway. Her medically induced coma has been lifted, so once the anesthesia wears off, she should wake up."

"Will you let us know how she's doing after the surgery?" Cat asked.

"Dr. Quinten rose to his feet. "Absolutely."

Billie lay on her back on her hospital bed and held hands with Cat. After Dr. Quinten left, she lowered the bed rails on the inside edges of both hers and Cat's beds, and then pushed them together. She would have preferred to lie in Cat's bed with her; however, Cat's leg was confined to a ramp-like traction device and she was concerned about hurting her.

"I like him, Cat."

"Dr. Quinten?"

"Yes. He seems to be a straight shooter, and he's pretty forthcoming about Tara. I appreciate that."

"Me too."

"I'm worried about Tara, Cat. What if the bleed is coming from her heart?"

"We'll cross that bridge when we get there, Billie. The important thing is to locate *where* the bleeding is coming from and then to stop it. She could bleed to death otherwise. If it's her heart, it will be more complicated, but not impossible."

# CHAPTER 20

Billie pushed the door open to the ICU and slowly walked in. The ICU was laid out with the nurse's station in the center, and several small rooms surrounding it in a spoke-like formation. Billie approached the desk and cleared her throat.

The attending nurse looked up, and couldn't hide the shock on her face when she saw the large, purple bruise on the left side of Billie's face where she had made contact with the rock.

Billie subconsciously touched the bruise. "Sorry. I was caught in the wildfires."

"How can I help you?" the nurse asked.

"I'm here to see Tara Charland."

"Relative?"

"I'm her mom…well, one of them, anyway."

"She's in room three."

"Thank you," Billie said.

Billie's heart was in her throat and her hands shook when she pushed the door open to Tara's room. She wasn't prepared for how fragile Tara looked. She stood just inside the room and leaned against the door to prevent herself from fainting. *Keep it together, Charland. She needs you to be strong.*

She took a deep breath and walked to Tara's bedside where she pulled a chair close to the bed. She sat down and took Tara's hand in her own. Billie swallowed and looked intently at her daughter. She was hooked up to several monitors. Her leg was in a halo-type device with pins protruding into her skin. The tear in her thigh where her fractured femur had torn through was angry looking, and the purple hue on the side of her face from her head injury pretty much mirrored her own, except her right eye was swollen shut. What she couldn't see was the incision in her abdomen through which the surgeons had repaired blood vessels

202

in her liver that were bleeding into her gut. For that, Billie was thankful. At least it wasn't her heart. Cat and Billie had been given the news the previous afternoon that the source of the bleeding had been located and that the surgeons were confident the repair had been successful.

For the better part of an hour, Billie was unable to speak. She just watched her daughter sleep, while she chided herself for being the reason Tara was in the condition she was in. The logical part of her mind knew better, but her heart told her otherwise. Her heart told her she failed to protect her child. Logic told her she couldn't fight the power of nature…that there was no way she could have saved Tara from being pulled under the water, but her sense of duty dictated she take responsibility.

Billie composed herself and then leaned in close to Tara. "Hey, Tare. It's Mom. I want you to know that we love you, sweetie, and we will be here for you. You need to fight, kiddo. We are all rooting for you…me, Mama, Seth, Sky, Karissa, Steve, Jen, Fred and Kelly."

Billie was startled when Tara squeezed her hand. She looked at Tara's hand, and then back at her face. "Tare, can you hear me?" No response.

Assuming the gesture was simply a muscle spasm, Billie continued. "Mom is doing pretty well. She has a broken leg…just like you, but otherwise, she's okay. Seth pretty much survived with just a few scratches. Oh, and Aunt Jen flew all the way from Albany just to be with Skylar while we were still lost in the wildfires. Seth and Skylar went home with her a few days ago. Jen said Karissa and Kelly were really worried about you."

Again, Billie felt her hand being squeezed.

Billie had a hunch. "Everyone is excited about you coming home soon…especially Kelly."

At the mention of Kelly's name, Tara squeezed her hand again, and then lifted it off the bed.

Billie leaned in closer. "Tara, if you can hear me, please squeeze my hand.

Billie's eyes grew wide when Tara complied.

She lifted Tara's hand to her mouth and kissed it.

Tara moved her fingers to touch Billie's lips.

Billie's gaze shot from Tara's hand to her face and she looked her directly in the eyes. Billie smiled through her tears. "Hey, baby girl," she said softly.

Tara tried hard to grin and struggled to keep her eyes open. "You look like hell, Mom." Her voice was raspy.

Billie couldn't stop a chuckle from escaping despite the tears that filled her eyes. "You don't look so hot yourself, Tare," she joked back.

"Where is Mama?"

"Confined to bed. Like I said, she has a broken leg as well."

"How?"

"She and Seth were caught in the wildfires too. They dug a hole in the ground and covered themselves with dirt while the fire passed over them, but after it was over, they tried to hike out, and a branch fell from a burned-out tree and hit Mama. Seth had to leave her there to go for help. Anyway, her leg and ankle are broken and her foot is crushed, so she's in traction for a few days."

"Tell her I love her."

"Would you like to tell her yourself?"

"How?"

Billie pulled her cell phone out of her pocket. "With this," she said. Billie dialed Cat's phone number and pressed the video call icon. Cat's face appeared on the screen.

"Someone wants to say hi, Mama," Billie said and then she pointed the camera in Tara's direction.

Tara raised her hand and rested it on Billie's wrist as she held the phone in front of her.

"I love you, Ma," Tara said.

Billie waited to hear Cat's reply, but it didn't come. She looked at Tara with her eyebrows raised high.

"She's crying," Tara said.

Billie moved so that Cat could see both of them at once. "Are you all right, Cat?" Billie asked.

Cat nodded and wiped her eyes. Finally, she found her voice. "I love you too, Tara. I am so happy to see you awake. You're going to be all right, love. We all are."

"I want to go home."

"We'll go home as soon as you're strong enough to fly, love."

"How long?" Tara asked.

"That's up to you, sweetie," Cat said. "Your body has a lot of healing to do. I'm anxious to go home too, love. We both need to work hard to make that happen."

"I miss Kelly."

"And Kelly misses you. I have that directly from her. Mom and I talked to her this morning. She really is a special young lady," Cat said. "She's anxious to talk to you when you're strong enough."

Tara nodded and closed her eyes. Her head rolled slowly to the side and then jerked back. She opened her eyes again.

"You look exhausted, sweetie. I know how taxing this is for you. Sleep now, love. It will help you to heal," Cat said. "I should be mobile in the next few days, so I'll be able to visit you in person. Until then, you'll just have to put up with Mom," Cat teased.

"Oh, goody!" Tara quipped as her eyes dropped again.

Billie took the phone from her daughter. "Cat, I will come back to the room when Tara drops off for a nap. I think her surgical team will be here soon, so I want to meet with them for an update. I'll fill you in when I get back."

"Okay. Point me in Tara's direction again," Cat said.

Billie turned the phone.

"I love you Tara. Fight like a girl, sweetie. The faster we heal, the faster we get to go home. I'll talk to you a little later."

Tara opened her eyes part way. "Love you too, Ma." She immediately closed her eyes again.

Billie returned the call to audio and held it to her ear. "It looks like she's drifting off. I'm kind of surprised she was a awake for as long as she was."

Cat's voice broke. "It breaks my heart to see her like that, Billie. When you first turned the video on her, I felt like I had been punched in the stomach. When I think of what she went through…"

Billie watched her daughter sleep. "I know, love. I know. I wish I could have saved her from that," She said softly.

"She will heal, Billie, and we will put this behind us. We can only move forward from here."

Billie's attention was drawn to the door. "Cat, it looks like her doc is here. I'll get an update, before I return to your room. I'll see you soon."

Billie hung up and met the doctor halfway across the room. She extended her hand. "Billie Charland. I'm one of Tara's moms."

Tara's doctor was a middle-aged woman. She shook Billie's hand. "Nice to meet you. My name is Dr. Kittle, but you can call me Mary. So, are you the doctor?"

Billie grinned. "No, that would be Tara's other mother, Cat. I'm a lawyer. Tara and I were actually together when the wildfire hit. We both took a pretty traumatic ride over a waterfall. Unfortunately, Tara didn't fare as well as I did." Billie rubbed the large bruise on the side of her face.

"Did you just say you went over a waterfall?" An astonished expression crossed the doctor's face.

"That's exactly what I said. We were kayaking and had to flip our kayak and hide under it while the fire crossed over us. When it was over and we climbed back into the kayak, it was dark and smoky, and by the time we saw the falls, it was too late to avoid it. I will never forget that nightmarish ride."

"Well, that helps to explain some of Tara's injuries."

"Dr. Quinten told us the bleeding was coming from her liver."

"Yes. Luckily, we were able to seal off the blood vessels. She lost a lot of blood and needed a transfusion, but we should see only improvement from here in that respect. My only other concern is the head injury. It looks like her skull may have been fractured. We'll need to assess whether she'll have any permanent disabilities because of it."

"You mean like, seizures, depression and aggression?" Billie asked.

Dr. Kittle cocked her head to one side. "Yes, those are some potential side effects, as well as Parkinson's Disease and even Alzheimer's. I take it you know something about TBI's?"

"A little," Billie admitted. "Actually, a lot, but that's a story for another time."

"I'm more concerned about immediate physical problems, like paralysis or other physical impairments. Her involuntary reflexes are good so far, but we'll have a whole battery of tests to determine if other problems exist after she is well enough to participate."

"So, she's going to be okay?" Billie asked hopefully.

"In my professional opinion…yes. If she continues to improve, we should be able to move her out of the ICU in a day or two."

Billie let out the breath she didn't realize she was holding. She shook Dr. Kittle's hand again. "Thank you. I can't tell you how much I needed to hear that. Cat will be thrilled as well. I'll let her know when I go back to her room."

Dr. Kittle frowned. "Her room? Is she here as well?"

"Yes. She was hiking with our son when the fires hit and was trapped under a fallen branch. She's in traction with a broken leg."

"And your son?"

"He's okay. Thank you for asking."

Dr. Kittle squeezed Billie's arm. "Well, someone was looking out for you. Tara has a long road ahead of her, including rehab, but she has youth in her favor." Dr. Kittle took the stethoscope from around her neck. "I'll take a quick look at her vital signs, but I'm certain they'll be fine. You said your wife's name is Cat?" Dr. Kittle withdrew a small notepad from her pocket.

"Caitlain Charland. Cat, for short. She's in room 349 in the orthopedic wing."

Dr. Kittle wrote down Cat's information. "Okay. I'll drop by to introduce myself to her after I examine Tara."

"Thank you. Well, I guess I'd better get back to Cat. If Tara wakes up while you're still here, could you tell her I'll be back soon?"

"Will do!"

Billie nodded and left Tara's room with her heart a little lighter than it had felt for days.

# EPILOGUE

Billie and Cat sat solemnly in the boarding area of the Cody Wyoming airport while they waited for their flight.

"I'm looking forward to going home," Cat said.

"You and me both," Billie agreed. "It's been a long road."

"It has. If anything, it has taught me to cherish every moment we have together. You could lose it all in the blink of an eye."

Billie took Cat's hand and held it close to her heart. "I will never again take what we have together for granted, Cat. As much as we went through, we are the lucky ones, and I thank the heavens above that we were spared. The Robertsons weren't so lucky. I can't imagine huddling with your wife and kids in a cave and thinking you're safe, only for all of them to die from smoke inhalation. As awful as it was to be in the path of the fire, at least we were all out in the open."

"It was touch and go for a while with Tara. I don't know what I would have done if we had lost her, Billie. I think I'd want to lie right down beside her and die."

Billie lowered her chin to her chest. "I'm so sorry, Cat. I wasn't able to protect her. I will never forgive myself for what she went through."

Cat turned in her seat to face Billie. "Billie, look at me. How many times do I have to tell you that what happened to Tara is not your fault? Sweetheart, you did the best you could under the circumstances. We all did. It happened three months ago. Please stop beating yourself up over it."

Billie nodded. "I'll try."

"It certainly was a harrowing experience, but oddly, one filled with moments of joy and pride. Billie, Seth was amazing. I wouldn't be here today if it wasn't for him. He kept his head even when I went off the deep end. I am so proud of him. He is truly my hero."

Billie smiled. "The moments I remember most were when I first saw Seth and Sky at the infirmary in the Ranger Station, and when you and I were finally reunited in the hospital emergency room. As horrid as the previous twenty-four hours had been, those two moments made everything better. That, and the moment we realized that Tara was going to survive."

"This is certainly one vacation I'll never forget," Cat said. "Especially since it was spent almost entirely in the hospital."

"I was only there for two days, but you and Tara weren't so lucky. You were there for about a month—right?"

"It seemed like forever!" Cat replied. "You were certainly the lucky one among us. You and Tara both went over the falls together, yet you basically ended up with a concussion and multiple bruises, while Tara nearly died."

Billie frowned. "I would have willingly traded places with her, Cat."

"I know you would, love. I know you would. I'm not being critical. I'm just amazed at the differences in your injuries when you basically lived through the same experience."

"I can't explain it, Cat. On the plus side, my quick recovery made it possible for me to sit by Tara's bedside during the days while you were in traction with your leg. It felt good to be there with her."

"I was so happy to get out of that contraption," Cat said of the traction she was in for the first half of her hospital stay. "It was great to be able to use a wheelchair and to finally visit Tara, although I have to admit, seeing her for the first time in person was traumatic. She seemed so fragile and small in that bed…and it didn't even look like her with all the bruises. I know we did the video call after her surgery, but it did nothing to prepare me for seeing her up close. My heart hurt so much for our baby girl." Cat wiped the tears from her eyes.

Billie squeezed Cat's knee. "Are you all right, love?"

Cat nodded. "I'm fine. It's just that when I think of how close we came to losing everything we loved..."

"I know. I know. Luckily, someone was looking after us."

"I had a lot of time to think while I was laid up in traction, Billie. I came to realize just how blessed we are. I mean, look at what we went through, and we all came out of it alive in the end. Damaged, maybe...but alive. I also realized that we have our own personal angel—Jen. No one asked to her fly to Wyoming to be with Skylar. No one asked her to take Seth and Sky home with her while you and Tara and I recuperated. She was supposed to be taking her certification class, but she dropped everything to be there for us. Thank God the school system still allowed her to begin teaching and to finish her training in the evenings."

"You are spot on, Cat. Angel is a good way to describe Jen. We share a level of love and emotional intimacy with her that usually only happens on a romantic level. It's like we live inside each other's skin and breathe each other's air. We share a heart and a love too profound for words. I am honored to be her friend."

"While I was laid up, I also thought a lot about Tara, and I've come to realize that my fears are unfounded," Cat said.

"How so?" Billie asked.

"I've realized that Tara's preferences in life are part of who she is, and after staring death in the face, I have to admit that we have no other option except unconditional love and support. We can't live our lives in fear. Hell, that's not living at all."

Billie grinned. "I agree. You know, Tara's a tough cookie. Seeing her fight for her life made me realize she's stronger than we knew. I think she can handle anything life throws at her relative to her lifestyle."

"That, she is!" Cat said. "This bump in the road made me realize that Tara doesn't need our permission to be true to herself. She needs only our love and acceptance."

Cat resettled herself on the hard and uncomfortable airport chair. She groaned when she repositioned her leg.

"Still hurts, huh?" Billie asked.

"Yeah. I think it will for a while yet, considering how much damage was done by the tree falling on my foot—not to mention the broken tibia. I'm actually lucky they didn't amputate it. I think if I had stayed trapped under that tree for much longer, there would have been a very different outcome. Thank God Seth was able to find help when he did. As it is, I'm looking at several more surgeries and rehab before I regain total function again."

Billie bumped shoulders with Cat. "Do you think you'll be able to stand at the stove long enough to cook? Otherwise, the family will have to eat *my* cooking."

Cat raised her hands into the air. "Heaven forbid! I will do my best to avoid *that* catastrophe!" Cat laughed.

Billie chuckled at their running joke and then checked her watch. "They'll be boarding us soon. I'd better find the bathroom so I don't have to use that broom-closet size bathroom on the airplane."

While Cat waited for Billie to return from the bathroom, she thought back to when they had brought Tara home after a full month in the hospital in Wyoming. Jen picked them up at the airport.

Unbeknownst to them, Jen had arranged for a small gathering at Cat and Billie's house to welcome the three of them home. Their family was waiting for them as they pulled into the driveway. Seth, Skylar, Fred, Karissa, Steve, Kelly, Doc and Ida were all there and all were very excited to welcome their loved ones home.

Jen pulled the car to a stop in front of the garage. Both she and Billie climbed out—Jen to assist Cat, and Billie to retrieve a wheelchair from the trunk for Tara.

"Let us help you with that." Seth and Steve offered to transfer Tara from the car to the chair. "Put your arms around our necks, Tare. There you go." Seth looked at Steve. "On the count of three, we lift and gently put her in the chair, okay? One, two, three!" With one swift movement, the boys had Tara comfortably seated in the chair with her broken leg extended straight out on the leg rest. "Easy peasy!" Seth said. He bent down and planted a quick kiss on Tara's cheek. "Welcome home, sis."

Tara struggled to hide her tears. "Thanks, bro." She looked at Steve. "Thanks to both of you," she added.

"I've got your crutches, Cat. Here, give me your hand." Jen offered her hand for Cat to anchor against in order to pull herself out of the car without putting too much weight on her bad leg.

Jen handed Cat's crutches back to her and closed the car door behind her just as Doc and Fred approached to escort her to the party.

As the group circled around the car toward the yard, Billie thought it was curious that Ida, Jen, Kelly, Karissa and Skylar were all standing in a straight line in front of the stairs. She stopped and looked at the group. "Why do I think you guys are up to something?" she asked.

"Surprise!" they yelled as the group parted to reveal a wheelchair ramp the guys had constructed especially for them.

Tara grinned and Cat cried as they each reacted in their own unique ways to the gesture of love before them.

"Cool! That'll be fun to freestyle down in the wheelchair!" Tara exclaimed.

Billie stood beside Cat. She leaned down to whisper in her ear. "That's our girl. Tara the Terrible is back!"

Cat laughed and elbowed her in the ribs.

After countless welcome home hugs, the family dispersed to the backyard where Ida and Jen had prepared a picnic lunch.

Billie pushed Tara nearly halfway across the lawn toward a shaded area of the yard when she suddenly realized Kelly was walking a short distance away. Billie stopped and looked at Kelly. "Hey, Kelly? Wanna do me a favor and push Tara into the shade over there?" She pointed to a secluded area of the yard where years earlier, she'd built a bench that completely encircled a shade tree.

Kelly eagerly took over the controls and soon, she sat on the bench, under the shade tree with Tara.

The girls sat in total silence for several long moments. Neither knew how to start the conversation. Finally, their eyes met and they both giggled and blushed deep shades of pink. Before long, Kelly offered her hand to Tara, who took it willingly.

"I missed you," Kelly said softly.

Tara could only nod. Her throat was constricted with emotion.

"I wanted to die when I heard you were hurt," Kelly continued. "I have never felt so lost and sad in my entire life."

Tara locked gazes with her friend for several long moments. Her chest ached with penned up emotion. Finally, she raised Kelly's hand to her lips and kissed the back of it. "I'm sorry," Tara said hoarsely. She blinked rapidly and tears gently cascaded down her cheeks.

Kelly touched the side of Tara's face. "Don't be sorry. It wasn't your fault."

Tara's insides felt like mush and the warmth she felt in her abdomen spread through her entire body. She had no idea what to say or do. She was powerless to look away as Kelly's gaze saw deep into her soul.

Kelly slid down the bench so she was close to the side of Tara's wheelchair and then, without warning, she leaned in to delicately kiss the tears from Tara's cheeks.

Tara closed her eyes and released the breath she was holding. She smiled and blushed in embarrassment at Kelly's gesture in front of her family.

"Oooo! Tara and Kelly sitting in a tree. K-I-S-S-I-N-G," teased Seth and Steve.

"I'm gonna kick your ass, Seth!" Tara yelled while trying to fight the grin on her face.

"Tara Charland! Do you eat with that same dirty mouth?" Cat yelled from across the yard.

"Sorry, Mom, but he started it!" Tara called back.

At that moment, Jen walked by, carrying a salad from the house to the picnic table. "I see things are back to normal," she joked without stopping.

Billie stood behind Cat with her arm draped around her waist. They watched the teenage girls from across the yard. Cat pressed her head into Billie's chest. "They're cute together," Cat commented softly.

Billie kissed the side of Cat's head. "Yes they are," she admitted. "They kind of remind me of us."

Cat chuckled and thanked the heavens above that their lives had been spared and that they would have many more opportunities to share moments such as these.

"Ladies and Gentlemen in the gate area. We will be boarding flight D324 to Albany, New York in a few minutes, beginning with those who may need assistance, active duty military and families with small children under the age of two."

Cat was snapped out of her reverie by the sound of the PA system. She sighed heavily and anticipated putting this chapter of their lives behind them. Physical injuries aside, the most devastating experience any of them endured by far, including Skylar and Jen, was the emotional turmoil as each of them realized how fragile life was. They came so close to losing each other forever. The devastation at Yellowstone made them realize how precious family is, and how quickly life can be snuffed out.

Never was that so evident than in the death of Jack Kilburn, who died saving Cat from a certain death. He made the ultimate sacrifice by giving his life. It was a sacrifice he knew he could be called upon to make, but never in his wildest dreams, did he believe would ever happen. Cat was tormented by grief and guilt for weeks following his death.

It was because of Jack's death that Cat and Billie were in the Yellowstone International Airport on this day. They had flown home with Tara two months earlier, but had returned for a special occasion: a memorial service honoring Jack Kilburn and the other firefighters who had given their lives during the Yellowstone Wildfires.

Cat would carry the vision of Jack dying before her eyes for the rest of her life. It was a death that was the result of courage, conviction and dedication to duty. He was truly a hero. This, she shared with his family and she hoped it brought a measure of comfort to their grieving hearts.

Cat looked around the gate area and noticed Billie walking her way with two cups of coffee. She smiled broadly. "You read my mind!" Cat said and she gratefully accepted the coffee while Billie sat beside her. "They'll be boarding soon," Cat said.

"I heard the announcement," Billie replied.

Cat shifted uncomfortably in her seat and manually repositioned the walking splint that encased her foot.

"Are you okay?" Billie placed a comforting hand on Cat's leg.

"Yeah, it's just a little uncomfortable dragging this thing around all the time," Cat complained.

Just then, their flight home was announced over the intercom.

Billie stood and helped Cat her to her feet. She handed Cat's crutches to her, took her coffee and then followed her as she hobbled to the gate for early boarding. Billie stopped just before entering the gangway. She turned around and scanned the seating area with a bittersweet smile on her face.

Once settled in their seats on the plane, Cat looked at Billie who appeared to be deep in thought while she stared out the window.

"Billie," Cat said softly.

"Huh?" Billie replied.

"Are you all right?"

Billie looked down at her hands folded in her lap and she nodded. "I'm fine."

"You look preoccupied."

Billie smiled. "No. I was just thinking about how excited I was when we first landed here several months ago," she explained.

Cat nodded as she recalled the feelings of excitement.

Billie reached for her hand and brought it to her lips. She kissed it tenderly and then looked Cat in the eyes. "Do me a favor, Kitten?" she asked.

"Anything." Cat was mesmerized by the powder blue orbs looking back at her.

"Never promise me a disaster-free vacation again. Okay?" Billie grinned mischievously.

## The End

Photo Credit: Song of Myself Photography

See Karen's author page at www.karendbadger.com

# About the Author

Karen D. Badger is the author of *On A Wing And A Prayer, Yesterday Once More* (a 2009 Golden Crown Literary Award winner for Speculative Fiction), *In A Family Way, Unchained Memories, Happy Campers, Collective Identity, Sweet Angel, and Relative-ly Speaking, Tailspin* and *Flashpoint* (Books I, II, III, IV, V, VI, VII and VIII of the Commitment Series), *The Blue Feather, All My Tomorrows* (sequel to the 2009 award winning *Yesterday Once More*), and *1140 Rue Royale*...all of which have been released by Badger Bliss Books, which Karen co-owns with her wife Barbara Sawyer (aka "Bliss').

Born and raised in Vermont, Karen is the second of five children raised by a fiercely independent mother, who remains one of her best friends. Karen earned her B.A. in 1978 in Theater and in Elementary Education, and in 1994, earned a B.S. in mathematics. In addition to her novels, Karen is the author of many technical papers on photomask manufacturing, which she has presented at numerous semiconductor industry conferences, and is the holder if several technical patents. Karen is currently in her 41st year as a Principal Member of the Technical Staff with a prominent semiconductor manufacturer in Vermont.

Karen and her wife, Barb (a retired Lt. Col., US Air Force) live in the beautiful state of Vermont—home of Ben and Jerry's. They spend their spare time with family as well as doing home improvement projects on both their homes in Vermont and New Mexico. They also enjoy camping, kayaking, motorcycling and singing Karaoke.

Please take a moment to visit Karen's author website at www.karendbadger.com, or the Badger Bliss Books website at www.badgerblissbooks.com. Also like us on Facebook!

# TITLES BY KAREN D. BADGER

www.badgerblissbooks.com

*On A Wing and A Prayer*
First edition published by Blue Feather Books, Sept, 2005
Second edition published by Badger Bliss Books, Sept, 2014
Third edition published by Badger Bliss Books, August, 2016
ISBN 13: 978-1-945761-01-0, ISBN 10: 1-945761-01-6

*Yesterday Once More*
First edition published by Blue Feather Books, July, 2008
Second edition published by Badger Bliss Books ,Sept, 2014
Third edition published by Badger Bliss Books, August, 2016
ISBN 13: 978-1-945761-02-7, ISBN 10: 1-945761-02-4
2009 Golden Crown Literary Society Award - Speculative Fiction

*In A Family Way – Book One of the Commitment Series*
First edition published by Blue Feather Books, March, 2010
Second edition published by Badger Bliss Books, Sept, 2014 Third
edition published by Badger Bliss Books, August, 2016
ISBN 13: 978-1-945761-05-8, ISBN 10: 1-945761-05-9

*Unchained Memories – Book Two of the Commitment Series*
First edition published by Blue Feather Books, Oct, 2011
Second edition published by Badger Bliss Books, Sept, 2014 Third
edition published by Badger Bliss Books, August, 2016
ISBN 13: 978-1-945761-06-5, ISBN 10: 1-945761-06-7

*Happy Campers - Book Three of the Commitment Series*
First edition published by Blue Feather Books, Sept, 2013
Second edition published by Badger Bliss Books, Sept, 2014 Third
edition published by Badger Bliss Books, August, 2016
ISBN 13: 978-1-945761-07-2, ISBN 10: 1-945761-07-5

### The Blue Feather
First edition published by Blue Feather Books, July, 2014
Second edition published by Badger Bliss Books, Sept, 2014 Third
edition published by Badger Bliss Books, August, 2016
ISBN 13: 978-1-945761-04-1, ISBN 10: 1-945761-04-0

### Collective Identity – Book Four of the Commitment Series
First edition published by Badger Bliss Books, January, 2015 Second
edition published by Badger Bliss Books, August, 2016
ISBN 13: 978-1-945761-08-9, ISBN 10: 1-945761-08-3

### All My Tomorrows – Sequel to Yesterday Once More
First edition published by Badger Bliss Books, May, 2015 Second
edition published by Badger Bliss Books, August, 2016
ISBN 13: 978-1-945761-03-4, ISBN 10: 1-945761-03-2

### Sweet Angel – Book Five of the Commitment Series
First edition published by Badger Bliss Books, June, 2015 Second
edition published by Badger Bliss Books, August, 2016
ISBN 13: 978-1-945761-09-6, ISBN 10: 1-945-761-09-1

### Relative-ly Speaking – Book Six of the Commitment Series
First edition published by Badger Bliss Books, March, 2016 Second
edition published by Badger Bliss Books, August, 2016
ISBN 13: 978-1-945761-10-2, ISBN 10: 1-945-761-10-5

### 1140 Rue Royale
First edition published by Badger Bliss Books, Sept, 2016
ISBN 13: 978-1-945761-00-3, ISBN 10: 1-945761-00-8

### Tailspin – Book Seven of the Commitment Series
First edition published by Badger Bliss Books, December, 2017
ISBN 13: 978-1-945761225, ISBN 10: 1-945761-22-9

### Flashpoint – Book Eight of the Commitment Series
First edition published by Badger Bliss Books, December, 2018
ISBN 13: 978-1-945761249, ISBN 10: 1-945761-24-5

## COMING SOON FROM KAREN D. BADGER AND BADGER BLISS BOOKS

### www.badgerblissbooks.com

### *En Garde!*
Expected release:  Summer, 2019

Makaya Kapule and Spencer Bennet are from vastly different backgrounds...Makaya from Hawaii and Spencer from Vermont. They met and fell in love as members of the US Olympic Fencing Team.  On hiatus from their grueling training schedule, Makaya and Spencer fly to Hawaii to attend her sister's traditional Hawai'ian wedding, at which, Spencer meets Makaya's family for the first time.  While there, Makaya's brother takes them water skiing, and an over-confident Spencer finds herself in danger when she fails to anticipate the raging fury of ocean whitecaps. She wakes up some time later to find herself alone on a deserted beach and with her world about to be turned upside down.

# En Garde!

𝓑

A BADGER BLISS BOOK

By

## Karen D. Badger

# CHAPTER 1

"Spencer, it's time to get up."

"No!" Spencer grabbed the edge of the sheet and pulled it over her head.

"Spencer. Don't make me break out the claw."

"Just a few more minutes," Spencer whined.

"I'm warning you!"

Spencer peeked out from under the covers. "You don't scare me."

"You asked for it. The Claw!"

In the nick of time, Spencer threw back the sheet, grabbed her assailant around the waist and slammed them onto the bed. She then proceeded to sit on top of her attacker, and pinned their arms to the bed by the wrists. She leaned in so close, her nose nearly touched that of the person trapped beneath her.

"Nice try, Makaya. You should know better than to threaten me with the claw. So now it's *you* who will pay!" Spencer formed both her hands into claws and unmercifully tickled Makaya as she squirmed and squealed beneath her.

"No! Stop! Okay. Enough! You win." Makaya tried to get away.

At one point, Makaya managed to free one leg and flipped Spencer onto her back. She took advantage of her sudden freedom to scurry off the bed. She grabbed a pillow and began to beat Spencer with it. "You little shit!

Spencer grabbed the other pillow and fought back. "If you play with fire, sooner or later, you'll get burned," she said.

After a few more swipes, Spencer grabbed Makaya's pillow and yanked her down onto the bed. She landed with a thud on her back. In a split second, Spencer was on top of her and once again, face to face.

Makaya panted heavily as she stared into Spencer's eyes. "You can be so infuriating," she growled.

Spencer narrowed her eyes, but never broke eye contact. "It's what you love about me most. Don't deny it."

"And you're cocky too," Makaya added.

"I'll show you cocky."

Spencer slipped one hand under Makaya's neck and tilted her chin upward while placing feather-light kisses on the corners of her mouth.

"You're also a tease," Makaya whined.

Spencer devoured Makaya's mouth and forced her tongue deep inside. A shudder contracted Spencer's abdomen as she felt Makaya press herself against her. She moaned when Makaya dug her nails into her buttocks.

"I want you," Spencer hissed.

"We'll be late for practice, Spence."

"Fuck practice."

\*\*\*

"Makaya, Spencer, on your starting marks," the coach called from outside the sparing area.

Both women struck their starting pose and waited for the buzzer signaling the start of the match. When it came, Makaya immediately attacked, extending her arm and continually threatening Spencer's target areas.

Spencer counter attacked by quickly moving back out of the way and evaded Makaya's aggression by turning to the side and grazing her blade. She was able to effectively deflect it so that it missed its mark. She followed the defensive move with a lunge and thrust while she extended her front leg with a slight kicking motion and propelled her body forward with her back leg.

Makaya executed a parry and blocked Spencer's weapon and then followed the move with a riposte attack. Once again, Spencer successfully deflected the counter attack with circle parries and was able to catch Makaya's tip and deflect it away.

The coach suddenly stopped the match. He ran his hands through his hair and then put them on his hips. Makaya and Spencer stopped and removed their helmets. Spencer frowned impatiently as she waited for him to speak.

"Come on, ladies. If you want to be taken seriously as Olympic fencers, you need to be more aggressive. You are my top two students. You should be going after each other like you really mean it. Now put your helmets back on and show me what you're made of."

Spencer looked at Makaya and whispered "He can be a real asshole," before she shoved her helmet back on and went to her end of the sparing area.

"All right then. On your marks!"

As soon as the buzzer sounded, Spencer aggressively executed a beat attack and disturbed Makaya's aim. This allowed her to successfully hit Makaya's arm and draw a high outside parry. She effectively scored first blood.

"That's more like it!" the coach yelled.

Makaya tore her helmet off and glared at Spencer. A hint of mirth filled her eyes and a thin smile formed on her lips. Spencer cocked an eyebrow and grinned.

The coach was immediately on her case. "Put the helmet back on, Makaya. If you do that in a match, you will be disqualified."

With both fencers on their marks, the buzzer sounded the start of the next round.

Makaya tore out of her staring mark and executed two feints, followed by a continuous barrage of attacks. She targeted Spencer's high line above her bellguard and then followed it with a low line attack. She pivoted her blade under Spencer's weapon and tipped her target; scoring a point of her own.

"All right ladies, next point wins. On your marks!" the coach shouted.

Spence came off her mark with a thrust attack and extended her arm to continuously threaten Makaya's mark. Makaya countered with a point-in-line position to disturb Spencer's aim.

After several parries and ripostes, Makaya flicked her blade and caused it to bend such that she was able to score a point against the back of Spencer's shoulder.

Spencer tore off her helmet and threw it on the floor. "Ahh!" she screamed in frustration.

"Great job, Makaya. You too, Spencer. I have a good feeling about you two. You'll be a force to reckon with in the next Olympics. That's enough for today. You can hit the showers," the coach instructed.

Spencer watched the coach walk away and then turned to Makaya. "That was dirty pool," she said.

"No—that was a legal move. Spence, you let your anger get the best of you. Hot heads don't win matches. Calm execution does."

Spencer stood with her hands on her hips. He gaze was directed at the floor.

Makaya rubbed her arm. "How about that shower? I'll wash your back for you."

Spencer grinned and shook her head. "Why can't I stay mad at you?" she asked.

"Because you can't resist my beauty and charm." Makaya picked Spencer's helmet up and handed it to her. "Here. Let's go get naked."

***

Spencer leaned against the locker room wall and watched Makaya disrobe and walk into the shower. She couldn't get enough of Makaya Kapule's beauty. Her long dark hair and Pacific-Islander features turned her insides to mush every time she walked into the room. Her native Hawai'ian heritage was displayed proudly in her demeanor and in the way she interacted with people. Spencer fell hard for her the moment they met more than a year earlier. She thanked the gods every day for her decision to join the fencing team. She would have never met Makaya otherwise.

Spencer Bennet was aware of how stark the differences were between herself and Makaya. Where Makaya was dark skinned and had long black hair, she wore the mantel of her Irish heritage, with fair skin and asymmetrically boy-cut auburn hair. Makaya was curvy, with full breasts and hips, while she was pretty much straight up and down. In fact, she had been called 'sir' may times in her adult life. The only thing they really had in common was their age. They were both in their early thirties and were in fact, literally born just a few days apart, but on completely different sides of the world...she, in Vermont and Makaya, in Hawai'i.

Spencer was deep in thought when a wet wash cloth hit her on the side of the head.

"Hey! What was that for?" Spencer protested.

Only Makaya's face was exposed from behind the shower curtain. She threw the curtain open, exposing herself in all her glory. "I can't wash your back if you're out there—and still dressed, I might point out. Now get in here...preferably naked."

A grin split Spencer's face as she tore the remainder of her clothing off and joined Makaya in the shower. She pulled the curtain closed behind her and backed Makaya against the side of the shower stall. The high-pressure spray pummeled her back. She placed one hand against the wall on each side of Makaya's head and kissed her passionately.

Spencer's mouth moved to Makaya's neck, exposing Makaya to the spray of water. "Damn, what you do to me," Spencer said.

Makaya's arms circled Spencer's waist and Spencer felt herself being pulled further into Makaya's embrace. "I need more," Makaya whispered into Spencer's ear.

Spencer reached for the soap and lathered her hands, then slipped one hand in between Makaya's legs. Makaya pressed the back of her head into the shower stall. "Oh, my God, Spence," she moaned.

"You like that, huh?" Spencer asked. Spencer watched Makaya's face as she slipped three fingers inside. The desire on Makaya's face nearly drove her over the edge. An intense heat built in her own abdomen and she felt herself shudder. The hot water spraying on her back only intensified the feeling and she struggled to control herself while she focused on Makaya.

Makaya matched Spencer's thrusts and Spencer felt her lover's muscles tighten against her fingers. She knew it wouldn't be long before Makaya went over the edge, and the closer she got, the harder it was to control her own climax.

"Mak…Mak, touch me. Please. I don't think I can hold it back," Spencer rasped into Makaya's ear.

Makaya's eyes flew open and she stared directly at Spencer at the same time she slipped two fingers into Spencer's folds.

The sultry look in Makaya's eyes, combined with the caress of her fingers, drove Spencer over the edge at the same time Makaya reached climax. It took all her might to hold them both upright as their bodies succumbed to carnal desires.

When it was over, Spencer leaned against Makaya. Her weight alone held them up on shaky legs. Spencer leaned her forehead on Makaya's shoulder. "Damn, woman. I have never felt like this for anyone in my entire life. I love you, Mak."

"I love you too, Spence."

Spencer's head snapped up as she heard the door to the shower room close. She looked at Makaya and grinned. "I wonder how many we've scared away in the last few minutes?"

"Fuck'em if they can't take a joke," Makaya replied.

Karen D. Badger